AN OLD SOUL

AN OLD SOUL

M. KEVIN HAYDEN

MUSE
of the MOON
BOOKS

First edition
ISBN: 979-8-9927805-6-7

Developmental Editing by Eva Maria Dietrich Carreño
Copyediting by Melanie Scott
Proofreading by Robin Schroffel
Cover art and interior design by Barış Şehri

THERE'S STORY IN THE MUSIC.

 Amazon Music  Apple Music

 Spotify YouTube

Part One

"Synchronicity is an ever-present reality
for those who have eyes to see."
    – Carl Jung

Chapter One

The heat clamps down as the door clicks shut behind him.

"Shi–!" Isaac mutters, cutting himself off. Even his breath seems to drop in front of him, swallowed by the humidity.

It's a sweltering Chicago June, 1996–the kind of heat that turns the air thick, syrupy, pressing in from all sides; barely breathable. The pavement ripples in the distance, the streets shimmering with the promise of more misery. Isaac wipes his brow, hoping this summer won't be a repeat of the last–the hottest on record.

No car–but with the streak of luck he's been riding lately, who needs one?

Right on cue, a white CTA bus, striped in red and navy, exhales a plume of exhaust as it lumbers east on 87th toward the Dan Ryan.

Lately, buses have been arriving for Isaac at just the right moment. It's a strange kind of luck, one he hasn't quite figured out. But on days like this, he doesn't question it. Anything that saves him from roasting in this asphalt oven after a long shift at Big Shoulders Video feels like a small miracle.

Work had dragged, stretching out like molasses, yet now it feels distant–blurred, insignificant. As if today, everything that truly matters is only just beginning. The sensation is fleeting, slipping away as fast as it arrives, but it leaves something behind–a quiet, lingering echo just beneath his thoughts.

As he walks, shuffling footsteps scuff the concrete behind him—faint yet close. Isaac stops, scanning the parking lot. Nothing. He exhales, shakes it off, and keeps moving.

Two steps later, the sound returns—closer this time, but from no clear direction.

"What the f—" Isaac spins to his right.

A gaunt man in ragged clothes shuffles toward him, already too close. Isaac flinches. It's as if the man stepped out of the thick, humid air itself.

"Oscar, sir." The man extends a trembling hand, his arm thin and warped like a splintered broomstick. "My brothaaa! Please, I'm down on my luck!" Oscar's voice cracks, gravelly and desperate. "If you could spare even a coupla cents. I'm hon'gree, brotha... please, find it in your heart..."

Isaac fishes in his pocket, hearing Grandad's voice: *The opportunity you don't want to miss is the chance to help someone in need.*

Fifteen bucks. That's all he has until payday, and he's saving for a computer. Without realizing, Isaac pulls out the ten-dollar bill instead of the five. He watches as the bus stops, then continues eastward down 87th—he's missed it.

When he looks down and realizes which note he's handed over, he winces. *Damn!* But he doesn't ask for it back.

"Thank you—MYYY BROTHAAAA!" Oscar shrieks, his voice echoing throughout the heavy air. He does a little jig with his newfound fortune, then lunges forward to bear-hug Isaac.

"Yeah—you're welcome!" Isaac says, half-smiling, nearly knocked back by the man's ripe odor. Sweat pours off both their faces. Oscar grins widely with a total of four teeth: two on top and two on the bottom.

Isaac continues his sticky, heavy trek, now just steps from the bus stop. Another bus so soon? Unlikely. But then again... *I am Isaac André—The Chariot Conjurer.*

Behind him, Oscar toddles away, triumphantly waving the ten-dollar bill in the air. Ahead, a second bus glides to a stop.

Isaac smirks. *Not complaining!*

A sudden *tsssssssshhhh* sound cuts through the air as the bus doors swing open with a mechanical clap. A wave of cool, musty, air-conditioned relief washes over Isaac, evaporating the sticky sheen of sweat clinging to his brown skin.

Isaac climbs aboard, then drops his tokens into the fare box, which makes a satisfying clink that tickles the senses. No transfer needed today—straight to Tommy's barbershop on 87th and Morgan.

Tommy's shop and Isaac's apartment are both in Auburn-Gresham, on Chicago's Southside. This short bus ride from Big Shoulders Video—a VHS rental store in Chatham—is a familiar routine. Isaac is one of two head clerks at the video store. The pay is terrible, but it's a job. For now.

College isn't for everyone—that's what he hears, and it's what he's come to accept. Grants weren't enough to cover tuition, and when he needed a co-signer for a private loan, his cousin Pete was rejected for bad credit. So he dropped out of the School of the Art Institute after one semester.

His grandmother had offered, but Isaac refused to risk her finances, despite her insistence.

Dropout, regroup, then go to community college for a bit. That was the plan—six years ago.

Now, Isaac lives in a small studio apartment, which is a converted attic in a Chicago bungalow just two blocks from his grandmother's.

He stops by daily to make sure she has eaten or check if she needs the garbage taken out. If she hasn't eaten, they'll share dinner and a conversation. If she has, they'll still sit and chat before he heads home. Every time Isaac meets Grandma, the first thing she asks is, "Have you found *Her* yet?"

Isaac's paternal grandparents raised him from a young age. His mother died in a freak accident at an Indiana steel mill when he was just shy of three years old. He doesn't even remember her face. Sometimes, he gets fleeting, indistinct impressions—a soothing voice, the warmth of breath against his cheek and neck. Are they memories of his mother? He doesn't know. Like the strange coincidences that pepper his life, these mysteries remain unanswered, lingering like fragments of a puzzle he may never solve.

Isaac has never met his father. He left before Isaac was born, vanishing from his life. In this neighborhood, that isn't unusual. Isaac feels only a faint curiosity about the man—content in the love and care of his grandparents.

The glimpses of his mother, if these are of her, are fleeting. Granular. He can't piece them together into anything concrete. Dreams don't help either, if he dreams at all—he never remembers them.

Whatever granules flicker across the screen of his unconscious mind always scatter, drifting away before they can solidify into anything resembling a dream.

****

Arriving at Tommy's always feels familiar, like stepping into a rhythm you didn't realize you missed. The subtle scent of aftershave drifts through the air, mingling with the steady hum of a wall-mounted fan that provides a pleasant chill.

Scattered piles of coarse dark hair pepper the floor, marking the day's work. A grey Montgomery Ward black-and-white TV sits on a wooden shelf—volume dialed to zero. It's a silent presence, its flickering images unnoticed beneath the sound of the radio playing post-bop jazz softly in the background—familiar tunes woven into the life of the shop.

Isaac has a healthy obsession with jazz music. His grandad, also Isaac André, left him with this respect, and also a sizable collection of old vinyl records of the best.

There is chatter among the patrons of the busy shop. One of the sickest drum solos recorded by Art Blakey accompanies the loud talk.

Tommy looks up as the bell alerts him to Isaac's entrance. He bellows out, "Isaac—Get yo ass in here, boy! Let me at that head—out there waving around like a stalk of unpicked cotton in the wind!"

Tommy, aka Phil, is the sole proprietor, as he often reminds all who can hear, of Tommy's Barbershop. His given name is actually Phillip. He bought the business in 1982 from the prior operator, Thomas Prince, and since then, everyone has come to know Phillip as Tommy.

Tommy is missing the tips of his middle and ring fingers on his right hand, the result of an old amputation. He always jokes, "The sugar took my fingers, but I tell folks I lost 'em in a toothed sugar bowl." Of course, he's referring to a certain part of the female anatomy.

Tommy loves raising that middle nub when talking shit with the regulars. His half-hearted flip-offs never fail to draw laughter from everyone, including himself. It's a signature move—nobody takes his signed 'fuck you' seriously.

This doesn't slow him down. Tommy can still lay down a crisp fade, especially for an old-timer. Isaac's grandfather used to bring Isaac here every other Saturday, starting when he was seven. It became a tradition, one they kept until Grandad passed from cancer two years ago. Now Isaac comes alone, usually with a book in hand.

Isaac used to sit back in the waiting chairs, watching as Tommy reclined Grandad's chair and performed a meticulous face shave—hot towel and all. The precision, the care, the slow rhythm of the blade—it was calming just to observe.

At twenty-five, Isaac doesn't have much facial hair to speak of. Tommy usually just sheep-shears his sparse stubble with clippers, the whole process over in seconds. Every once in a while, Isaac jokingly requests a proper face shave, just to see what Tommy will say. And without fail, Tommy banters back with a grin something like, "I'll take your money if you want me to... but boy, there ain't shit there to shave."

Isaac strides into the shop, his usual near-confident yet quiet swagger in full display. The hum of clippers and low chatter greets him, blending with the faint crackle of the radio. As he enters, he stretches out a closed fist, exchanging a quick bump with one of the shop regulars. Without breaking stride, he steps up to Tommy's chair and settles in, pulling his retro Walkman's orange headphones behind his neck, a casual gesture that feels second nature. They come to rest at the base of his unkempt mini-afro.

Isaac always has a book in his grip, usually a well-worn library copy of something by Philip K. Dick or a similar author; strange fiction, full of warped realities and impossible questions. It resonates with him in a way he can't quite explain, like a half-remembered dream he's still trying to piece together.

Today, Isaac's paint-stained fingers grip a tattered, half-read copy of *Ubik*. Last time, it was *We Can Build You*, also by PKD. Tommy picks up the book, turning it over in his hands.

"Her 'fro looks better than yours!"

Isaac replies, "Whatever—old man. Low taper—and clean up my face while you at it."

Tommy tosses the book onto Isaac's lap, and with the same hand, flips him a sawed-off bird.

"I got your taper. Watch who you talking to, boy! I won't cut too low. You ain't got no sense up there as it is; why would I take more off of that head?"

The two of them break out into exaggerated laughter, along with the rest of the shop patrons. The usual shop vibe.

Another shop-goer, Cleon, sitting in the chairs, adds to the banter. "That nappy rock head you got!"

"Easy, son!" Tommy interjects. "You don't know him like that!"

Everyone stops in awkward silence. Tommy breaks it with his trademark half-assed middle finger at Cleon. Relieved laughter resumes among all in the shop.

On this balmy day, Isaac is sporting baggy denim shorts and an oversized Chicago Bulls jersey, with a white T-shirt underneath. The bottom of the jersey nearly reaches his knees. Of course, the jersey is none other than the number 23.

Isaac differs from most of his peers, especially those from the Southside of Chicago. Most don't share his interests in jazz, sci-fi, and art. Still, he isn't an outcast. He receives more admiration from the local female persuasion than he even notices, but they aren't usually interested in discussing his interests, such as the tropes of writers like PKD. Sitting back and chatting about these and other topics is something he would love.

He isn't in a steady relationship, even as he approaches the age of twenty-six. Grandma tried to set him up at church, but to no avail. This is why she jokingly asks every time they greet, "Has *She* found you yet?"

Tommy takes a moment to switch off the radio. He walks over to the high-perched TV above the mirror and twists the volume dial. The tail end of a sports segment on WGN flickers across the screen—something about the Cubs. What a terrible year.

One thing Isaac inherited from Grandad was a love for the Lovable Losers. Tommy, a rare Southside Cubs fan, shares the same affliction.

The ten-year-old TV struggles to hold a steady picture, its screen trapped in a rhythmic, hypnotic loop—bouncing up and down, rolling side to side—pausing in brief clarity before slipping back into its usual jitter.

Tommy's clippers *click-clack*.

A commercial for Empire Carpets flickers through the static, its iconic jingle filling the shop.

"Empiiiiire," one of the waiting patrons sings along, flipping through a *Jet* magazine. As the commercial fades, so does his voice. He lingers on the Beauty of the Week page, eyes skimming the prose—*Yeah, right*.

A WGN Chicago's Very Own bumper fades out to a commercial showing an unknown black teen clad in flannel, baggy jeans, and backpack, boarding a public transportation bus. As he walks to the rear of the bus, he belts out the Coca-Cola jingle, while everyone else on the bus looks at him with wide eyes and smiles. He makes it to his seat, finishes the jingle, and pulls off his headphones—just in time to grin as a cute girl flirts with him, herself gripping a glistening glass bottle of Coca-Cola.

The next commercial fades in through the static. It's for Silicon City, an electronics chain that specializes in computers. A new store recently opened at Evergreen Plaza on Western Ave.

The Silicon City commercial draws Isaac's full attention. He's been coveting a computer for a while now, saving every extra dollar. But last week, Grandma's AC unit went out, and there was no way he was letting her sit in that heat. He dipped into his savings, picked up a new unit from Sears. A setback, but necessary.

He still plans to surprise her with three new rosebushes for her flowerbed. Every summer, they plant something new—mostly annuals, since she loves the change. But last week, she had casually mentioned, "You know what would be nice? Some roses."

The entry-level PC system from NewBell usually ran for $1,750, but Silicon City has it marked down to $1,299.

Monitor, keyboard, mouse—and a free compact disc to upgrade the OS to Portals 97. A Summer Save Final Days deal.

Owning a computer would change everything. The internet—this vast, growing thing—feels like something pulled straight from Arthur C. Clarke's pages. Sending mail electronically. Video phone calls. Information at the click of a button.

Even socializing. Usually, people around here weren't into things like that. But someday, the borders of community will disappear. No more limits to social circles based on geography. Grandma always jokes about some imaginary girlfriend waiting for him; maybe she isn't that far off. At the very least, a computer would expand his world. Maybe it could even help him find answers.

He just needs Ron to agree to advance his paycheck tomorrow morning. Ron's never done that before. No one's ever asked.

The TV flickers.

A second of static.

Tommy's clippers *click-clack*.

A commercial for Empire Carpets flickers through the static. "Empiiiiire."

The same patron sings along. The same *Jet* magazine. The same page.

Not this!

When this happens, Isaac feels a sense of existential fragility. Reality already feels like it hangs from a taut string, ready to break.

He glances around. Tommy doesn't react. No one does. Just the soft hum of clippers, the murmuring voices, the smell of aftershave and powdered necks.

Isaac shifts in his seat, flexing his fingers against his shorts. *Maybe the heat. Maybe it's nothing.*

The feeling lingers—something slipping just beneath the surface of his thoughts.

Something feels off.
Today feels off. Today feels new and old at the same time.

****

Today's shift will be short, hours considered. It's Sunday and BSV closes early at 7 p.m. This is also the day Ron, the owner, routinely comes in to collect the cash from the safe after the Friday-Saturday rental rush. He is often in and out before Isaac gets there to open up.

Isaac plans to catch Ron this morning by getting to the store earlier than his 7 a.m. shift start. Thankfully, and expectedly, a CTA bus steams in the direction of 87th and Morgan as he foots toward the stop.

The air is sticky but there is a slight breeze—and the temps have yet to climb. The sun is just an hour above the horizon in the east. This is the direction Isaac is heading, from Gresham to Chatham, a ten-minute bus ride. He intends to catch Ron before he closes that safe and jets out of the store.

A brisk wind slaps Isaac in the face as the CTA bus squeals to a stop. Bluish-gray exhaust trails behind. The bus doors flap open, and Isaac ascends the rubber-coated steps. He drops a token in the slot—no transfer needed, as he slowly and rhythmically dips his head up and down to the Miles Davis classic *All Blues*, playing through his bright orange foam earphones. Inside his Walkman, the cassette tape spindles spin slowly, pushing the melodies through the circuits, into his skull.

He passes a beautiful Latin woman in her mid-twenties sitting at the front of the bus, her eyes trained on a novel. She briefly looks up at Isaac and smiles as the two make eye contact—then flips her hair. After the short non-verbal signaling, she returns her gaze to her dog-eared checkout lane romance novel. This one has the image of a shirtless, buff, long-haired man toiling away in the middle of a wheat field. An oval cut-out frames the illustrated man on the cover of the book. When opened, the oval gives way to a full picture with a wider view of his surroundings—the sun beating down on him.

Isaac feels no connection to those stories. Without judgment, he moves on, steadying himself by the overhead railings. He maintains his near-confident stride, but he isn't going to croon the *Always Coca-Cola* jingle. There are no mouth-breathing riders in awe. There are fewer well-groomed persons asleep against the windows. Others stare down into their Sunday papers, or into thin air, as if in trance. The cute girl here is gripping a Jewel-Osco bought romance novel, not a refreshing Coke.

He walks past the collection of sleeping or tuned-out folk toward the rear, stumbling backward into his seat as the bus accelerates. Even the fall is near-confident—neither cool nor uncool.

Someone on the bus smells amazing. A delicate and intoxicating scent takes him over. Isaac notices a woman holding up a magazine in front of her face. The artwork on the cover appears futuristic, bearing the headline 'Who is Carolyn Faber?' A woman wearing suspenders and a button-down shirt stands in a resolute pose, her gaze fixed skyward. She appears intrepid and charismatic, surrounded by people with upheld fists, holding picket-like signs—most of them scrawled with 'Scientia Mater' or 'SOMA'—whatever that means.

The girl reading the strange periodical appears to have sandy brown hair, but the magazine, which she holds up for the entire ride, obscures her face. This intrigues Isaac, but he isn't sure why. It's not even the techie font and artwork but something else. A part of him wants to ask about it. Or maybe just to see the person holding it. The surreal artwork, the scent hanging in the air—it all teases at his curiosity. Nah... he hesitates. Instead, he exhales, pulls out his battered copy of *Ubik*, and drowns his curiosity in Miles Davis.

Of course, he keeps an eye out for an opportunity to see the person behind the veil for the rest of the ride, hoping to get a glimpse of her. He is certain the sweet smell is from her–gardenia, maybe?

Isaac arrives just as Ron's chair scrapes against the floor inside his closed office. The wonky wheel screeches like chalk on a board. 6:35 a.m. Perfect timing–or terrible, depending on Ron's mood. Ron is the owner and manager of this BSV as well as two others in the city.

Isaac feels his stomach knot over five times; his mouth is dry. Ron is in a clear hurry. Just as he exits the office, they meet face-to-face outside the office door. A brief awkward silence plays out, as Ron and Isaac stand facing each other in silence. Ron has nothing to say, and Isaac can't get out what he has come to ask.

Isaac finally gets his question out, knowing it's his only shot. If unsuccessful, he'll have to wait a week–which means he'll miss the sale.

"Yo, Ron, what's up?"

Ron's forehead wrinkles in surprise at Isaac's atypical behavior.

"Nothing, Isaac, how are you this morning?" Ron asks in his Southside Irish accent. He has a chewed, unlit cigar in his mouth.

"I was wondering if I could get an advance, just of next week's check? I still got three shifts on this pay period, but you know I'm good for them. I wouldn't even ask if it wasn't important. For real, though."

Two thick, raised brows frame Ron's face. His forehead wrinkles, then smooths as he exhales slowly. That slow exhale. Isaac has seen it before. When Ron has it out for someone, it's not yelling or threats–it's the cold, indifferent stare. The kind that makes you feel like dirt.

He usually is rush-rush, but Isaac's request has caught him off-guard; Isaac rarely asks for favors, and is dependable. More than the other head clerk, Wayne. Isaac works the morning shift, and 'Lazy Wayne' comes in for the evening shift.

"Sure, kid. That's fine. You know I don't do this shit, so this is the first—and last time." He pulls his cigar from his lips, and a small smirk appears in the stained corner of his left lip. "I'm serious, Ike, I'm not doing this again."

"Yes, sir!" Isaac exclaims with a grin on his face. He nearly bounces. The image of a six-foot-one-inch, slim but athletic black guy bouncing in joy would be a sight. It would probably even pull a rare laugh from Ron, but that won't come today. Isaac remains elated.

Ron pulls out a small spiral notepad from his back pocket, thumbs it open, and examines rows of names and numbers.

"So, three more shifts this week. You got the long morning today, Wayne the later shift. And then Friday last week." He traces numbers in the air to figure out how much to pay Isaac, excluding deductions, and it figures to— "Two hundred-eighty three and fifty-seven cents."

Ron unzips the cash sack, peeling off banded stacks with practiced efficiency. He counts out the bills, slaps them into Isaac's palm, and mutters, "Keep up the good work, Ike. See you next week." His voice is flat, dry—transactional.

He turns to leave but stops mid-step. "Oh—forgot the fifty-seven cents."

With a sigh, he drops the bag onto the red countertop, rummaging through another sack filled with rolls of coins. "I ain't re-rolling this shit. I owe you fifty." He holds up a warning finger. "And Ike—this doesn't get out. Tell no one."

Their paths rarely cross. Ron only fills in when one of the head clerks is off, or when he's picking up deposits. That distance has always made moments like this feel like an exception-not a rule.

As he reaches the door, Ron stops again. Slowly, he pulls the cigar from his lips, inspecting the shredded end like he's contemplating something.

Then, without looking up, he mutters, "I may or may not be calling in a favor for this later."

The cigar lands in the trash bin with a dull thud.

He walks out without another word.

****

Shortly after Ron leaves, Sharika, one of Isaac's coworkers at Big Shoulders Video, approaches the door and slap-knocks loudly with her open palm. Isaac walks out from behind the counter area, which is shaped like a square-bottomed letter *U*, with a single opening. This serves as an island where the clerks can serve from either side. At the entrance of the store, there is a large opaque protective glass window—only clear enough to see the outline of Sharika's short bumpy hairstyle as she waits for him to come around and let her in.

Sharika days are usually not fun for Isaac. She seems to take many opportunities to insult Isaac for his taste in movies and books, or just for who he is. She constantly reminds him she likes "thugs," which certainly isn't Isaac. Why she does this is confusing, as he isn't fond of her either. For some reason she appears to think the opposite, and this is her tactic to remind him that she is off the table. A difficult person indeed. Isaac's temperament allows him to take a great deal, but every once in a while he has to practice slow breathing, or remove himself from the store floor when she really digs in.

Isaac makes it from around the counter to the entrance corridor of the store, clicks open the deadbolt, and goes to politely open the door for her. She snatches it outward quickly from his hands.

Sharika grunts, "What took you so damn long? You too slow! It's hot as a motherfucka out here!" She scoffs again, "... And my hair is sweatin' out!" Isaac's face is unchanged, so he thinks, but an eye-roll does escape.

Sharika stops when she sees this. "T-uh? What? Got something to say?" she challenges with a decreased pitch in voice, almost masculine.

Isaac wishes he was working with Tamika, one of the other clerks. She is usually more agreeable but doesn't hold conversations during slow periods in the store. She laughs at every joke Isaac makes, and even when he isn't joking, as if her amusement is not genuine. Pity laughs, when she clearly didn't get the joke. He considers her a cute girl, but he truly longs for someone who understands him. This is difficult for most, if not everyone. That's how he feels. Like an alien in his own world.

Sharika continues into the store. She pats the side of her frosted head with the same open palm she used to knock, albeit with less force, to quell an itch. Her short haircut is virtually plastered in place with hair products to produce something called finger-waves. She rolls her eyes when she looks up at the display screen and sees *2001: A Space Odyssey*. It's playing simultaneously on all six screens scattered throughout the store. Isaac loves this film, one of his favorites.

Sharika scoffs, "Fool—you and this corny shit! Why are you always watching this garbage?" She points at Isaac's copy of *Ubik* and continues the tirade. "These books too! You are weird as shit! See, you can't take care of me. I need a thuggish man. You ain't it!'

Her animosity toward Isaac remains poorly understood. While Isaac has a penchant for science fiction and things considered nerdy, he doesn't fit the description of nerdy. Despite his reserved nature and difficulty in getting angry, his commanding presence is undeniable because of his height at six feet and one inch.

He is usually oblivious to any attention he receives. No flirt-radar. Besides being humble, he is usually in his head, pensively pondering over something. He would miss the flirting, even if it were recognizable.

Sharika deliberately takes slow and short steps to the back of the store to stash her belongings. It'll take her twice as long to return to the floor to work. The smell of strong and cheap perfume trails behind her. This overpowers the smell of plastic and cardboard of the VHS tapes and covers, most of them dusty, except for the new releases displayed on the wall shelves.

Isaac intends to fill the day with busywork, like dusting the cases which were supposed to be done by Sharika weeks ago. He plans to catch his predictable 87th Street CTA bus straight over to Evergreen Plaza and Silicon City later to get his first personal computer. He has the cash now.

****

As anticipated, Isaac's shift drags, despite the self-imposed busywork and the steady customer stream. People are returning VHS tapes from Friday and Saturday night, and some enter to rent again after their drop-offs.

Half of the tapes that are returned are not rewound, so Isaac and Sharika have to slide them into an automatic rewinder before placing them back into their cases and putting them onto the shelves. Sharika has a habit of putting them into the rewinder and leaving them, instead of doing the rest of the return process. This leaves Isaac having to return them to the case, then place them on the floor, in addition to the ones he rewinds. Isaac would normally call her out on this, but today he wants no more friction. He just wants to get through this day, which would also include a visit by Creepy Teddy. This rude, thirty-something store regular always shows up wearing the same dingy Transformers T-shirt and disappears into the curtained Adult section for at least thirty minutes.

It's a policy to peek in when someone spends too much time in the Adult section, to prevent theft, but no one fancies having to check in on Creepy Teddy, loathing the idea of finding him in a compromising situation. He also has a short temper, prone to blow up for the slightest reason.

Teddy takes a little longer today. Isaac looks over at Sharika, who kisses her teeth and turns away. Again, he doesn't want friction, so he heads to the rear, just as the black curtain flies to the side rapidly. Teddy emerges with a copy of *Slap That Ass* sandwiched between two other mainstream tapes: *Mannequin Two* and *Naked Gun 2½*. He will likely be back tomorrow claiming all three tapes are malfunctioning despite using the tracking control, and he'll be telling the truth. This can happen after VHS tapes have been played hundreds of times, as the older mainstream movies were. It's usually not the case for newer releases, unless they are of the Adult genre. *Slap That Ass* was released a just few weeks ago and is already in bad shape.

Teddy walks over to Sharika's side to check out, as he always does. He puts the cases onto the counter with a contemptuous slam. He rolls his eyes at Sharika, beating her to the punch. It's like a sport for these two. Isaac finds this hilarious but puzzling. He thinks, *People can be strange... but maybe this is all normal, and I'm the strange one.*

The workday crawls to an end. Wayne walks into the store lackadaisically to work the backend. He takes his time as he strolls to the back of the store, and Isaac finishes balancing his cash at his terminal. Sharika does the same as Tamika walks in shortly afterward.

Wayne walks up with two cash register drawers in hand for Tamika and himself, and holds out his fist for Isaac to give him dap, saying, "Whaddup, son!"

Isaac reciprocates the greeting and the dap, gives Wayne the rundown, and collects the registers for himself and Sharika. He can now get his self onto the bus, which will be waiting for him when he approaches the 87th and Dan Ryan stop. Very fortunate and strange this bus thing is to Isaac.

****

Isaac rides the 87th Street CTA bus westward. On the ride, he passes the stops for his apartment and Tommy's shop before he arrives at Western Ave. Once there, he transfers to the Western Pace bus down to 95th Street. Why walk when you have his luck?

Evergreen Plaza is an indoor mall located at 95th and Western Avenue. The Pace bus trucks to a stop. The doors open and the heat immediately rushes into the previously cool bus. It's 6 p.m., yet the heat and humidity still presses.

Isaac steps down, then walks across the large parking lot from the bus stop as beads of sweat collect on his brow. He walks through the entrance at the east side of the mall, a refuge. He is overcome by cool air scented with the smell of popcorn and sweet concessions.

As he advances down the long corridor entrance past a large retailer, the smell fades and gives way to one of various colognes and perfumes. Elevator music is heard on the overhead Muzak system.

Isaac passes by a dark replica statue of Ousamequin, a celebrated Native leader of early America. The figure cradles a sword across his forearm, his gaze fixed on the distant yonder. Isaac walks toward that imagined horizon, his steps deliberate as he approaches the indoor entrance of Silicon City.

The moment he steps inside, a cacophony of sound greets him—multiple demo TVs blaring at once. The largest floor models dominate the space, their screens glowing faintly. Most boast rear-projection technology, their images soft and vague compared to the crisp definition of old-school CRTs. At least, that's how Isaac feels about them.

He pauses briefly near the audio section, just steps beyond the televisions. The portable CD players catch his eye, sleek and compact, promising hours of music on the go. Miles Davis, Coltrane, even A Tribe Called Quest—all without the hassle of rewinding.

Isaac lingers, tempted. But practicality nudges at him. I can play CDs on the new PC for now, he thinks, then save up again for the portable player.

He mentally runs through his priorities. Rent paid? Food in the fridge? Grandma set?

For a moment, doubt creeps in. Wait—the rent *is* paid, right?

He reassures himself quickly. *Of course it's paid. I've been hyper-focused on this new computer, but I wouldn't let that slip.* Even with his excitement, Isaac knows his responsibilities come first.

With a final glance at the CD players, he turns and continues toward his goal.

A short-statured salesman notices Isaac approaching the floor-model PCs and steps away from a standing computer terminal to meet him. His neatly ironed, carnation blue, short-sleeved button-down shirt is tucked crisply into pleated khaki pants.

The Silicon City logo is affixed to his right shoulder, while his name, Robert, is stitched in tidy white letters over the left chest pocket. A pen juts neatly from the small pocket on his right side, completing the uniform's utilitarian look.

Robert appears to be in his mid-thirties, with dark hair tied back in a sleek ponytail. His face is framed by a prominent mustache, balanced—or perhaps contrasted—by a soul patch centered below his lower lip.

Robert approaches with his right hand extended dramatically, far ahead of him, ready for a handshake well before he's within range. Isaac steps forward and meets him halfway, returning the gesture with an awkwardly unbalanced but firm shake.

"Welcome to Silicon City! I'm Robert, your PC sales specialist today!" Robert says, enthusiastically and rehearsed.

Isaac responds with a casual upward nod. "Hey—whaddup? Isaac."

Robert sizes him up quickly, his hands settling on his hips as he surveys the small sea of computers on display in the center of the store. "So—" he says, tilting his head slightly, "which one are you buying?"

Isaac points toward the computer section. "I was hoping you all still had that sale going on—the NewBell PC? With the monitor and everything included?"

Robert pretend-cringes as he emphatically drops his hands to the side. "I am so sorry, chief, we sold the last one last night. They went fast with that deal..." He lowers his tone. "... and that was a good deal! We won't be doing a deal like that again for a while!"

Isaac's spirit drops visibly. Robert looks around sneakily, as if he has some secret. Then he says, "Check this out, chief. We do have an open box—good as new—NewBell CX3000, which is newer and more powerful than the model you were looking at. I'll talk to my manager—see if we can just throw in the monitor and other stuff! We still need to get rid of those monitors and it shouldn't be a problem. We gotta clear those puppies out of here too!"

Robert sizes up Isaac again and continues. "It is an open-box item though, chief. That means it was already opened for whatever reason. It's a better system overall, but I can probably get it to you for only one hundred bucks more than the thirteen-hundred-dollar deal on that other crap."

Isaac takes a moment; he rubs his hands together. Robert extends his right hand for a shake. He asks, "So—whaddya think, Isaac? Much more bang for just a little more buck!"

Isaac doesn't take long to ponder. His mind is made up, but he tries running through the economics of the purchase one more time.

Robert reassures him, "Again, it is open-box—but this puppy has been fully inspected and is basically brand-new. It's the CX3000! The processing power is above and years ahead of that other one! It's also a newer model, so it already has the Portals 97 operating system installed too, chief. That other one—entry-level stuff. You know, grandmother saving her recipes and keeping tabs on her checking balance. The CX3000 is the next level." Robert shakes his closed fist. "If you want to use it for any other reason, this is your guy!"

Isaac has enough to cover this and is excited at the prospect of owning a more powerful, up-to-date model. Buying it won't leave him much money for anything else, though. Thankfully, it comes loaded with the new Portals 97. He asks, "And y'all will throw in the monitor, keyboard and mouse?"

Robert waves his hands and puffs his lips. "Psssh—of course! I'm telling you this is a steal!"

Isaac nods and says, "Cool!"

He spots another customer, a man appearing to be listening in—ready to pounce with *I'll take that deal*—so Isaac quickly accepts the offer with a stiff handshake. He notices Robert's palms are sweatier than before.

Robert grunts playfully, "G-oooh! That's some grip you got there, big guy!" He bends slightly at the waist and points dramatically toward the rear of the store.

"Lemme go get the goods! We'll get you home and online in no time, bud!" he says with exaggerated excitement. As he walks away, he stops abruptly, spinning around to point his finger at Isaac.

"Isaac—you're getting yourself a NewBell, bud!" he exclaims, grinning broadly.

Robert shoots Isaac another playful finger gun before wiping his sweaty forehead with the back of his hand. He adjusts his long, damp ponytail, flicking it over his shoulder before disappearing into a swinging door marked Employees Only.

Isaac watches him go, and a thought strikes him—*How the hell am I getting this thing home on two buses?*

Robert brings out multiple boxes on a dolly and parks it near Isaac. Isaac exhales sharply, but relief washes over him as he remembers. Pete.

Pete, his cousin, works right here in the mall and is getting off soon. His ride? A beat-up 1986 Buick Skyhawk he scored at a police auto auction for $500. The car has its quirks—most notably, a hole under the passenger-side floorboard, hidden by mismatched brown carpet. When it rains, the entire interior reeks like a dead carcass for days.

But quirks aside, Pete's Buick is a godsend on a hot, humid day like this. Isaac needs to get everything back to his tiny studio apartment on Morgan Street, and lugging it onto public transportation is not an option.

Pete finishes his shift at Waggies around 7 p.m. He works as a clerk in the pharmacy-slash-convenience store attached to Evergreen Plaza, right at the northern entrance of the mall. Perfect timing.

Isaac steps up to the payphone outside Silicon City, across the mall from Waggies, and dials Pete. He needs this favor, but the problem is, Isaac only has $30 left, and Pete immediately asks for gas money to seal the deal.

Pete isn't trying to be shrewd or greedy—he genuinely needs the gas just to pick Isaac up, get them home, and then make it back himself. He has a bad habit of driving until the tank is nearly empty, neglecting refills until he's down to fumes.

This habit often coincides with him being out of cash entirely.

More than once, Pete has been spotted in the Evergreen Plaza parking lot, steering from outside the driver's side door as he pushes the depleted Buick Skyhawk to a gas station—or at least closer to the mall entrance.

After a brief back-and-forth, Isaac agrees to spot him ten dollars, which should more than cover the trip. Regular unleaded is going for ninety-five cents a gallon, and even Pete can make that stretch.

Isaac says to Robert, "Is it cool if you hold this while I get my cousin and his car? It's right across the way, and I won't be long."

"Yeah... yeah, sure, Isaac," Robert says as he twists his wrist to check the time, forcing a smile.

A little after 7 p.m., Pete steps out of Waggies Pharmacy, tugging at his bright royal-blue smock vest. He sees Isaac waiting by the Skyhawk, a large box perched on its rusted trunk.

"Whaddup, fool!" Pete hollers, wiping his sweaty forehead with the edge of his smock as he approaches.

His voice carries a mix of energy and mischief, the kind that always promises a story—or trouble.

Isaac smiles and silently raises a fist to return the greeting. They put this single box, which contains the large and heavy CRT monitor in the backseat; it doesn't fit into the trunk. The computer and peripherals are awaiting Isaac at the store's pickup area. They race over to pick them up, driving across the parking lot before the store closes.

Robert stands expectantly at the outdoor entrance of Silicon City awaiting them. He has two boxes on a dolly. They find that the box containing the computer won't fit in the trunk, but they are able to squeeze it into the backseat with the monitor by adjusting the passenger seat forward. The driver's seat was already pulled forward with the monitor box behind it. Pete's legs are considerably shorter, as he is five feet seven in height, so it isn't a problem. Isaac, however, will have an uncomfortable ride, which he of course doesn't mind considering the circumstances.

The smaller box holding the mouse, keyboard, and other discs fits in the trunk easily. The inside rearview mirror is obscured by the boxes and Pete's passenger-side mirror is missing. However, they feel confident in taking on this tight and potentially dangerous Chicago drive as it's a short distance.

****

Isaac and Pete make a quick stop at Grandma's on Carpenter Street, less than two blocks away from Isaac's apartment on Morgan Street. He always checks on her after work to see if she's eaten or needs anything, and today is no different, despite his excitement to hit the Information Superhighway.

The Skyhawk slowly parks in front of Grandma's brown-brick Chicago-style bungalow. There is a brown aluminum awning suspended over crystal-clear windows. The poured concrete steps end in a porch at the top, all covered with brown outdoor carpeting. A heavy white screen, installed in the 1980s and which often malfunctions, hangs slightly open.

Isaac and Pete ascend the stairs. Isaac walks unassisted, while his cousin slowly and cooly walks up holding onto the wobbly thin steel banister, looking around in all directions for any potential female observers.

At the top, the screen door makes a scuffing sound as it scrapes the step to get inside. Isaac corrects the screen-door quirk by adjusting the sliding mechanism on the door hydraulic, and it shuts completely behind them as they step inside. Grandma's sweet voice is heard from the entrance.

"Isaac?"

"Yeah! It's me, Grandma! Pete too!"

Pete yells, "Hey, Grandma!"

Grandma calls back joyfully, "My babies! Come on back here! I'm in the kitchen."

Isaac had come to make sure she had eaten dinner and, if not, offer to go grab takeout from someplace, but the two young men are suddenly overcome with the smell of sweet and savory goodness in the air. They walk through the front living room, which is just off to the left, into her dining room. The kitchen is just on the other side.

Grandma stands at the stove, stirring a pot of collard greens. Her long silver-streaked dark hair is tied back. She has multiple pots going at the same time. She wears her ever-present smile on her light caramel-brown face. Her kind eyes pair with her smile.

Steam rises into the cozy air. It's warm in her kitchen but tolerable. A rotating fan sits in front of the rear kitchen door, which opens into her air-conditioned den. The fan is circulating some of the cool air from her window AC into the humid cooking space.

The sweet smells are from her dinner rolls, rising slowly. These are the Grandma version of croissants. Buttery, flaky, and soft when bitten into. They hit the tastebuds perfectly when paired with her oven-baked macaroni and cheese. This is not the stuff you buy in a box—it's a culinary delight.

Pete grabs his stomach and points with his other hand to the heavens. He is fortunate to not have to spend money for dinner tonight, having spent most of his last paycheck from Waggies on a subwoofer for his car. That sound system cost more than his car alone at this point. Listening to Tupac with the bass rattling your chest makes it worth it to him.

Isaac and Pete both walk over to their smiling grandmother and kiss each cheek in succession. Isaac has to bend down, being taller; Pete, of course, doesn't.

First, Grandma asks Isaac, "Did you find *Her* yet?" For some reason, she only does this to Isaac, not Pete.

Isaac blushes. "Grandma!"

She laughs, swats softly on his shoulder. She then talks a bit about her day. Her Louisiana accent always commands attention, even through what would otherwise be boring anecdotes.

Grandma is excited to be hosting a dinner at her home with the pastor from her church next weekend and asks if someone can get her list of groceries. She pulls the neatly creased list from her apron pocket, which Pete reaches and grabs before Isaac can. Pete insists, "I got it, Grandma! Don't worry, cuz, it's easier for me with the whip." Isaac smiles, nods, and offers his fist for a bump, which Pete returns. He is relieved. He has a busy week, and he wanted some time to mess around with his new toy. He would have done the errand without batting an eye, but he is still relieved. Living the closest, he does a bit more for Grandma—but deep down, he knows she has others that can step in.

Grandma says to Pete, "Thank you, Petey!" This name always makes Pete blush as Isaac usually teases him immediately after. This time, he doesn't.

She looks over at Isaac. "I'll see you tomorrow?"

It's nearly time for Grandma's flowerbed and garden work, a part of his busy week, but one that is welcome.

Isaac always does the heavy work for her. This time, he went and got her flowers ahead of time. He lugged them home each day last week from the nursery by BSV.

"Of course, Grandma, I got a surprise for you too! I'll be here before you even wake up!"

The three rosebushes he has bought her are to symbolize himself, Grandma, and Grandad. He knows just the place to put them—against the house at the base of the rear window. His grandparents used to let him sleep in on Saturdays.

He didn't sleep in long; they were early risers, but when he woke up to a seemingly empty house, he would find relief when he peered out of this window to find them in the garden. A nervous relief each time. An anxiety that hasn't dissipated over the years.

Chapter Two

The door of Isaac's dark studio apartment opens. He catches the large box containing his computer's base—with a plate of Grandma's cooking resting on top. He had been bracing it with his knee against the door prior to turning the key. He places the box into the entrance and clicks a bronze-toned light switch, revealing his place.

Pete carries the boxed monitor up the rear stairs to the only entrance to Isaac's apartment. He hands it to Isaac as he stands at the door and runs back down the stairs to his car, which is parked in the alley behind the home. Isaac follows behind and is handed his final box of computer peripherals.

Isaac and Pete slap hands, holding to pull each other into a side hug. Isaac says, "Man, I really appreciate all of this, not just the ride, but always having my back with Grandma." Pete looks at him and says playfully, "Stop all of this soft shit, cuz—Ah! Sike! For real, kid—I got you. I'm about to get on something tonight; may be some females there. You down?"

Isaac has the next day off but would rather get inside with his computer and see what the next level of technology will bring. Besides, he has to wake up early and help Grandma in the garden. He replies, "Nah, cuz. Imma just hang back tonight. Worked with Sharika today and I'm straight exhausted."

Pete interjects, "Say no more, fam. That girl got issues. I'll hit you up later, aight?"

"Aight, cuz, peace out."

Pete steps into his car. The door doesn't catch closed initially, requiring a second slam. As he turns the engine, it makes a loud and grating sound. He needed to replace that muffler some time ago. A dog bark rings down the empty alley. As he pulls off, the car lets out a gurgling roar. His left tail brake light doesn't work at the end of the alley as he taps the brake. The car screams as he turns onto 86th Street.

Isaac heads back up to his apartment. He puts Grandma's extra plate in the refrigerator; he'll likely want that in the middle of the night.

The interior of the apartment is one room, longer than it is wide. The kitchenette consists of a stove and refrigerator, both flanking the entry door, the only two walls that will fit them, as the ceiling slopes downward on the lengthwise walls. A person of Isaac's height can really only stand straight in the center. There, in the center of the apartment, his bed spans half the width of the space. Beside it, a small table serves dual functions as a place to both work and eat.

Across from the bed, there is a low-profile wide bookcase, which is stuffed with hardcover and paperback books on one side. The other holds an impressive vinyl record collection—part of his collection, that is. There are also stacked milk crates to the side of the bookshelf containing even more wax classics.

On the top of the bookcase, there is a Technics turntable with two speakers, connected to a stereo set. At the bottom of the receiver, there are two cassette tape decks side by side. These can be used to make dubbed copies of cassettes. Next to the stereo, a thirteen-inch Sears-branded color TV set rests. He rarely watches it.

There are no framed posters of any kind hanging on the walls of Isaac's apartment. Instead, they are painted an off-white at the base and otherwise completely covered in an elaborate mural, which Isaac painted himself. What's there was done over a period of months. It's his attempt to collectively piece together his fractured visions. The mural has three parts, all with randomly appearing themes. The most striking is that of a grassy meadow. The sun is drawn in a fiery manner, with multicolored coronae stretching over the landscape. In the center of the meadow, a male silhouette painted in black lies looking upward. Sitting with the male is another silhouette, a female, cradling his head in her lap.

The sun's coronae thin out and stretch toward the two human figures like fine tendrils. Each filament is a different color; some shimmer in the light. Isaac used fine wires of different types, some painted in metallic golds, silver, and copper—eye-catching.

This part of the mural is on the sloped ceiling across from Isaac's full-size bed. He looks up at it nightly. This is the one he fixates on. It seems to have the most significance to him, even with that significance being unknown. Two other paintings flank the central mural. To the left, Chicago's skyline. The one to the right is a futuristic looking city, with windowless skyscrapers.

****

Isaac grabs a utility knife and slices through the tape of the first box with cautious ease. The light-gray computer tower rests snugly inside, cradled by Styrofoam. A faint smell of newness drifts up as he lifts it free, placing it carefully on the cleared table—his newly designated workstation. He sets the monitor next to the tower.

With a low click, the computer powers on, its internal fans humming softly. Isaac presses the monitor button, watching as the yellow indicator light shifts to green. For a moment, he pauses, anticipation rising as the machine whirs to life.

The screen flickers, stabilizing on a black background with the NewBell logo displayed in bold orange. Beneath it, the model designation CX3000 appears alongside a scrolling list of specs. Moments later, the stark display dissolves into a clean blue desktop, framed by soft clouds and crowned with the Portals 97 logo.

A single piano note booms from the speakers, rich and resonant, accompanied by a swelling crescendo of strings. The sound fills the room, both majestic and surreal. Isaac's eyes widen slightly and his lips curl as he gives a soft nod of approval. The machine's startup earns his silent acknowledgment.

He picks up a stack of CDs from the peripherals box, flipping through them until he finds one labeled Columbia OnLine (COL). A trial offer for internet service—just what he needs to get started. He presses the button on the CD-ROM drive, and it ejects smoothly. He sets the disc into the tray, presses it closed.

Click.

The disc spins to a hum.

Isaac finds the included phone cord and plugs it into the LINE jack on the back of the computer. The other end replaces his telephone connection at the wall jack, linking his system to the outside world through dialup.

The installation finishes, and the Columbia OnLine dashboard loads onto the screen. Its elegant green calligraphy and spinning globe animation look modern and futuristic. Below the logo, tabs labeled Sign On, Settings, and Help hover in clean rows.

He clicks Sign On, skims through the standard disclaimers, and clicks 'Accept' after noting the fine print about recurring fees. He inputs his details—name, address, phone number, and credit card—before clicking the glowing 'Go Online' icon.

****

Eleven rapid beeps sound from the computer tower as the modem dials in. It then springs to life, emitting a chaotic symphony of hisses and whines.

Pwwwwsssssshhhhhhhhhhhhhhhh.

After a few seconds, the dashboard refreshes to a deep, pleasant male voice: "Welcome!"

A series of faint clicks echoes from the computer's base—then the same pleasant voice exclaims:

"You have messages!"

A small mailbox icon flashes in the top-right corner of the COL dashboard.

The dashboard itself looks like a snapshot of the city: the *Windy City Tribune* dominates the center, its headline shouting, 'Let's Do It Again!' above a photo of Michael Jordan and the Chicago Bulls mid-game. Below this, local weather updates, entertainment news, and world headlines populate the screen.

On the left, an icon labeled 'www' catches Isaac's eye. He clicks it, and a portal window pops open. At the top, an empty text box with a flashing cursor waits for input. Isaac hesitates briefly, then types:

www.sciencefiction.con

The modem buzzes loudly, the computer's fans revving as the page begins to load. A deep orange background crawls into view at a snail's pace, inching its way down the screen. Stars and planets appear first, scattered like breadcrumbs. Then, the top of a head—forehead, eyes—gradually emerges. By the time the full image appears, it's unmistakably William Shatner as Captain Kirk from *Star Trek*.

Below, a collage of iconic sci-fi characters slowly materializes: Luke Skywalker, Ellen Ripley, and more. On the left-hand side, a vertical menu offers categories: Books, Film, TV, Animation, and others. Isaac clicks Books, triggering another sluggish load.

The new page is sparse—a simple black background with floating blue and gray text links arranged alphabetically. He scrolls, scanning the list for Philip K. Dick, then clicks the name.

The modem stirs to life again, fans whirring louder as the page begins to load. The screen shifts to a blank orange background. Then—

Server Timeout.

A lone Home button appears in the center of the screen. Isaac clicks it, and the Shatner collage begins to reemerge, starting with his forehead.

"Man, this is whack," Isaac mutters under his breath, shaking his head.

****

Isaac heads back to the COL home dashboard. On the left-hand pane, he notices an icon of two smiley faces tilted toward each other, their wide grins almost mischievous. He clicks it and enters the world of online chat for the first time.

The screen populates with links for countless chatroom sections. There's a category for romance, which leads to subcategories, many organized by location. But Isaac isn't here for romance. He clicks on the Interests tab and selects The Grassy Knoll, a chatroom dedicated to conspiracy theorists.

Lately, Isaac has been experiencing an increasing level of synchronicity, what Carl Jung would describe as meaningful coincidences. His fascination with Philip K. Dick's writings stems from a shared sense of unease—Isaac feels watched, guided, even manipulated. At times, it's as though something is trying to communicate with him. His segmented visions, lack of dreams, and unusual streaks of luck only deepen his suspicion. There's also the nagging feeling of displacement. Like Marty McFly in *Back to the Future*, Isaac sometimes wonders if he's living in the wrong timeline and needs to fix it.

Inside The Grassy Knoll, the user interface is simple but alive with activity. A column on the right displays a list of at least thirty usernames. Some are original and clever, others less so. One in particular makes Isaac laugh out loud: ErnestGos2sht.

"T-HAAA! Ernest goes to shit! That's some funny shit!"

For now, Isaac watches the conversation unfold, the screen scrolling slowly upward with each reply:

> UFOHunter23: Man this just blew my mind. What else are they hiding from us?

> MoonLandingWasFake: More than we even realize. They're probably watching this chat right now. If I suddenly disappear, you'll know why. lol

> ErnestGos2sht: Moon, do you think the feds monitor these chatrooms?

> MoonLandingWasFake: I know they do! Last month, I got into a debate with some dude about car phones. I went deep on specifics... cuz I got specifics... and boom, I got punted offline.

> ErnestGos2sht: Damn... crazy shit, dude!

> ElectricSheep7: Hello

> UFOHunter23: Yo, new guy! What's up?

> MoonLandingWasFake: Welcome to The Grassy Knoll. Watch your back.

ElectricSheep7: Man, y'all are really bugging out in here. haha. What do you all think about synchronicity? Strange stuff that happens at random, but can't be random.

UFOHunter23: Synchronicity? Like Carl Jung, right?

ElectricSheep7: Yeah, exactly.

UFOHunter23: Carl Jung was onto some deep shit!

MoonLandingWasFake: Yo! Language! We're being monitored, remember?

UFOHunter23: MoonLanding, yeah, by the government, not your priest!

ErnestGos2sht: lol

MoonLandingWasFake: Who do you think finances every major world government? The Pope... duh!

FlatEarthDude: You all just gave me the bedtime warning. Later, peeps!

MoonLandingWasFake: lol... Later, Flat!

Isaac watches the conversation unfold, a mixture of paranoia, humor, and scattered musings filling the screen. He leans closer, his fingers hovering over the keyboard, feeling like he's stumbled onto a portal of minds just as scattered as his own.

****

The chatroom goes back and forth, with hilariously outlandish claims and replies. A new person pops into the chat:

BirdGurl9: Hey all. :)

UFOHunter23: what's up Bird girl!

FlatEarthSurfer: Welcome to the madness. lol

MoonLandingWasFake: Hey hey! You missed the talk about how the moon is a giant hologram. ;).

BirdGurl9: Haha, you all are a trip. So, what's the topic today?

ElectricSheep7: I was just asking about coincidences. Ever have something happen that felt too strange to be random?

BirdGurl9: Oh, all the time. But I don't think anything is truly random, you know?

ElectricSheep7: Yeah, but how do you explain those crazy moments where it feels like the universe is messing with you? Pulling strings around you. Maybe the universe isn't real, like Phillip K Dick used to say.

BirdGurl9: I think everything is more connected than we realize. Like, there are forces we can't see that are guiding us.

We just have to be open to it. Fighting it may cause anxiety. Maybe we should be more open to be along for the ride. That ride might take us on a crazy and beautiful journey.

ElectricSheep7: Sometimes I feel like I'm in the wrong place. The wrong time or something, like in the movie **Back to the Future**.

BirdGurl9: That's interesting—maybe. I never considered that was Marty's MO, very interesting take, ElectricSheep7. You mean like you are in the wrong timeline?

FlatEarthSurfer: I love classic Philip K Dick. He always talked about another layer on top of us, which itself may not even be the real world.

ElectricSheep7: Yeah BirdGurl9... It's crazy!

BirdGurl9: We just don't always understand it right away. Sometimes, it takes time to see how everything fits together.

MndControl42: That sounds nice and all but I think it's all about control. They gotta shuffle us into a pile before the new world order takes place.

BirdGurl9: Well, I don't know about all that, but maybe not everything is a conspiracy. Sometimes it's up to us to find meaning in things. Go along for the ride, then your world can actually become your world.

ElectricSheep7: Meaning is hard to find. In anything.

BirdGurl9: Just gotta keep your eyes and mind open.

FlatEarthSurfer: I'm with you MndControl. It's either the government, or some futuristic human civilization playing us like an arcade game lol.

ElectricSheep7: What does lol mean.

FlatEarthSurfer: LOL

ErnestGos2sht: lol

MoonLandingWasFake: LOL DOOD!

On Isaac's screen, a portal pops up:

BirdGurl9: Hi!

Accept or Decline?

Isaac clicks Accept. He is taken from The Grassy Knoll chatroom into another room with only two users. Himself and BirdGurl9.

ElectricSheep7: Hello

BirdGurl9: Hi!

Isaac, being new to the online experience, didn't know you could break out into private rooms.

ElectricSheep7: What's up BirdGurl. What's this?

BirdGurl9: It's a private instant messenger. Cool name btw

ElectricSheep7: What's btw?

BirdGurl9: By the way. Lol is (laughing out loud) btw.

ElectricSheep7: lol. I'm new to this.

BirdGurl9: I can tell. I like your name. Do Androids Dream of Electric Sheep. Philip K. Dick right? Blade Runner is one of my favorite adaptations of his.

Isaac feels his face flush in excitement.

ElectricSheep7: What you know about that? You're into sci-fi?

BirdGurl9: My best friend is my pet bird. Her name is Sarah Connor. That answer your question? ;)

ElectricSheep7: Woah! Terminator?

    BirdGurl9: Yup

Isaac has no idea who this person is or what she looks like, but he feels the pull—immediate and undeniable. It's like stepping into a memory he's never had, a déjà vu with no past. Like he was always meant to meet her.

Plus—she knows who PKD is. *Where has she been all this time?*

    BirdGurl9: So tell me about your
    synchronicities. Let's share stories.

Isaac grins. His fingers hover over the keyboard, frozen. It's not nerves—it's something deeper. Like a force pulling him forward, or holding him back. She's incredible. Too incredible.

He does not want to mess this up. An hour ago, he had no idea who this was; now, he is wondering if this is *her.*

    BirdGurl9: Well. Guess I'll sign off if
    you're tired.

    ElectricSheep7: No. Don't leave yet! I'm
    up. I'm just surprised, very surprised about
    this whole exchange. Let's get into it!

    BirdGurl9: Lets! btw... my name is Noa.
    What's yours?

The two go on for hours into the night, before Isaac remembers he has to wake up early to be at Grandma's. He mentions the need to sign off for sleep, but the conversation resumes for another hour before he finally does at 3 a.m.

****

Isaac lifts his heavy eyelids. Time to get up and work the earth with Grandma. Despite being tired from chatting with Noa all night, this is a must-do. He wouldn't miss this, nor does he want to.

He has to make multiple trips to get the flowers over to her house. His plan is to walk the first pallet over, start turning the soil, planting each with each trip. If he's not efficient, this job will take all day.

Isaac showers, tosses on an old T-shirt and a pair of shorts. He shoves his socked feet into a pair of retired black Nikes, scoops up the first tray of flowers, and heads down his back stairs. It's already warm and the weight of today's heat will build up brick-by-brick, trip-by-trip.

At the foot of the stairs, he spies a shopping cart carefully positioned. He didn't put it there, but how helpful this would be instead of walking back and forth to Grandma's. Isaac has three rosebushes and four trays of annuals to transport two blocks over. The air is already heavy and will only get worse.

As Isaac examines the cart, he's tentative about using it. He stands at the foot of his stairs, with the first pallet resting over the corner of the shopping cart, which is actually in good condition. It's from Cub Foods, and all of the wheels are intact, and it is clean and free of empty beer cans. He hates the thought of running off with someone's cart; it's likely used by someone in need, with very few belongings, which they intend to store and move about the neighborhood.

A raspy yet jolly voice calls out behind Isaac.

"THANK YOU, MYYYY BROTHAAAA!"

He turns and sees Oscar, the out-of-luck man from the BSV parking lot. He struts away down the alleyway, in and out of view due to the early morning shadows cast by garages and trees.

Oscar toddles away as he slowly pumps an upheld fist rhythmically. In the other hand, he's gripping a half-eaten Mc-Donald's breakfast sandwich. There must be a song playing in his head, inaudible, but it seems calm and reassuring. For some reason, Isaac hears in his own head "Wake Up" by Harold Melvin and the Blue Notes. He smirks and shakes his head. He lifts his own right fist and matches the rhythm. In his other arm, he cradles the small crate of annuals. That accidental ten-dollar gift paid off.

Yes, Isaac will accept this reciprocated gift from Oscar. He doesn't question it. Only, how would Oscar have known Isaac needed this at this very moment?

Isaac rolls the full shopping cart down Grandma's gangway. He decides to set up before going inside to get her, but as he makes it to the backyard, he finds her already turning the soil with a hoe. She is wearing a straw hat with an oversized brim.

He's never beaten her to garden day, but he keeps trying. Just like when he was ten, he's relieved to find her there. He wishes he could find Grandad leaning against a pitchfork. He doesn't take these moments for granted.

Grandma hears him rolling the cart. "Well! My goodness! Where did you get those?"

"A friend!" Isaac jokes.

Grandma hurries over. "Are those little rose bushes?" She shakes her head, smiling as she waves him off. "My goodness... you boys always take care of me."

She tilts her cheek up, and Isaac kisses it.

"Yeah! I was surprised they even had 'em. I had to go right after opening the store all last week—trying to catch the good stuff."

Grandma waves her hand again. "They never stock much anyway. You have to go out to the suburb nurseries to find this kind of quality. It was meant for you to find them."

Isaac unloads the cart as Grandma excitedly scampers back toward the garden. She steadies her hat over her silver-streaked hair, held in a ponytail, extending mid-back.

"Let's put 'em over here, baby! Against the wall by our gardenias. And you got three of them?" She claps her hands together once.

"Yeah, one for you, me, and Grandad."

Grandma's eyes mist. She pulls Isaac into a hug.

"He was always so proud of you! He would be today!" She points at the repurposed shopping cart and winks.

Isaac shakes his head. He digs the first hole in the center. "Not after dropping out—getting stuck at that video—"

Grandma cuts him off with a point of her finger. She gently replies, "Isaac—you are exactly where you are supposed to be in this world at this moment. It doesn't mean that you are supposed to be there forever." She smiles. "Your Grandad was always proud of how special you were."

Isaac protests again. "Special? Ha!"

Grandma giggles. "Yes, baby—special!"

Isaac digs into the second hole for the bushes.

Grandma continues. "Do you remember going to the drive-in with Grandad to see that movie with that Michael J. Fox boy?"

"*Back to the Future*!" Isaac pauses his shoveling, staring off as he reminisces.

"Four times! You had him take you back four times!" Grandma grins and looks up at Isaac endearingly. "We thought it was because you liked some cool car going back in time!" She twirls her finger and shakes her head. "Uh-uh! You were fascinated by the fact that the boy..."

Isaac finishes the sentence. "...Didn't feel his world was right—but he went back in time and fixed it."

Grandma slaps his forearm playfully. "Boy, don't cut off

grown folks." She giggles. "Well... that was your take on it, and a good take at that."

They both chuckle.

Isaac finishes the second hole and starts working on the third hole for the roses as he picks back up.

"I always felt like him. Alone... different, like everything is out of place..." He shrugs his shoulders. "I just can't figure out what those differences are."

Grandma grabs his wrist. He stops shoveling, plants the shovel, and rests on its handle. "I'm sorry, Grandma. I got you and Pete—that's not what I meant."

"I know, baby—I know you feel alone—because you are. You are special, and there is a special person that will erase that feeling. I don't think you have to find her—she may find you. She may crash into your world and change the face of it forever and you both will be whole. Grandma chuckles. "I like teasing you about it, and it's only because I know she is out there, and you will find her soon—if she doesn't find you first."

Isaac tongues his cheek in disbelief. "Soon, huh?"

"Very soon!"

Isaac shrugs. "We'll see!" He wonders if this mystery BirdGurl9, aka Noa, is a candidate. He starts digging the third hole for the roses, blushing slightly, which Grandma notices. She tilts her head and smirks.

"Well—that reaction was different!" she says.

"I don't know what you talking about."

He doesn't want to seem like he's acting strange or admit he's even having thoughts about this person he met online being *Her*. He also feels too embarrassed at the moment to say he may have met someone in a computer chatroom. For one, Grandma wouldn't understand. Two, he worries she may think less of someone he met online. It feels like meeting someone on one of those 1-900 adult party lines.

Grandma and Isaac plant the entire flowerbed, rosebushes included, as the sun rises higher into the sky, and the temperature rises with it. They finish it off with a cool watering from the hose. The hose gives off a strong plastic smell in the heat.

A ruckus of cheering and laughter flies in the air over the bungalow from the front. The sound of screaming children accompanies the sound of rushing water. Splashing and joyous laughter are heard from all directions. Isaac and Grandma head down the gangway to the front of the house.

The people on south Carpenter Street are all watching, celebrating as most of the neighborhood children, and even some of the adults, run in and out of the flowing deluge from an illegally opened fire hydrant. Gallons of cool water spray relief from the scorching heat. Some slowly drive their vehicles through the water for quick and free car washes. The Chicago Fire Department will come shut this all down, but after the fun is had.

Isaac grins as Virgil, an eight-year-old kid from the corner, does an impressive backflip in the flowing water. "Ha! You see that?!"

Grandma nods. She looks up at Isaac. Tears form in her eyes. She places her hand on his shoulder, then leans her face against his arm. "Yes, dear heart—that's something else, isn't it?"

****

Isaac's computer boots up. He double clicks the icon for COL— followed by the Sign In button.

The fan of the computer *burrrrrs*, accompanied by the rapid *beep-boops* of the modem dialing up. A fleeting silence makes way for the handshake sound between his computer and the COL server in New Castle, Indiana: *Beeeeep... Krssssshhhh...buzzzz...ksssshhhh...buuurrrr.*

Once the connection is established—silence. A large blue COL logo pops up center screen; it disappears and that friendly voice alerts him, "Welcome... You've got messages!"

That greeting is an instant dopamine hit. What a letdown it would be to sign on to only *Welcome*!

Isaac immediately clicks the mailbox-shaped icon in the upper left corner. It's from her: BirdGurl9. He was hoping to hear from her again. He has never had such a connection, and this is just from chatting all night; he wonders how she'd be in person.

The single message in his inbox is titled: Hey!

```
From: BirdGurl9 at 12:00PM CST


Hey handsome! I don't know what you look
like, but after last night's convo, I just
assume you are handsome. You have a handsome
brain at least lol... laughing out loud,
remember? Well anyways, I hope you got some
good sleeps and had a good time with Grandma.
I would love to reconnect at some point cuz
I feel we were connecting. I should be on
here later tonight as well, we can pick back
up on your theories about synchronicity.


Ciao,
Noa
```

One of Isaac's old-school self-made mix tapes is playing in the background: "Computer Love" by Zapp and Roger. He did not consciously play this song. He didn't time it to play now; it just happened to be next after "Misled" by Kool and the Gang. Synchronicity indeed, for those that can hear.

The song is the perfect backdrop as Isaac peers into his friends list, finding that BirdGurl9 is online. His eyes widen. He wonders if he should send an email, or maybe invite her to a private chat. He doesn't want to seem desperate. So he decides to play it cool and wait a few minutes, but an immediate harp tone rings and a PIM box pops up:

    BirdGurl9: Hey you!

    Accept or Decline?

Without a thought, Isaac's mouse darts to and clicks Accept:

    ElectricSheep7: Hey! What's up?

    BirdGurl9: Been waitin 4 u.

    ElectricSheep7: Really now?

    BirdGurl9: yup ;)

    ElectricSheep7: So—how you figure I'm handsome?

    BirdGurl9: I can tell. Maybe I'm psychic. Wooooweeewooo

    ElectricSheep7: lol

    BirdGurl9: Look at you, learning the lingo!

    ElectricSheep7: So tell me more about yourself... what do you look like... beautiful.

BirdGurl9: Stop that… I'm okay. I'm about 5'6", with a slight tan.   Light brown eyes. Funny how you call me beautiful and ask what I look like in one thought lol

ElectricSheep7: What nationality?

ElectricSheep7: Or race rather

BirdGurl9: Well… my nationality is Canadian… I don't believe in the construct of race. It just causes division. That's the only reason it exists. Would any of that affect our friendship?

ElectricSheep7: No, I guess not. Don't matter to me.

Isaac is nervous he may have insulted her with that line of questions. His gut is full of regret—they were getting along so well, connecting. Noa chimes back in:

BirdGurl9: If you're curious about how I look, let's meet.

Isaac is taken aback by this. He didn't expect her to suggest meeting. He hasn't even spoken to her on the phone, and just met her online last night. Still, something tugs at him. He quickly responds, almost involuntarily.

ElectricSheep7: Yeah! Sure, we can meet.

BirdGurl9: Good. Let's get pizza. I have

been wanting to try this place. Pequod's up north. Being from Canada, we don't have access to good pizza like you… LUCKY!

Isaac grins. He strokes his barely there mustache.

ElectricSheep7: That's right… you are living in Chicago at the moment. cool… when you trying to meet up?

BirdGurl9: Lets meet tomorrow! At the Fullerton L station? It's public so you can feel safe.

ElectricSheep7: Whatever. lol

Part Two

Chapter Three

Isaac arrives at the Fullerton 'L' stop. He steps off the train onto the damp platform, slick from a brief rain shower. Noa hasn't arrived yet—or at least, he doesn't think she has. She isn't late. Still, his nerves insist this meeting is the only thing that matters today, and they convinced him to show up an hour early.

He has some idea what she looks like from their COL chats, but she's been deliberately vague about her ethnicity. To her, it's no big deal, but in his world, race feels like a constant lens people see through. Is Canada really that progressive? Could race truly matter less where she's from? He's never even met anyone from Northern Lights, Canada, before, and the thought intrigues him as much as it baffles him. He's traveled to Louisiana plenty of times but never crossed the U.S. border.

Forty-five minutes crawl by before the rattle of an approaching 'L' train pulls him from his thoughts. The train screeches to a halt, but as he scans the windows, there's no sign of Noa. His hand moves to his Walkman, flipping the cassette door open and closed with a soft click-click. His right leg bounces with restless energy, anticipation pushing him closer to the edge of his seat—or in this case, the platform bench.

The train screeches to a stop. The doors facing the platform frame the faces of passengers in waiting. Almost violently, the doors open. Noa Gayle steps off among a squall of other riders—one black Doc Marten boot at a time steps onto the wide blue painted line of the platform.

She walks toward Isaac as if she knows him. Isaac's breath pauses momentarily; despite never seeing her before, he recognizes her. He whispers to himself. "Damn! That's... her!"

He is an artist in awe of a masterpiece fashioned by another hand. Isaac loves jazz because of the melodic complexity. Noa Gayle approaches as a melody: Miles Davis' "Générique."

She is wearing a solid off-white linen pinafore dress, which falls right above her knees. The breeze teases a delicate but curved figure as the garment tenses against her narrow waist. She has an alluring gait, accentuated by her perfectly curved hips—but not so undulatory that she appears to be attention-seeking.

Isaac's gaze doesn't linger on her body—those eyes of hers command him back. They are a rich brown, similar to an expensive cognac, unlike any pair of brown eyes he has ever seen.

She has sandy brown hair, worn in a bob cut hovering just above her delicate shoulders. Her olive skin tone radiates her already vivid aura. Faint, tiny brown freckles adorn the bridge and sides of her slightly upturned nose. One can only see the freckles when up close.

Visually, it's difficult to categorize Noa into a specific race or ethnicity—and based on her COL profile and conversations, she seems to abhor the idea anyway. Being racially ambiguous is not just how she appears; it's also a part of her worldview. Isaac still can't classify her into a race, and at this point, it doesn't matter. It never did.

She scans Isaac from a distance with her wide, entrancing eyes. There's a cute shyness about her, almost as if she is every bit as nervous as Isaac.

As Noa draws closer, her freckles become visible to him. The gravitational pull increases as every inch of distance is closed. As she comes within a few steps of him, she waves bashfully, and tries unsuccessfully to restrain a grin.

"Isaac?" she asks.

He loses his cool internally. The question registers, but it takes his brain a few seconds to remember his own name.

"Yeah," he rasps.

Isaac gives a brief, unheard scolding to his vocal cords and tongue for not following instructions. This scolding may be unheard, but seen in his demeanor—*Dammit!* He wants a do-over.

Noa giggles—blushes. She appears just as nervous, but her confidence appears to get an ever-so-slight bump in reassurance from Isaac's visible jitters.

He reattempts his reply, this time he taps his usual near-confidence. "Yeah—yeah. Isaac is me." Not quite near-confident.

"Well, hello, Isaac—I'm Noa!" She extends her feather-soft right hand toward him. Before he registers Noa's handshake offer, Isaac's trajectory was to come in for a hug. He felt they had reached at least side-hug status from the long chats on COL; still, status is nebulous.

They both awkwardly cycle between hug versus shake. They bask in the same awkwardness—but it feels right.

Isaac takes the leap and goes in for the hug, wrapping his arms carefully around her torso. She leans right into the hug, giggling softly. Noa takes a deep inhalation as she pulls herself up into him a little tighter—standing tiptoed as she presses her neck against his, arms encircling. She then exhales with, "Hi, Isaac."

They hold this hug for a few moments—atypical for what is virtually a blind date. Just before release, they both take a slow, deep breath—and mutually giggle.

Isaac takes in her scent, which pairs cosmically with Noa Gayle and is the perfect accompaniment to the warm embrace he is experiencing. Not overpowering in the slightest. Although Isaac lacks expertise in fragrances, he detects gardenia and citrus, softened by subtle vanilla.

Noa steps back and emphatically looks him up and down. "Wow, exactly how I expected you to look—handsome."

Isaac man-blushes, tries to think of a smooth reply, but comes up with, "Exactly, huh?"

She rubs her hands together playfully. "Almost exactly. How's that?" Noa says, "Just a hunch." She pulls at his Walkman. "Whatcha listening to?"

"Ah... just some Miles Davis."

Noa nods, smirks. "Okay—Okay... An old soul. I like that!"

Her sandy-streaked brown hair brushes her shoulders as they start their walk toward the stairs of the 'L' stop. From here, they will take a short walk to the bus stop and ride the 74 bus over to Pequod's Pizza on Clyborn.

Noa has been in Chicago over the last three months since starting her position at Lincoln Park Zoo but has never had deep-dish pizza and is excited.

Isaac, in gentleman form, allows Noa to board the bus ahead of him. She climbs the steps, and of course he takes an opportunity to check out the remainder of her.

So far, Isaac is enamored by everything about Noa; there's not a blip of anything off-putting yet. Her hair gracefully sways over the olive skin of her neck, which curves upward to her perfect earlobes, studded with emerald earrings.

Isaac presents his paper transfer ticket to the bus driver, who clips it with a handheld punch and hands it back. Isaac also drops two tokens in the slot to cover Noa's fare. She replies, "Thank you, handsome."

"Don't mention it—radiance!" Smooth, he thinks.

Isaac smirks, and that near-confident swagger builds. He gestures to her to go ahead and she leads them to an empty row. She slides in first by the window, grasping the small handbag slung over her shoulder. Isaac sits beside her as the bus roars off in a jolt.

Isaac tries to take a discreet peek over at Noa, as her head turns toward his. Those brown eyes catch him. She blushes, giggles softly, then turns her head to look out of the window—her attention is still clearly on him.

As Isaac sees her smile in a subtle reflection in the bus window, he nods his head in a perfunctory gesture to himself. *This feels right!*

****

Isaac and Noa arrive at Pequod's Pizza after a brisk walk from the bus stop, the kind that makes the city feel alive. As they approach the restaurant, a green monk parakeet flutters down onto the sidewalk in front of them. The bird tilts its head, looking up at Noa with an expression that seems almost sentient, as though it's saying hello.

Noa smiles, crouching slightly as she greets it with a smile and a cutesy high-pitched tone. "Hey, you!"

The bird regards her for a moment longer, then flaps its wings and takes off, disappearing into the canopy of streetlights above. Isaac watches the exchange, his brow furrowing slightly. He finds the interaction peculiar—not just the way Noa spoke to the bird as if it might respond, but the bird itself.

He's never seen monk parakeets in this part of the city. They're typically found farther south, near Hyde Park or along the Skyway, where their colonies thrive despite Chicago's brutal winters. Originally from Argentina, the birds are strangers here, transplants in a world so unlike their own—yet they survive, even flourish.

The thought lingers as they approach the restaurant entrance, but Isaac lets it go, deciding not to ask about the odd encounter.

A haze of cigarette smoke greets them at the door. Two men

stand just outside, their conversation halting as they notice the couple approaching. Each holds a cigarette, the ends glowing faintly in the evening air. One man flicks ash to the ground before popping his square back between his lips, while the other steps forward to hold the glass door open.

"Thanks, man," Isaac says with a polite nod, gesturing for Noa to go first.

She floats past the threshold with her characteristic ease, her hair blowing slightly as she steps inside. Isaac follows close behind, a small sense of pride swelling as he trails his alluring date.

Pequod's is dimly lit, exuding a warm, intimate vibe. A neon gray-blue whale glows faintly on the left-hand wall near the entrance, casting a soft, almost aquatic light over the surrounding space. The whale, Pequod's logo, is a clever nod to Moby Dick—an unmissable centerpiece that quietly anchors the room's charm.

The aroma of freshly baked pizza envelops Isaac, and his stomach churns in anticipation. The narrow walkway ahead is bordered by a row of booths on the right, each filled with patrons, and a lively bar on the left. The low hum of clinking glasses and overlapping voices creates a symphony of cozy chaos, one that feels quintessentially Chicago.

As they approach the hostess counter, a young woman greets them with a toothy grin that seems almost too wide for her face. "Hi there! Aren't you two just adorable?" she says brightly. "I'm Katie," she continues, her voice warm and slightly singsong. "Would you like a booth, bar, or table?"

Isaac raises two fingers, casually gesturing toward the booths.

Katie's grin widens even further as she pulls her hair into a ponytail, revealing the shaved and tattooed sides of her head. "Got it!" she chirps, grabbing two menus from a neatly stacked pile. With a playful twinkle in her eye, she adds, "Well, what are you waiting for? Come with me if you want to eat!"

She waves them forward with an exaggerated flourish, her energy as infectious as the aroma of the food waiting for them.

Katie's style is striking—rarely seen, but somehow perfect for her. She radiates confidence, her presence blending edge and warmth in equal measure. Her pigeon-toed strut as she leads the couple down the walkway only adds to her unique charm.

The place feels like Chicago in a way only Chicagoans understand. It's like stepping into the cozy, slightly chaotic home of an extroverted aunt who hosts parties every weekend; family and friends—each with distinct personalities—intermingling in laughter and lively chatter.

Friendly outbursts punctuate the air, cutting through the cacophony of overlapping conversations. It's loud, but it feels like community, like a shared experience in every sense of the word.

"Hand in My Pocket" by Alanis Morissette plays in the background, its jangly optimism weaving seamlessly into the room's atmosphere. The tables are full, the barstools occupied, and waitstaff bustle from one end of the restaurant to the other, balancing trays of deep-dish pizza and pitchers of soda. For a Tuesday night, the place is buzzing—alive with vibrant, unmistakable Chicago charm.

Noa peers around the restaurant, looking up and down. She examines the people with the smile of a child watching other kids playing at the park. It's as if she is excitedly exploring a distant planet for the first time. Isaac finds this strange but adorable.

"No pizza pubs in Canada?" Isaac snickers, but displays a raised brow.

"What—ever!" She playfully and gently slaps his shoulder.

They slide into a mid-row booth, sitting across from

each other. The varnished wood tabletop reflects their faces as they take each other in. Isaac is impressed. Maybe Noa is too.

They sit in silence for a moment, still looking into each other's eyes until the waitress, who is actually Katie again, asks, "You guys still figuring things out? With the food!" She winks at Noa. "I think the rest is already figured out."

Isaac, still looking into Noa's eyes, replies, "Nah, we're ready." He orders while looking for Noa's approval. "Ten-inch pan? Mushroom and spinach, right?"

Noa grins, impressed at his memory that she is vegetarian. This was a brief mention during one of their online chats. Isaac winks in debonaire fashion and says, "My favorite!"

Katie grins. "Anything besides water?"

"Water's fine—oh, and girl, I love your look!" Noa says, flashing a smile.

Katie's grin widens. "Thanks, girl!"

You can tell she doesn't get many compliments—this made her day. Noa scans Katie as if she has never seen a tattooed blonde with gauged ears and an undercut hairstyle. A stark difference these two ladies are. Both are beautiful, but Isaac's attention is squarely on Noa.

Isaac orders. "Orange pop?"

Katie winks and nods. "I'll be right back with your slice—handsome!"

Noa snickers as Katie walks away. "I was right, wasn't I? Handsome!"

"Why vegetarian?" Isaac says as he blushes.

"I love my critters!"

Isaac keeps returning to Noa's eyes. It's not just their golden-brown hue tinged with subtle specks of red—it's the life in them. The soul. Isaac doesn't mind being lost there. At the risk of appearing creepy or weird, he decides to stay lost a little longer.

Noa holds eye contact a bit longer as well. Her head involuntarily tilts slightly—as her full, soft lips crease at the corners. She can't restrain the smile that follows, so she looks away for a split second—then returns her gaze to his face—followed by another smile that she covers with her hand.

Isaac is smitten by her beauty. He wonders if she is out of his league. He may be a tall and handsome twenty-five year old, but he hasn't dated or even spoken to a woman this *fine* before. What intrigues him further is that Noa doesn't seem to realize her own beauty and carries herself in a very down-to-earth manner.

He focuses his attention to her lips, then scans upward, noticing her perfectly shaped eyebrows. Down—their eyes meet again. He smirks, and Noa's eyes squint as she blushes. She says playfully, "Be careful with that!"

"With what!" Isaac sniggers.

"With that look—that look is dangerous!"

"I don't know what you talkin' about," Isaac says, now flattered. He looks down momentarily, then back at her.

Noa sighs. "That right there. When you look at me like that—you remind me of someone, that's all."

A tiny sizzle of jealousy creeps into Isaac's psyche. He wonders if she is talking about a past relationship. They never delved into each other's love lives. He chooses not to pry and leaves it at that. He doesn't want to invite internal comparisons in his own mind. This insecurity, though not heavy, still feels disproportionate for a first date, but this may be love at first sight.

Isaac takes a solid breath and asks, "So. It's over?"

Noa looks down at her palms, examines and flips them over. She looks up at Isaac. "Yes—yes, it's over."

"My bad! I'm sorry—I shouldn't have!" He feels a flash of remorse over his unintentional interrogation.

Noa holds her right hand up to reassure Isaac. "It's okay. It's a fair question." Using the same hand, she dabs a tear before it breaks free from the corner of her eye.

"Fuck. I'm sorry, Noa. For real, though!" He looks around. "Noa. I mean... shit!"

"It's okay! Isaac— It's okay!" she says with moistened eyes.

Katie returns with their ten-inch pan pizza. The deep-dish pie is carried with a clamp on the pan's edge, then placed onto a wood board at their table. Steam dances from the red-sauce-smothered surface.

Katie scoops out a slice and places it onto Noa's plate first, skimming the string of melted cheese with the spatula. Red sauce drips into the pan underneath. She places Noa's pizza in front of her, then does the same for Isaac—who politely thanks her with eye contact.

Noa smiles at Isaac's manners. Her head tilts as she braces her chin on her palm, and affectionately watches Isaac open his napkin and place it on his lap.

She turns her attention to her plate and follows suit. She gently unfolds her napkin and places it daintily on her lap. She gazes again at Isaac, who waits for her to taste first. She micro-frowns, not out of anger but stronger attraction at his manners. She picks up her fork and knife and starts to cut into the thick pan pizza. She smiles. "Down the hatch, right?"

After taking a bite of the piping hot pizza, Noa's eyes widen in amazement. She says with a hot-potato voice, "Oh! My—goodness!" She tries to cool the hot cheese sitting centrally on her tongue by sucking air in. It's hot, but her eyes close as she chews slowly. "This is the best thing ever!" Noa exclaims.

She cuts another bite of the pie. This time, she can manage the temperature. She closes her eyes again as she savors every cheesy morsel and the rich red sauce layered on a very well-done crust. She has never had anything like this.

****

It's now dark outside. Noa and Isaac exit Pequod's onto Clyborn Avenue. The smell of car exhaust replaces the smell of baking burnt-cheese crust. The music in the restaurant, "Tell Me" by Groove Theory, is drowned out as the door closes. Isaac holds a box of extra slices they had left over after they stuffed themselves full.

Isaac lets Noa walk out first, and she slings her small purse over her shoulder and across her chest. Her sandy-brown wavy bob-cut hair brushes against her nape from the slight air gradient moving from inside to outdoors.

Isaac eases the door shut behind him, his movements deliberate, his back turned to Noa, who's already outside, just ahead. When he finally turns, she's facing him. Their eyes meet, and her smirk ignites something deep within him. It's subtle but charged, as if her expression says: *I like you.* Maybe even asks: *Do you like me?* Isaac can't be sure, but it's what he hopes she's thinking. Time to escort the lovely woman home.

Isaac offers a small, gentlemanly wave, motioning for Noa to take the lead. She smiles, her gaze dipping shyly to the ground before she begins walking at an unhurried pace.

Their conversation flows easily as they delve into the future of computers and the internet, each exchanging ideas and theories with an almost childlike curiosity.

Isaac chuckles, his hands casually tucked into his pockets as they walk. "I wonder how long the internet will be a thing. Who knows, right? It could just be some fad. Honestly, other than the chats, it's nothing like I thought it'd be." He lets out a short laugh, shaking his head.

Noa turns her gaze toward him, watching the way his expression shifts as he strolls. She appears lost in thought. There's a spark of amusement in her eyes, but something softer too.

She shrugs lightly, her tone playful. "You never know. I think it's gonna be one of the most important tools people use. Who knows? Your grandma might order meals online someday!"

Isaac's face twists into a skeptical micro-frown. "I don't see how. It's pretty whack right now! You imagine it being all grand, full of information at the click of a button—bam. Nah, it ain't that at all!" He gestures vaguely, his tone laced with doubt.

Noa shakes her head, a playful grin spreading across her face. "It'll get better," she says with quiet confidence. "One day, it might be a network of all things—all places." She pauses, her grin widening as she teases, "All times."

Isaac glances over at her, caught between amusement and disbelief. "All times? You're wild," he mutters, but her certainty stirs something—just enough to make him wonder if she might be right.

He feels Noa's left hand brush lightly against the back of his right as they walk. The first time, he dismisses it as accidental. The second, he wonders. By the third, each touch punctuating her episodic stutters as she explains her thoughts on the internet, he's sure it's deliberate.

Isaac gently scoops her delicate hand into his own. The action halts her mid-sentence, her words suspended. She glances up at him, a small smile curling at the corner of her mouth.

His hands are warm—too warm, damp with sweat. He wonders if this exposes his nerves. Noa's fingers curl slightly around his, and her touch feels reassuring.

The slowed pace of walking purposefully prolongs the journey home. Isaac doesn't want the night to end—but her apartment is only a few steps away. She points up at her apartment window, from which a warm light pours out. "Well—that's me right there."

Isaac glances up at the window, where movement inside catches his eye. "Somebody home? Wait—is that a bird?"

Noa giggles. "Nobody's home—well, not a human. That's Sarah Connor, my monk parakeet. She's been with me a long time—that's my kick-ass girl that will rise up against the machines!"

Isaac smiles and nods. "That's right. I remember you mentioning her."

That feeling hits him again. The eerie sense of synchronicity rushes through his circuitry, like an invisible thread pulling him toward something unseen, untethering him from what is.

Isaac recognizes the monk parakeet immediately. It's the same type of bird they saw earlier tonight—rare to spot, yet somehow, he encounters two in a single evening. One of them is her pet.

His mind lingers on the connection, mentally tying this quirky Canadian woman to the exotic birds at Lincoln Park Zoo. The sheer improbability of it renders him visibly pensive—not uneasy, but thoughtful.

Noa giggles, catching his expression. "You okay?"

"Yeah, I'm good!" He shrugs, a half-smile forming. "Just thinking about the bird thing. What are the odds, right? That—"

"Well... I had a nice time!" Noa interrupts, her voice rising with nervous cheer. She cringes inwardly at the cliché, knowing it punctuates their arrival at her place—and the end of their night.

Isaac micro-frowns, starting to ask, "See you ag—?"

She cuts him off again with a playful grin. "Tomorrow morning, handsome—11 a.m.!"

"O—kay... tomorrow?" Isaac's eyes widen, then he nervously looks down. He is virtually broke after this date. His recent computer purchase has set him back. But it's okay—it seems to be paying off in an unexpected way. Without it, he wouldn't have met her. So far, he feels the gravity of Noa Gayle. She just may be *Her*. But Isaac anxiously asks himself, *Where am I going to take her with thirteen duckets?*

Noa scans Isaac's face and his attempt to hide his embarrassment. "My treat!" she says as she chases his eyes up with her own.

"Nah, I got—"

"My treat, handsome! I insist!"

Isaac accepts, half relieved on the inside. "Aight, Tomorrow morning—11 a.m.?"

"Can you meet me at Navy Pier? I want to do one of those boat tours. Then you can show me around. I haven't explored much since I got here two months ago."

"Of course! Tomorrow—11 a.m.!" Isaac restates.

Noa turns slowly toward her building. She breaks eye contact, then reestablishes it as she still holds his right hand. Isaac tightens his grip slightly and asks, "Hug?"

She pulls herself toward him and stretches up to his neck on tiptoes. Isaac wraps his arms around her waist as she pulls up into his chest. They both inhale deeply. Noa's eyes close as she takes in his scent. Like the look she nearly swooned over, this *reminds* her of someone.

As they slowly release from this very intimate hug, Noa's right cheek brushes Isaac's. Isaac feels her rose-petal lips approaching from the side. Her feather-soft skin presses more firmly against Isaac's face. He feels her warm breath on his neck as well. This is spine-tingling. This is familiar.

They both stop here for a moment, feeling each other's chest move back and forth. Just a few more centimeters and her soft lips will be pressed against his. Noa hugs him tightly again, exiting the trajectory of that near kiss. She says, "Goodnight—handsome!"

"Goodnight—beautiful."

Noa turns away, smiling. She says, "Wow! See you tomorrow." She walks away, fanning her face. She then playfully spins around and giggles. "Hey, Isaac!"

Isaac lifts his eyebrow, barely seen under the amber street-lights. "Yeah, Noa?"

"It's our world! We can do whatever we want!"

She giggles as she twirls around and walks to her door.

Isaac waits for safe entry. She slides a silver key into the brass lock on the outer apartment door. Once inside, Isaac watches her through the glass door as she ascends the stairs to her second-floor apartment. He collects himself and thinks, *Wooo!*

As his stride down Southport Avenue begins, Isaac wonders, *Why did she come in on the northbound Red Line when she lives here in Lincoln Park?* His pensive brain starts up again.

Isaac pulls his orange foam headphones over his fro and ears. The soft pads squeeze his ears gently and the ambient noise is lessened—but still audible. He starts to press play on his cassette, but instead flicks the switch to radio, which is already tuned to 107.5 FM, WGCI. The song playing is Blackstreet's "Before I Let You Go."

Wow! This is going to happen, and the word 'synchronicity' will be worn out. Apologies in advance.

****

Noa opens the door to her one-bedroom apartment. She hangs her purse on the doorknob as she closes the front door. She leans against the door momentarily, then walks over a rustic-appearing tan jute rug toward Sarah Connor's perch stand at the front window.

Noa strokes Sarah Connor's tiny green head as the bird tilts it to look into her eyes. Noa looks out of her window to watch Isaac slowly walk away in the distance down her residential street, towards the Red Line L. She says, "It's our world."

Sarah Connor makes happy trilling sounds, bouncing playfully.

****

Isaac enters his apartment. With a flick of the bronze-toned wall switch, warm white incandescent bulbs illuminate his elaborate mural. He walks over to his console underneath. He places an old LP on the turntable, then carefully lowers the needle. A pop and sizzle precedes Lee Morgan's version of "Since I Fell for You."

He lies back in bed, grabbing his copy of *Behold a Pale Horse*, a conspiracy book written by Milton William Cooper. Isaac reads anything and everything he can to find answers about his confusing existence, but right now he can't concentrate. He tosses the book to the side and stares up at his mural, specifically, the section with the silhouettes lying in the empty green meadow. The sun is now painted in scorching orange, beautifully contrasting the multicolored coronae and tendrils. He added this coloration prior to leaving for his date today. After said date, he sees the mural in a different light but can't put his finger on it.

Maybe the answers are coming. Perhaps Noa Gayle, mysterious and beautiful, holds them in her cosmic eyes. Maybe Noa is *Her*, the person Grandma predicts will bring his meaning.

Now Isaac must get out of his shift tomorrow, because he has his second date tomorrow morning. No time to build himself back up, mentally work through his bumbles to avoid them again. No, the second date is in less than twelve hours.

Using his two-toned gray plastic cordless phone, he calls Ron at home. He makes up an excuse so he can get out of tomorrow's shift. He knows the sooner he gets through to Ron, the better the chance he can get the coverage before someone else needs him to cover at one of the other stores.

Ron answers after three rings. Isaac reluctantly uses the excuse that Grandma has an emergency tonight. He is nervous and nearly hangs up. It's late and he already feels guilty as-is.

"You're one for favors these days, aren'cha?" Ron pauses. "Shit—I'm sorry, Ike." Pauses. "Is she going to be okay? What happened?"

Isaac is disgusted with himself; he closes his eyes. He refuses to put the bad juju on her by making up something too serious. He fidgets his fingers, his right leg bounces.

"Yeah! I don't want to go into too many details, but it's an emergency."

Ron pauses again momentarily, then replies. "Sure, Ike—I'll cover. I'll have to leave one of the regular clerks in charge alone at the Northside store." He sighs. "She can handle it!"

"Thanks, Ron. I owe you!"

"Don't mention it. Take care of your grandmother. Don't worry about the shift right now, but you still owe me an extra one after the advance. We'll settle up later. Goodnight, Ike."

"Later, Ron."

Click—buzzzzzz.

Isaac holds the phone against his temple, listening to the dial tone for a moment. This gripes Isaac's stomach, more than he expected.

After a bit, a swarm of butterflies eclipse his guilt when he thinks about Noa. Imagining a kiss from her soft lips silences his conscience. Not that he's expecting one, but he is hopeful.

Isaac tosses his phone next to him in bed and clicks the switch on his nightstand lamp, turning the room a dark gray. The sloped ceiling mural is still visible from peeks of light from the streetlights, which sneak through the slits of his mini-blinds.

This piece of his is vibrant, colorful, and complex. He doesn't see it this way, but it's a vision to behold. In the right mindset, one might imagine themselves climbing directly into it. He sometimes imagines himself lying in that meadow, hearing the breeze blowing through distant trees just prior to feeling it. These thoughts calm him and help him sleep; it's the closest thing to a dream his mind can produce.

Isaac has been fascinated with painting murals since his teenage years and idolizes Gregory Spain, a famous artist who got his start painting full murals guerrilla-style in the eighties here in Chicago.

Usually, Spain's murals are whimsical and fun, but he suggested in a magazine article that there are hidden meanings behind each, his unconscious mind trying to speak out with a voice he can't produce. There is an urban legend of a secret mural painted by Spain somewhere in Chicago—its location kept hidden for unknown reasons.

Isaac himself is trying to do that with his visions through these paintings. The only problem is, he doesn't know the meanings, and after working on this one for months, he still doesn't even have a clue.

As Isaac closes his eyes, he swears his eyelids are lit from the outside by the sun in the mural, but only for a brief second. He opens his eyes to see the painting unchanged, then writes it off as a hypnogogic hallucination. He finally dozes off.

****

Tuesday morning. Isaac's alarm clock screeches at 8 a.m., jolting him from his dreamless slumber. Damn, he thinks, finding himself drenched in sweat. His window AC unit was not blowing cool air overnight. He peels his white tank-top forward, away from his toned chest, as he swings his legs over the side of the bed. He feels chilled until he peels the clinging shirt over his head, a more difficult mission than it seems.

Isaac slings the heavy, wet shirt over his table chair and realizes he has to get himself going. Taking the Red Line downtown, then walking over to the lakefront will take some time.

He doesn't want to lose a second of staring into Noa's eyes. They are otherworldly, and worthy of the hyperbole. Mesmerizing.

He turns on the radio for background music. 107.5 WGCI, of course. The song queuing up is Mint Condition's "Breakin' My Heart." *Of course.*

Isaac brushes his teeth, then stretches as he walks toward his two-level refrigerator. He grabs a bottle of Nourish, a nutritional supplement drink. It provides high levels of protein, as well as electrolytes. It's breakfast for Isaac this morning, and on most other mornings. He usually works the opening shift at BSV, so he would rather have something quick to grab instead of a full breakfast. He wants something quick now as well.

****

Dressed, Isaac starts his walk at a hurried pace. This trip will take at least an hour, so he has to get going. Thankfully, he approaches the eastbound 87th Street stop at 9:45 a.m. Of course, the CTA bus approaches him as he gets there.

As he dials through his Walkman's radio tuner, he passes through the station identification for WNUA 95.5, which is a pleasant female voice singing and sounds like "W-N-U-Ayyy Ninety-Five point Fiiiiiive."

Isaac finds this identification calming, always has, but he can't stand the smooth jazz usually played on the station. He loves jazz, but can do without its annoying little brother. This should be reserved for elevators and department stores.

The hulking blue-and-red-striped bus squeals to a stop in front of Isaac. He sees a pair of familiar eyes staring through the closed glass doors. They catch his eyes.

His breath pauses as the doors flap open. Noa is there—wearing a half-smirk and biting the corner of her lower lip. The rushing cool air blows her hair forward.

Those butterflies stir up in Isaac's mid-section, and his spine, and his head. He feels weightless, held afloat by the euphoric aura extending outward from her petite body.

Isaac momentarily wonders why she was on the eastbound 87th Street bus coming from Lincoln Park; it should be the other way around. Then again, *why is she here at all?* He is also mystified that she arrives just as he was about to board the bus, the exact bus. He wants to write this off as one of his usual synchronous moments, but no, this is different.

It takes a moment for Noa's scent to reach his consciousness. Other than his sight, the surge of electricity from beholding her has knocked his other senses offline.

She is wearing a sleeveless linen dress with thin shoulder straps. This dress has a different build but is a bright orange and appears just as breezy as the one worn last night. There are lines of color streaking across the sloped chest-line, which reveals a perked cleavage. She is wearing a pair of braided hemp open-toed sandals.

Isaac is still stunned by this moment. She steps off of the bus, and he stands speechless. He forgets they need to catch that same bus for the Red Line and Navy Pier. It revs away, leaving a faint blue cloud of exhaust behind.

Isaac raises his arm to signal the driver to stop—but Noa gently grabs his arm. "No—it's okay!"

"I thought you wanted to do the boat tour?"

"No, I changed my mind." She smirks. "Good morning, handsome."

"Good morning, celestial being!" He feels this is less cliché than beautiful.

"Wow—Smooth, you are."

Isaac lifts his eyebrow. "Okay, Yoda!" He snickers. "Whatchoo wanna get into?"

Noa bites her bottom lip gently and smiles. "It's our

world, Isaac. We can do whatever we want. You weren't paying attention in class, handsome."

"Ahhh—you got jokes!" He looks around. "You kinda caught me off-guard."

"I *grok*..." She winks. "...but I wanted to keep you on your toes."

Her *Stranger in a Strange Land* reference impresses Isaac, and he feels a sense that it's more relevant than a playful retort.

"Hold up! You gon' just hit me with an 'I *grok*' like that?"

Noa giggles as she looks around at the littered corners of 87th Street, at the small Mexican restaurant on the northeast corner, the blue-and-red neon *ESP Reader and Advisor* sign in the window of the bottom apartment in the neighboring building. She peers at the abandoned gas station on the opposite corner, and down west 87th Street.

A pensive expression slowly develops on Isaac's face as he tries to conjure a shotgun itinerary.

Noa reaches for Isaac's pinky with her own. "I wanna get to know you, Isaac. Show me your world. Maybe I'll show you mine someday."

There's a plan. Let's show her Isaac. His limited world of sci-fi, jazz, Big Shoulders Video, Tommy's Barbershop, and maybe his apartment. Too soon for the apartment. *Don't even go there*, Isaac thinks. Actually, that's the furthest thing from his mind right now. He wants to get to know Noa Gayle as well, more than anything. He hasn't had this much excitement over a person or thing in some time.

Noa stands there—waiting and looking directly into Isaac's eyes with a playful grin. She intermittently bites her lower lip. It's adorable on her and doesn't appear contrived. As she does this, her eyes dart to Isaac's lips—then back to his eyes. Her eyes with their super-bright whites and cognac-brown irises dilate, peering deeply into him. Her hemp braided sandal is tensed from her standing on the edge of her right foot.

Isaac says near-confidently, "Okay! Let's go!" He challenges her hypnotic eyes with his own gaze.

She breaks her stare, backs down. Her voice lowers to a whisper, "Whoa. I told you about that look. You are starting something you can't finish!"

The two walk east on 87th Street. Isaac's pensive expression returns as he looks over at Noa. He is confused that this Canadian native, in Chicago for three months, has this deep knowledge of the city. It's not like she was up all night studying CTA map pamphlets. "Soooo–how'd you know where and when to pull that stunt?"

Noa titters. "I know a thing or two, handsome!" She disarms him. "Oooh! Can we get ice cream too?"

****

Isaac walks Noa through Gresham, leading her to Foster Park. The park is mostly empty except for a few kids playing basketball. When their ball rolls her way, Noa picks it up with a playful grin and lines up a shot. She drains it effortlessly.

"Can I get one more?" she asks, holding up a single finger.

"WHOAAAA!" one boy shouts, scrambling to rebound the ball. He bounces it back to her, and she sinks another long-distance shot–nothing but net.

She keeps going, sinking four shots in total, each one from beyond the three-point line. The boys erupt with excitement after every basket.

With her final shot, she leaves her right hand held high in the air. "Follow-through, boys! Always follow through!"

Isaac can't help but smile, impressed. But a seed of curiosity about Noa begins to sprout in his mind.

As they stroll further into the park, the kids argue loudly

over which one of them she liked best. "Not you, Telly! You a scrub!" the most boisterous boy taunts the quietest one.

Noa stops, turns back, and stops in front of Telly. She leans in and plants a quick kiss on his forehead, whispering, "It's your world."

Telly's light-brown face turns crimson as he looks back at his envious friends with a triumphant grin.

The date continues as Isaac and Noa leave the park and walk back to 87th Street. They catch a westbound bus toward Western Avenue, then take a short stroll to The Original Rainbow Cone.

At eighty-seven degrees Fahrenheit, it's not a terrible value, but the sixty-seven percent humidity makes it worse. Isaac feels sticky and uncomfortable. Noa, however, seems completely unaffected—not a single bead of sweat visible on her skin.

They emerge from the shop with matching cones, each stacked with rectangular slices of vibrant, multiflavored ice cream. It looks like a handheld rainbow and tastes just the same. They settle onto a small bench outside, sitting close, savoring their treat as the humid afternoon hums around them.

"Aren't you hot?" Isaac asks, wiping his forehead with the back of his hand.

"Nope. I love the heat. Being from Canada, I'll take it any day." She takes another lick of her cone, her eyes lighting up with excitement. "Oooh, you know where I want to go? The ocean. I want to see dolphins, watch their fins break the water. That's my wannabe happy place."

Her gaze drifts into the distance, cut short by the modest view of the country club grounds across the street from Rainbow Cone. Still, her expression suggests she's seeing something far beyond—a limitless expanse of blue waves and playful fins dancing in the sunlight.

"I've never actually seen an ocean before, not in person,"

she says, her voice softened, carrying a hint of wistfulness.

Noa takes bites of ice cream in between talking about her zookeeper work at Lincoln Park Zoo and her love of birds, when another monk parakeet appears, here in the Beverly neighborhood, where they are rarely seen. It lands on her outstretched forearm as if she were a fairytale princess.

"Hi, precious!" she says as the bird shimmies side to side excitedly.

Isaac winces in surprise, leaning back slightly. "Okay! You wanna let me in on the bird thing? At least the bird thing! Zookeeper trick?"

"No tricks," Noa says with a laugh. "I just have a special relationship with these guys." She squints her eyes dramatically and rubs her hands together like a cartoon villain. "Or—maybe they're really spy drones, and we're being watched."

A micro-frown passes over Isaac's face, just for a moment. It doesn't linger long and is barely noticeable before he laughs it off. "Jokes again, huh?" Slowly, he reaches toward the bird. To his surprise, it lowers its tiny green head and closes its eyes, letting him gently pet it.

Noa wears a slight smile, but her misty eyes hint at something deeper. "They like you too, huh?" she says softly.

She winks, causing her faintly freckled nose to scrunch. Then, almost imperceptibly, she turns her head, discreetly wiping away a tear before it escapes.

The parakeet tilts its head as if acknowledging the moment, then dips down and takes flight, heading northeast. Its green feathers catch the light, shimmering as it disappears into the sky.

The pair doubles back east on their tour of Auburn-Gresham, with the brief stop at Rainbow Cone now behind them. Isaac worries, a growing knot in his stomach. Is this boring her? It's starting to feel like an overly long, glorified walk through a community he's suddenly decided is uninteresting. Lincoln Park, Andersonville—hell, even Pilsen—he can think of so many other neighborhoods that would've been better, more picturesque.

Noa doesn't seem bored. Not even close. She's fully engaged, her eyes lighting up at every detail. She comments on the way the tree canopies form an intricate tunnel above them and notices patches of wildflowers poking up defiantly through the cracks in the sidewalk.

Isaac glances at the street, littered with empty potato chip bags and shattered beer bottles. To him, it looks like a mess. But Noa's gaze makes it seem like she's strolling through a scenic nature preserve, every corner a discovery. Her enthusiasm pulls him out of his own head, even if just for a moment.

This is what she came for. She wanted to learn about Isaac, and she wants to learn quickly, it seems. She won't learn about Big Shoulders Video today, though. Isaac has to steer clear of there and Ron.

Noa stops walking, softly grabs Isaac's hand. "I wanna meet Grandma!" She pauses. "Is that cool?"

Isaac doesn't question the rapidity of her request to meet his family. "Yeah. That's cool."

This female is different, he thinks. *The birds? Finding my location? And why does she act like she's new to this planet?* Then he remembers the cute "I *grok*" moment earlier. He's smitten, and the questions swirling in his mind are not winning this shouting match.

To Grandmother's house, we go.

As they turn back toward Gresham, Isaac goes quiet. The conversation lulls, replaced by the rhythm of their steps. His mind is a whirl of thoughts, trying to piece together the puzzle of Noa. There's something about her—a familiarity and strangeness all at once—that both excites and unsettles him.

Noa seems lost in thought too, though not in the same way. Every so often, she glances at Isaac when his head is turned, studying him intently. Her eyes trace his features—his expressions, his movements—as if she's trying to memorize every detail. She looks away each time he turns back, a small, secret smile tugging at her lips.

****

Noa and Isaac climb the outdoor carpeted steps to Grandma's front door. The heavy screen door squeaks as Isaac pulls it open, then he slides his key into the lock. Before stepping in, he turns to Noa with a sheepish smile. "Give me a second. I just want to make sure she's decent, okay?"

Noa nods, her smile easy. "Of course!"

From just outside, Noa hears Isaac's muffled voice, followed by Grandma's delighted response: "Tell her to come on in here, baby! Yeah, I'm decent! Oh boy!" Grandma's voice carries warmth and excitement, the joy unmistakable.

Noa can't help but snicker softly, charmed by the exchange. She steps back slightly, taking a deep breath to steady herself as Isaac reappears at the door.

Grandma rises and walks toward the front room, her long, silky black and gray hair partially braided—an unfinished task interrupted by the couple's arrival. Noa steps forward, extending her right hand. "Hi, I'm Noa. Isaac speaks so warmly of you!"

Grandma glances at Isaac, her eyes twinkling with approval. "I knew you'd be standing here soon. And here you are. Isaac, she's so beautiful!"

Noa blushes, her cheeks warming. She quickly pivots the conversation. "Grandma, your hair is so pretty! Let me finish that for you."

Grandma waves a hand modestly. "Oh, you don't have to

do that, baby." But she doesn't protest when Noa gently gathers a loose lock of hair and starts braiding.

"So," Grandma begins, her tone curious, "how did you two find each other?" She emphasizes the word *find* with a knowing smile.

"Well," Noa starts, her hands deftly working on the braid. "I'm originally from a city called Northern Lights, up in Canada, but I'm living here now while working at Lincoln Park Zoo. I study and care for birds." She glances at Isaac with a small, nervous smirk. "Actually... we met in an internet chatroom."

Grandma pauses, tilting her head slightly. "What's that, honey?"

Isaac stiffens, his nerves kicking in. Meeting a girl online wasn't exactly the most traditional story, and he wonders if it might come across as strange.

Grandma, however, doesn't seem to mind. "Whatever that room is—you are a doll and as sweet as pie," she says with a giggle, turning her head toward Isaac.

Noa stands behind her, twisting and turning Grandma's hair within her fingers, braiding it with careful precision. She glances at Isaac, her smile warm and full, her eyes carrying a soft glimmer that makes his heart skip.

Isaac returns the smile, his nerves melting away in the moment. Grandma catches the exchange, her sharp eyes sparkling with knowing. She winks at Isaac and subtly points at Noa.

"It's *Her*..." Grandma mouths silently, with a slight nod.

***

Isaac and Noa walk into Tommy's shop later that afternoon. It's not time for his ritual Saturday cut, but Noa insisted on coming along. She wants to see everything, she'd said with a playful grin that Isaac couldn't resist.

As Noa steps in ahead of him, all eight heads in the shop swivel toward her. The room goes momentarily still, save for the rhythmic hum of clippers. Tommy himself grins wide from his station, breaking the silence. "Isaac! Boy, get on in here—and you too, young lady! I heard so much about you!"

Isaac knows Tommy is lying; his barber's attempt at being a wingman is painfully obvious. Tommy's sharp eyes do, however, linger briefly on Isaac's empty hands. He's here without his usual book—a detail that doesn't escape Tommy.

A faint whisper snakes through the shop, barely audible over the clippers. "Damn, you see that? Pound to the ground. Wooo!"

Isaac stiffens, the twinge of possessive insecurity poking him square in the chest. He trusts Tommy, but he's no stranger to the barbershop banter. He knows what gets said when the clippers buzz and the chairs spin, and now, Noa is here in the middle of it all.

Cannonball Adderly's "Mercy, Mercy, Mercy" hums softly over the radio. The tiny black-and-white TV perched precariously on Tommy's DIY shelf is muted, the screen flickering with WGN News. An un-bespectacled Tom Skilling gestures animatedly through an unheard weather forecast.

Isaac excuses himself to use the washroom, weaving toward the makeshift curtain—a navy-blue pinstriped bedsheet—hanging at the back of the shop. Noa instinctively starts to follow, but Tommy intercepts her with a quick wave of his hand.

"Girl, he don't need no help in there—not yet, at least," Tommy quips, flashing a teasing grin. "You come sit your pretty self right over here."

He points to the empty barber's chair next to his own, where he's busy cutting hair. His clippers buzz rhythmically, blending into the shop's symphony of chatter and "Mercy, Mercy, Mercy." As the only barber here, Tommy commands the room with effortless charm.

All eyes are on Noa. Before their arrival, the group had been engrossed in typical barbershop banter. Some days it's boxing, others baseball or basketball. Today, they're debating the old urban myth about whether a man can kill another by punching his nose so hard it drives bone into the brain. No one provides solid evidence—just back-and-forth arguments and increasingly absurd analogies about why it could or couldn't happen.

From the bathroom, Isaac hears bursts of laughter and commotion, followed by Noa's voice cutting through the noise. "Well, actually, the nose is mostly cartilage, and the nasal bone is far too fragile to—" He couldn't catch the rest.

Curious, he quickly washes his hands but finds no towels. Muttering under his breath, he fidgets his way out through the pinstriped bedsheet, flapping his hands dry as he steps back into the shop.

The energy in the room is different now. Noa shakes her head with a playful smile, clearly enjoying herself. She sits slightly angled in the empty chair next to Tommy, her posture relaxed as she takes in the lively conversation.

Isaac glances around, trying to piece together what just happened. From what he can gather, Noa had weighed in on their urban myth, her voice apparently convincing enough to stir both laughter and agreement. Whatever she said, it's left an impression on the room.

Essentially, Noa debunks their myth with ease, backing it up with medical jargon that sails over most of their heads. Cleon, in particular, struggles, calling cartilage "cota-lege." The sheer contrast between his fumbling and her fluency adds weight to her explanation. The shop erupts in laughter, hands gesturing wildly as the men debate even more emphatically, clearly entertained by her sharpness.

Isaac had pulled back the curtain just in time to catch the commotion. Tommy pauses mid-cut, his clippers buzzing in place as he looks at Isaac. He points at Noa with an approving nod—an unspoken seal of approval, much like Grandma's earlier blessing.

But Isaac's amusement fades when he spots Cleon. The bigger, more muscular man is standing next to Noa, smugly invading her space. His left arm rests casually around her waist.

Noa, however, doesn't flinch. She doesn't even look at Cleon. Her composure is unshaken, her focus locked on the lively conversation around her. It's as if Cleon doesn't exist, which only makes Isaac's chest tighten with a pang of jealousy.

The surge of possessiveness catches Isaac off-guard—a rare feeling but unmistakable. It prods him into action. With a calm stride, he approaches Cleon and flashes a grin, his tone light but purposeful. "What's up, man?" he says, throwing Cleon a friendly high-five.

The gesture works. Cleon pulls back slightly, dropping his arm from Noa's waist, though he still lingers in her orbit. Isaac takes the opportunity to close the gap, stepping closer to her.

Noa notices. A subtle, surprised smirk spreads across her lips as she glances at Isaac. Without hesitation, she wraps her arm around him—a casual yet deliberate move that soothes the tension in his chest instantly.

Tommy, watching the whole exchange, breaks into a chuckle. He nods at Isaac, giving him a closed-fist dap. "There you go, son. Cleon, sit your ass down. I done told you about being disrespectful up in here!"

The shop erupts in laughter again, the tension defused, leaving Isaac standing tall and Noa comfortably by his side.

An hour passes. The late afternoon light starts to make way for the early August evening.

Tommy sweeps loose hairs into a pile as Isaac says, "Aight, Tom—we gon' head on out. See you Saturday?"

Tommy replies, "Oh yeah, we need to tame those whiskers of yours." He winks at Noa, who chortles.

Isaac says, "Oh, you both got jokes? I see you, Tommy. Be careful not to catch the rest of your fingers in them clippers." He laughs. "You can cut now, but whatchoo going to do when your hand is just a square palm, with no ability to lay down a fade, what, use your teeth?"

Tommy gives Isaac his signature sawed-off middle finger.

Noa laughs, then waves goodbye. "We'll see you Saturday, Tommy." Isaac looks at her, and back at Tommy, also surprised. He hasn't even kissed her yet—but somehow they have arrived at the *bring your girl to the shop* stage in the relationship.

Isaac blushes. "Of course. We'll... see you Saturday."

Tommy nods emphatically and snickers, waves them away. "I got you, son."

Isaac and Noa exit Tommy's shop. They stand before each other. Noa smiles at him, her eyes darting side to side. She asks, "Take me home, handsome?"

Isaac nods, and the eastbound 87th Street CTA bus approaches as he gestures to the stop outside of Tommy's shop.

****

Isaac and Noa sit side by side on the 87th Street bus, heading eastbound towards the Red Line. They sit in the same fashion as they ride the Red Line L northbound. As the L train goes into the darkness of underground, when it enters the Chicago Loop area, he looks over to see her reflection in the window as she peers into darkness. She knows he is watching—so she smiles and turns her head to look into his eyes. She reaches for his right hand, then squeezes it softly.

He feels a warm fluttery feeling take over his body. The feeling is familiar, but he can't place it. Isaac is falling. Falling toward

Noa Gayle at a constant acceleration.

She appears suddenly pensive to Isaac—as if meditating on something deeply. Something that makes her both excited but also uncertain. With a gentle touch of her right hand, she caresses her lips and the skin beneath her nose. She then places her right hand on top of Isaac's hand, already being held by her left. She smiles and lays her head on Isaac's broad right shoulder. The intoxicating scent of her hair momentarily stifles his concern.

With her head on his shoulder, Noa looks up at Isaac. "Were you surprised? That I came to you instead?"

"Yeah. How did you know where—?"

"It's our world, love; we can be where we want. I knew where you lived, and I felt a tug to come learn more about you."

"A tug? Explain," Isaac says, still slightly rattled by her unexpected presence this morning, as well as the tour of Gresham, which she seemed to take in excitedly. He would never bring a date to his neighborhood. If anything, he would have come up to her area in Lincoln Park. There are cool bars, music scenes, and walk-friendly streets. It's okay, he feels; at least now he doesn't have to feel embarrassed about his community. She seems to embrace him and it.

Noa and Isaac arrive at the Fullerton Red Line L station and exit the train together. Noa's wavy hair falls forward over her face when she looks down at her bag to see if she has everything. She grabs his hand firmly, looks him in the eye, and says, "Are you walking me home, handsome?"

Isaac says, "Yeah, of course."

The pair take a short walk from the L stop toward her apartment on Southport Avenue.

The sun has fully set at 9 p.m., and the air is about to become brisk—but it's absolutely perfect. Isaac's eyes are on Noa, rubbing her folded arms with her hands. To help comfort her, he wraps his long arms around her torso in an embrace from behind. They stop walking in this moment. Her hair smells intoxicating, and Isaac dips his head down to smell it directly. Noa takes a deep breath in, and out. She follows with, "This is nice. What's next?"

Isaac replies with a whisper, his lips now pressed against her left ear, "Yeah." This instantly makes her body tremble.

Isaac walks Noa to her apartment on Southport Avenue, as he did the night prior. He doesn't mind needing to double back home; he wants to be in her presence as much as possible.

As they arrive at her apartment, Isaac spies her bird indoors on a perch in the window. Sarah Connor walks back and forth on her perch in excitement, as she can see Noa has returned home.

There also appears to be a small flock of those monk parakeets in a tree right outside of her window. These birds are, again, uncommon outside a specific swathe over the eastern Southside. They are not native to Chicago, and no one knows exactly how they got there. They are very hardy birds, especially considering their survival in the Chicago winters for decades.

Isaac loves the vibe going in the moment, but his sense of connected-disconnection tugs at him. These have been increasing since meeting Noa, so there are questions on questions at this point. He can't let it go. *What is with these birds?* he thinks. He tries to inquire without a large shift in tone. "So, can you let me in on the trick?"

"No tricks here." She giggles. "These are my friends. I love them—they know it—and they feel safe. It's that simple."

Isaac isn't satisfied. It's not that simple. He loves plenty of things, and they don't just flock to him. Or maybe they do.

"Really? That's all there is to it?" A flicker of frustration rises. He's trying to get to know her, but she's holding back. It may seem harmless, but it nags at him. He lets it slide for now— t's early—but he hopes she'll open up. He's spent most of his life trapped in a vortex of uncertainty. The last thing he wants is for the girl of his dreams to pull him deeper into it, even if she's only being coy.

Tonight, he has the privilege of walking Noa right to her apartment. The hallway, like her place, carries the faint scent of her—gardenia and jasmine. Intoxicating.

Noa slides her key into the lock, jiggles it, and turns until the door creaks open. At once, Sarah Connor flits over and lands on her left shoulder. The grey-chested bird, with a tiny green head, nuzzles into Noa's neck. No ornithologist credentials are required to recognize the meaning: *Where have you been? I love you so, so much.*

Isaac smiles as Noa offers her finger, letting the bird step up. She scritches Sarah Connor's crown, pressing her nose to the side of the bird's face. She kisses her gently, both their eyes drifting closed.

Sarah Connor lets out a scratchy little squeak, then flutters back to her perch in front of the living room window, overlooking the front lawn and sidewalk.

Noa often leaves the television on for her when she steps out for errands. Tonight, *Wheel of Fortune* plays softly in the background, and the bird peeps whenever Vanna White turns a letter.

When Noa works at the zoo, she sometimes brings Sarah Connor along in a carrycase, settling her into a clean, spacious spare cage so she won't be alone.

Now, Noa hesitates, nervously holding something back. Then, finally, she speaks.

"I wanted to ask you about the Lincoln Park Zoo Ball. It's next month. I didn't expect an invitation—I mean, I'm just a lowly zookeeper—but somehow, I got tickets. It's a fancy shindig, full of wealthy donors and celebrity types, raising money for the animals and awareness about the challenges they face.

The idea is that the people with power will actually do something about those challenges." She exhales, almost laughing. "Honestly, I'm still shocked I got invited. Would you take me?"

"Of course!" He pauses. "I guess it's a dress-up thing?"

"Yes—it's a dress-up thing!" Noa says, giggling. "Black tie. Get a tux and be even more handsome for me?" she requests cheekily.

Isaac replies without batting an eye, "Fa-sho, I can do that. Just need to get my tux from my tailor."

Of course, Isaac doesn't own a tux. That will be something to worry about later. Right now, he is staring down the hypnotic tunnels of Noa's eyes and doesn't consider refusing.

She squeals in adorable excitement. "Good—date down, next—dress!" Her posture straightens with excitement. She asks, "Oh! What's your favorite color?"

Isaac replies, "Blue, sometimes green."

"Okay then, I shall surprise you. You like surprises?" Noa asked, raising an eyebrow.

Isaac replies with low conviction, "Yeah. I love surprises!"

Oh shit, Isaac thinks. *Playing the simp*—that's how he feels. He doesn't want to appear desperate. He tries to deepen his voice, stands taller. "Yeah. I guess I do like surprises. Depends." He shrugs.

Noa smiles. "There'll be many surprises coming, Isaac! Just stick with this girl, Noa Gayle. I'll learn ya something!"

Feeling confident from their playful exchange, Isaac laughs nervously and says, "Okay—we'll see about all that."

Noa continues, "By the way, I almost forgot. I have to go home tomorrow for a bit. I have to check and make sure all is well back there, then I'll head right back here for work, and you, handsome."

Isaac deflates. "Oh. Yeah. No doubt. I understand. So you'll be back, like, by Friday or so? I mean, Canada has got to be a hike." He stares at Noa, who returns him a sympathetic, pitiful look. This is off-putting for Isaac, because he does not want her pity. He doesn't want to come off weak or clingy, so he has no choice but to be supportive here. Even though it's a gut-punch to hear she has to suddenly leave the country.

She breaks her gaze now down to the ground. "I'm not sure. It will at least be a week, but I can't know for sure until I'm there." She asks Isaac if he can look in after Sarah Connor, her bird, while she is gone. He responds, "Fa sure! I can do that. What, just give her seeds? Talk to her?"

Noa snickers. "Come in." Isaac is tentative. She looks him in the eyes. "Come on in, it's okay!" She affixes a mellow smile and expression on her face, then heads to the kitchen. "I have a diet for her, and will give you instructions." She notices Isaac's overly attentive demeanor. "You're going to do fine. She will take care of you more than the other way around. She has always taken care of me."

Noa shows Isaac where the food is in the refrigerator. Seeing how well-prepared the bird's food is shocks him. There are fresh-cut fruits, mixed nuts, and seeds. There are also the pellets, which are her main nutrition source, and less impressive—little brownish gray things. Noa advises him to offer fresh fruit when possible. "Also, spend a little time with her if you have a moment each day. She'll love you for it—maybe I will too," she says with a wink.

Isaac thinks about his already busy week at the video store, and he also really does have to take Grandma to a doctor's appointment—this time it's true. Despite that, he wants any contact from Noa he can get, even if it's through her adorable bird.

Isaac agrees with the arrangement. Noa grins as she walks in front of him and peers up into his eyes. Her wavy bob-cut locks fall from her face to behind her ears as she presses her chest into his and tilts her head up.

He smells her; his heart pounds. Isaac can imagine her petal-soft lips pressed against his right now. She pulls him tightly. Isaac bends, places his cheek against hers.

Isaac whispers into her left ear, "Can I have a kiss?"

She trembles and arches her hips back. He notices.

Noa strokes the back of Isaac's neck with her hands, loosening the tension from their cheeks. Her head slides back to reveal her jewel-like eyes in front of his. Their noses brush at the sides.

Isaac feels her satin lips press against his, slowly increasing pressure as more of their lips come in contact. She gently parts her lips, and he tastes her sweet, prickly tongue brush against his own. Noa's brown eyes set under her olive eyelids as she closes them. He bends down, allowing her to plant her feet from her tiptoed stance, without breaking the kiss. His large hands grasp her hips as the heat increases. He feels her soft skin sliding underneath her sundress.

With mouths still in contact, her lip motion stops as she takes a slow breath—followed by a moan. She resumes her kiss and leans her chest and body into his. Isaac can feel her tremble subtly at the end of each exhalation, and her small hands press against his toned chest. Her lips stop and start again with their kiss. She whispers, "Mmm—okay."

She kisses him again, presses into him again—then her palms plant on his chest. She presses away gently. "Okay—wow—okay!" Her face appears between ecstasy and longing.

They stand before each other, her hands resting now on his upper arms. His hands gently encircle her waist.

The kiss seemed to last forever, but it was only a few moments. Noa slowly tiptoes back up to Isaac, and kisses him for another three seconds. That tongue of hers is just like a strawberry, both in taste and texture. Isaac feels himself becoming more *attentive.*

She releases Isaac's lips softly. They both look at each other again, then kiss once more. It's like they have never kissed before, and as if they'll never kiss again.

Noa slowly reaches her right hand toward his chest. She gently pushes away and whispers, "Isaac." They hug tightly, then she steps back farther into her apartment, and puts her purse on her entrance catch-all table. "Call me when you make it home?"

Isaac replies, "Yeah. Okay. Yeah—I will!"

"Promise?"

"Yeah. I promise. Unless you wanted company." *Don't push it,* he thinks.

"Good night, handsome."

"Good night—" Isaac pauses briefly to find something better than beautiful, or gorgeous, he's played them out. He's already used radiance.

"Goodnight, dream weaver!" Noa blushes. She shields her mouth, which is tight from her ear-to-ear grin.

"Hey, Isaac!"

"Yeah?"

"It's our world!" She tilts head adorably. "Goodnight, handsome!"

Isaac smiles as he pats his chest with his palm. He's unsure if she is being purposefully cryptic with this statement, or if there's some meaning that she is trying to communicate. He has no clue, but he is okay with going along for now.

Isaac steps out of the apartment and down a corridor of stairs to the first floor. Noa is looking at him from her open apartment door. She then goes inside once he exits the building. The building door closes in a low-pitched thunk. Isaac looks up from outside the building. Sarah Connor sits on a perch next to Noa and rocks back and forth on her feet.

Noa smiles at the bird, then at Isaac. Her apartment looks cozily dim from that distance. Sarah Connor does a shimmy dance as she bobs her head.

After looking down to slide a cassette into his Walkman,

Isaac looks back up–intending to initiate a wave goodbye–but Noa's apartment has gone completely dark. She and the bird are not visible.

Isaac feels a sudden sense of unease. The feeling points to someone toying with him.

He walks a short distance, then boards the Red Line L, which has an unusually low number of riders tonight. He stares from the window as the street-lit world zooms past.

He closes his eyes to think back on the night, but another one of his granular visions of the soothing female presence interrupts this. It overcomes him. The visions are still incomplete, but he feels an emotional response this time that he can't pinpoint. Sadness, longing, pain, happiness, anger–he can't isolate it, but the weight is heavy.

****

They summoned Noa for a rendezvous. She had to leave hastily–and hopes Isaac didn't notice from outside of her Northside apartment.

A black void.

All directions resound with a deep and clinical male voice.

"Noa Gayle."

Noa says, "Yes, I'm here as requested."

"You will be careful, Noa. We have discussed this–ad nauseum. We want you to experience this, enjoy your life–but understand the critical limitations we must hold on to."

"I understand, but–"

"If you continue with your risky activity, you will put yourself and SOMA at risk... I needn't say just how important you are to this mission... but you are not more important than SOMA."

"I understand. I will be careful–I can't lose him again."

"Ms. Gayle–we needn't remind you, he is not him."

Noa remains silent. Her face is not visible. Not a single photon penetrates this vast darkness.

"Are we in agreement about this mission?"

Noa replies, "Yes, sir. I'm sorry. I will be car–"

The voice interrupts. "You have to be more than careful– you must be vigilant. You must fulfill this mission, or not only will you lose what you want, but you will jeopardize many lives and the future of our planet. No singular person will take precedence over the mission of SOMA."

"I understand, but sir. May I–"

"Just be careful, Noa. We will contact you soon. Watch for further communications via your radio and ciphers, which will come more frequently as we draw closer. Patience, Ms. Gayle."

Noa says, "Can I go back? What's happening back here?"

Silence.

"Hello?" Noa calls out.

Silence.

"Please?" she tearfully pleads. "Please?"

Noa pauses. She then whispers, "Thank you–for everything."

Silence follows. She feels herself inhale–but it doesn't climax and return for an exhalation. It goes on until–*Pssssssssh.*

White steam billows out of a large glass chamber as the glass wall slides downward. It sits in the center of what looks like a main room in a sterile apartment.

Noa steps out, covered in beads of moisture. She pats herself dry, then grabs an oversized sweatshirt from the neatly folded stack on top of a kitchen counter–at least it looks like a counter. There are no stoves, refrigerators, or even a sink.

The walls are undecorated. There is an enormous wall, which appears like a window and video screen in one. A large digital clock reads:

03/09/2078–19:00

****

Five-thirty a.m. The screeching repetitive sound of his alarm clock jolts Isaac awake from his typical dreamless sleep. He has to work today.

He sits up in bed, bracing himself on his palms at his side. He stretches his chest to a grunt, rolls himself off the right side of his bed, then heads into the bathroom to get ready for work.

A short 87th Street bus ride gets him to BSV, where he opens as usual. Today, Tamika is waiting at the door for him to open. She's covering the morning shift, and she's always early.

Isaac spends most of his day thinking about Noa. That kiss has locked him in. It's a very slow Wednesday at the store. After shelving the returns and rewinding the un-rewound, there wasn't much else to do. Typically, he'd be sitting here listening to Sharika complain or spout negativity as he sketched in his book. Today, it's just silence. Tamika watches *The Lion King* for the twentieth time, holding attention as if it's her first time seeing it.

Isaac sits with his sketchbook, reading a poem he's just finished. He has his headphones on, listening to Miles Davis' "Générique," which he dubbed onto cassette from the mono vinyl record. This song is Noa. Her movement, her mystery.

The page reads:

The warmth of your eyes brings my blood to a simmer. The spark of your touch sets my soul ablaze. An inferno only quenched by the soothing cadence of your voice. Your warmth thawed my frozen heart, making it beat loudly into the surrounding void. A place otherwise without sound or light. You are not what you seem! You are not of this place!

Chapter Four

It's the morning of July 12th, 1996; the day of the Lincoln Park Zoo ball. Noa has returned to town, and she sounded excited about it on the phone. She had spoken little to Isaac while in Canada. He assumes she was taking care of family, home, or some other issue. He doesn't care to dig too much into this, even though he wants to know more specifics. *What if she is with this person he reminds her of? Secretly married?*

Isaac had searched desperately for a temporary vehicle for the ball prior to today. Pete agreed immediately to let him use his Buick; however, Isaac wanted to find a more suitable ride for the heavenly Noa Gayle, keeping Pete's Skyhawk on standby. Unfortunately, Isaac hasn't been lucky here, and Pete's hoopty is his only option. He nearly changes his mind to ride the CTA, but he wants more time with Noa alone. Also, he doesn't want Noa to be uncomfortable in her dress on the L and bus. It's a long commute.

Isaac and Noa spoke last night and they agree for him to arrive at her apartment at 5 p.m. From there, they'll drive over to the ball. To get there in time, Isaac has to fight rush-hour traffic. He plans to leave Gresham at 3:00 or 3:30 p.m. to be safe. Chicago traffic on a Friday afternoon—grab your chill-pills!

Isaac has a fresh haircut courtesy of Tommy, a low taper fade for his short mini-fro. He went this morning, a day earlier than his usual Saturday. Haircut came first; the afternoon was to get this car somewhat presentable for a beautiful lady.

Attentively, Isaac cleans the exterior and interior of Pete's Buick Skyhawk. He intends to make it clean and comfortable for Noa. He wipes down the console and sprays a light fragrance he bought from a street vendor. Isaac isn't a fan of the artificial-smelling oil, but it's better than stale weed.

Fortunately, it hasn't rained in the last week, so Pete's Buick won't smell like death today. Unless they drive over and splash through a large puddle, things should smell okay—not new, but they'll avoid the ass smell at least. Isaac points to the sky, thanking the heavens as if he is celebrating an MLB home-run.

After finishing the car the best that he can, he heads into his apartment. He unzips his rental tuxedo. It fits impeccably, perfectly baggy in the trousers and coat. He hangs it by a hanger on his bathroom door. Isaac starts his shower and primping, which will be twice as attentive as the care he gave Pete's car.

It's now 3 p.m., and Isaac finishes the detail of himself. He learned how to tie the perfect bowtie knot from Grandad. He picks and pats his afro, making sure no stray nap is out of place, and that it's not flat on one side. He grabs the hanger with the tux coat and heads out his rear door into a heavy humidity. Now he is really nervous about this car deal. Pete's AC doesn't always blow cold air.

Isaac stumbles down the gangway of his apartment home to the street, where the 1986 Skyhawk awaits. Yuck, it is not a pretty sight, even when cleaned.

At least he looks well put together, well groomed, and smells amazing. The juxtaposition of that with this hoopty-ride is like pairing caviar with Yoo-hoo.

He emerges from between two bungalows and walks toward the Buick. Approaching from his left, he sees a black shiny vehicle in his periphery. He hears, "Whoooooa! Look, y'all!" from a group of five neighborhood kids, who stop lobbing their football to and fro and watch.

Isaac looks in that direction, and he sees a piano-black stretch limousine slowly driving down South Morgan Street. It stops just in front of Pete's car, essentially blocking it in. A sharply dressed driver steps out and walks around to the door in front of Isaac. He slowly opens the door. The scent of gardenia gently escapes.

Noa! She is sitting in the passenger compartment in a stunning black slip dress. The material has a tasteful sheen. She wears a dainty black sheer lace choker with a dangling emerald gemstone and feather-shaped emerald drop earrings.

Along with the choker, she is wearing three tasteful silver necklaces of various lengths. The longest falls just at her perked cleavage, which is tastefully teased by the neckline of her dress. The mid-length necklace stops at the top of her sternal notch and has a clear crystal stone with an etched bird feather design. She steps out with the helping hand of the driver. She bows playfully at Isaac and bares a blushing smile.

The dress material is slinky and softly caresses her skin, accentuating her petite hourglass frame. That's his BirdGurl9. Everything is gorgeous on her. She is radiant, giving off a bright aura, which is visible around herself and around anyone standing near her.

Her smile, especially when she bites her lower lip, brings out those flutterbys in Isaac's midsection. She does this as she blushes over his excitement from her surprise. He is obviously surprised! His mouth is held open, and he is unintentionally mouth-breathing. He can't feel his face in this moment. It isn't the limousine. It isn't that his car problem is no longer a car problem. It is her—Noa, she is here!

In a trance, Isaac approaches her without thinking. His body is caught in the surreal gravity of her presence. He snaps to attention as her scent, paired with her eyes, registers.

Her familiar scent is there—only tonight, the gardenia blooms stronger, anchored by soft vanilla.

Isaac shakes his head slightly, hands stretched to his sides in disbelief. "I thought— How did you—?"

Noa sighs.

"It's our world, Isaac!" This is said in unison, Isaac joining in on her predictable mantra.

"I'm being serious, silly!" She tries to laugh it off.

Something about her sincerity strikes a chord with Isaac this time. Until now, he took that as some silly platitude like, *The world is yours.* No, this is something different. There was something about the sincerity in her eyes when she said this. Her more serious expression.

What is she involved with? he asks himself. He wonders if she's involved with unsavory characters. He considers the possibility that she is not who she says she is. This last thought stings, but this is Isaac in his head, not based on any observed reality. The musings of someone with deep-seated fears of loss.

Isaac's seeds of concern don't germinate here. He is pleasantly surprised, and he is smitten to an even higher degree with this woman. No need to throw ink on this beautiful painting, not tonight. She saved the day. She may be the one to save him.

At the limousine door, Noa lifts her chin upward and slightly pouts her lips. Her eyelids hang low, but the moment Isaac's lips touch hers, they close completely. He feels palpitations in his chest. His heart is racing, fueled by the raw energy of her, and this moment.

She opens her eyes. "Hi, handsome!"

"Hi?"

She playfully curtsies. "Your chariot awaits, milord!"

Isaac shakes his head, wearing a half-smile, as they share a chuckle. He takes her hand and assists her in first.

Inside, the humid haze of mid-July in Chicago is obliterated by the AC. The seating feels cloud-like; there are refreshments prepped on trays, and a stocked bar.

Noa sits next to Isaac and takes his hand. She smiles as his eyes and head dart around the luxurious ride. Something, or someone, is on her mind. Her smile briefly gives way to welled-up eyes, but she controls this and pulls it together. Isaac feels a tightening of her hand around his.

The driver raises the privacy panel after confirming with the two that they will go directly to Lincoln Park Zoo. Isaac reaches to his right and slowly increases the dial on the radio, which is tuned to 102.7 FM. "After the Dance" by Marvin Gaye is playing. Interesting, this musical synchronicity is.

****

Isaac and Noa arrive at the ball in the stretch limousine. They step out one at a time. Noa captivates all around with her beauty, while he is dapper.

The Lincoln Park Zoo grounds glow with multicolored spotlights. A grand white tent houses the opulent gala. Underneath the sprawling tent are islands of round tables and chairs dressed in crisp white linens. Spotless crystal glassware and silverware adorn the tables and sparkle under dreamy lighting.

The Pinks Sisters—a mostly female band, save a lone male bassist—sway in rhythm on stage. Two women lead the performance, wearing matching carnation-pink pantsuits, pink neckties, and fedoras, a nod to Chicago's own *The Blues Brothers*. The rest of the band, including three backup singers, wear similar suits, but without the hats. Their performance is surreal, almost trippy, as multicolored spotlights cast a dreamy backdrop from outside of the open tent. The girls swing and bounce in unison, filling the tent with their rendition of the Jackson 5's "Forever Came Today."

Isaac feels awed by the grandeur and slightly intimidated as a host seats him and Noa at their table with two other couples. The influential philanthropists Jan and Randall Bradley are already in their seats. Their name graces the halls of the Dorey Children's Hospital on South Lake Shore Drive. Their contributions to the institution helped to restore the voices of countless children at the Dorey Pediatric Vocal Infirmary. Children who would have otherwise suffered from a life of silence can now have the chance to be heard. Their charity doesn't end there. The Bradleys are remarkable people in every sense. Humble despite their great wealth, and generous beyond measure.

Isaac's eyes nearly pop out of his head when he realizes that he's also sitting with his idol, the world-famous muralist Gregory Spain, known for his thought-provoking murals throughout the city. His girlfriend, Teena, accompanies him.

Jan Bradley is already a few drinks in, and it shows. She bounces as the Pinks Sisters continue their funky Jackson 5 cover, her grey-streaked bouffant hairstyle swaying side-to-side. The large crystal swan brooch pinned to her pastel peach dress sparkles to the beat. The seemingly reserved Randy Bradley sits stoically beside her, eyes forward—chain-sipping his single-malt Scotch.

Just before Isaac and Noa can sit, Jan shakes her head and silently mouths, "Oh, no you don't." She tugs her husband by the neck of his tux and playfully gestures with her finger for Isaac and Noa to follow her to the dance floor.

Isaac bashfully holds his hands up in protest as Noa tilts and shakes her head at him. "Nope-nope-nope! We're going!"

The blood rushes to every inch of Isaac's skin. His heart pounds. He can't erase the grin on his face—which betrays him feeling ablaze in awkwardness. His idol is less than six feet away, still sitting, making this moment nearly overwhelming. Regardless, he can't help but follow Noa; he has no choice.

Randy Bradley, previously eyes forward, snaps to attention. His stoic demeanor falls off as his shoulders rock side to side. He willingly follows Jan to the dance floor, now bearing an unexpectedly toothy grin.

Shelwood, one of the Pinks Sisters' lead singers, points to the group and bounces and yells, "C'MON! Get on up HEAH!" Then she returns to belting out her breakdown of the song.

The two couples reach the empty dance floor, and pure, euphoric jollity takes over the event. More couples pour onto the dance floor.

Isaac is not a dancer, but he finds the rhythm. Noa looks paradoxically heavenly despite her dark dress. Her hips sway gently, her arms stretch upward. She closes her eyes as if the music is washing over her. She opens them in time to catch Isaac sporting a teeth-bearing grin. He dropped his awkwardness somewhere between the dinner table and the dance floor.

Noa's smile deepens, revealing a subtle left cheek dimple. Her cognac eyes squint playfully; her bob-cut swings from side to side with her emerald drop earrings, which glow and shimmer as if alive with magic.

Isaac blushes as he tries to match her seemingly more experienced movement. He's only got one good move and that's it. Noa giggles, hand over mouth. She dances toward him and places both palms on his shoulders—guiding him in step with her graceful motion.

The bassist of the band bops his head as he slaps the funky bassline. The backup singers belt out their part of the chorus as they wave their palms face-out to the audience and move their feet in unison.

The band finishes the J5 classic. Shelwood pulls the mic from the stand. "Welcome to the Lincoln Park Zoo Ball, you animals! Now we are pulling a dusty for you all by request!"

The band starts the song "BBL Drizzy" in the style of King Willonius.

Noa cackles, hiding her face. "Oh snap! This is an old-school banger right here!"

She grabs Isaac's hands and starts Chicago-style stepping, without missing a beat. Isaac lifts his brow in confusion. He asks himself, *Banger?* Also, *Where did this girl learn to step like this in Canada?*

The two pull closer together in an embracing motion. They match each other perfectly. No one is leading at this point. Isaac' hands rest gently on Noa's hips as she places her face against his chest. As Shelwood croons out the silly and seemingly meaningless lyrics, Isaac feels Noa's face move with laughter. This starts a slow buildup of his own laughter as well. Before long, they are both caught in hysterics—which spreads to the now full dance floor. Who requested this song and why is a mystery, and would remain as such.

Isaac and Noa head back to their seats, giggling together. She leans into his torso as he wraps his arm around her waist.

Isaac and Noa are making their way through the maze of tables when Noa spots her boss from the zoo, Larry Renzi. Unknown to Isaac, it was Larry who gave her the invitations for the ball.

Whisky sour in hand, Larry ambles toward them. He stretches out his right hand, wearing a smarmy grin. "OH HI! You must be—" He makes exaggerated air quotes. "–the friend!" Larry takes a swig of his drink, swallows carefully with his teeth bared. "Yeah—the friend!"

Isaac glances at Noa, who flushes—not in a cute way, but with a look of disgust.

Larry continues. "You are one lucky sonofabitch for getting this one's attention! She's all work and no play around the zoo—and the labs!" His gaze slides down to Noa's hips. "She's got the males of multiple species doing their mating dance!"

This encounter lights a pilot in Isaac's stomach. His blood simmers and his jaw tightens.

Larry does an embarrassingly off-rhythm dance—biting his lip and rocking his pelvis awkwardly. On stage, the Pinks Sisters launch into "Let's Groove" by Earth, Wind & Fire. The bassist uses a Talkbox to start the song off appropriately. The Bradleys are still on the dance floor—and Jan is killing the footwork. *Where did* she *learn to step?* Isaac wonders absently, his attention distracted briefly from the cad standing before him.

Larry sizes up Isaac, stiffening his posture to appear taller. He is six foot one but appears much shorter than the one inch deficit between the two of them. He turns his attention back to Noa—his eyes crawling up and down her figure before freezing at her chest. He wipes the corner of his mouth.

"So, whadya do, Isaac? For a living?"

Isaac shrugs, feeling a wave of heat on the back of his neck. "Well, at the moment—right now... management." Isaac cringes at his embellishment of his head clerk position.

Larry smugly lifts a brow, smirks. "Oh yeah? Management? Where at?" He takes another swig.

Isaac shrinks. "Big Shoulders Video... right now... at the moment."

"Video store, huh?" Larry smirks, his eyes snapping back to Noa, finally looking at her face.

Before Isaac can say another word, Noa reaches for Isaac's hand with a firmness he hasn't felt before. She interlocks her fingers with his, anchoring him. Isaac feels an instant shift—a sense of grounding.

Noa stares Larry down with a sharp and defiant expression, the corners of her lips tugging into a self-assured smirk.

Larry sneers back at Noa. "Well, I AM glad you could make it, Noa! Looks like you're enjoying yourself—I knew that you would—which is why I got YOU the invitations. For you and..."

He lifts his glass dramatically, lips puffed to make a *pfffft* sound. "...a friend." He stumbles off with his half-empty glass.

The stench of whisky and Larry's slurred speech lingers on like an insult in the air. It's clear that he is beyond his fourth whisky sour. It's also clear that he has a thing for Noa. He seems to think his indirect objectification of her isn't noticeable. He seems to lack any sense of decency and doesn't seem to care.

Suspicion gnaws at Isaac, building on insecurities and questions he had already been burying. He recalls Noa saying, "I don't even know why I was invited." *Did she really not know?*

Isaac's simmering blood is near boiling as his mind races. Mostly because he pictures Noa enduring this constantly. Her passion for her work constantly interrupted by unwanted advances and slimy men like Larry—this infuriates him.

Little does Isaac know, Noa has everything under control.

****

The couple returns to their seats. Gregory Spain and his girlfriend, Teena, remain quietly seated. They avoided the dance floor but watched with quiet, smiling faces.

Spain, nearly as tall as Isaac, sports a well-groomed silver beard and strong hands, paint speckled beneath his fingernails. His black tuxedo is pristine, but paired with an old pair of navy-blue Chuck Taylor Converse sneakers—also bearing paint stains in varying hues. The faded blues and grays suggest his favorites.

Teena appears ten years younger than Spain—an attractive strawberry-blonde in her mid-thirties. Her hair is worn in a single braid, which is pinned up in a bun with an iridescent colored butterfly clip. Her deep-blue chiffon dress mirrors her azure eyes that appear to hold the sky, as if it spilled into them long ago when she first looked upward.

Spain is a man of few words—a sharp contrast to his art, which is unapologetically loud, demanding the eyes to linger and notice. The recurring subjects of his murals are a stray dog named Artemis and an escaped circus elephant, Luna, depicted in various scenes across Chicago. Artemis often serves as a guide for the hopeful yet displaced Luna, the two of them exploring the city with a sense of wonder and playfulness.

Last year, a building bearing one of Spain's murals sold *as-is* for a record amount. Without the mural, the building itself held little value; it would've likely been abandoned and eventually condemned. Legend has it, that building once housed his favorite childhood candy store—a place long since closed.

Spain deliberately kept his secret mural under wraps, insisting it should only be seen at the right time, by the right people. His reasons for keeping it concealed remain unknown.

Isaac has seen all of Spain's murals across the city—except for the secret one. In his junior year of high school, he skipped class with Pete to see a new mural painted right before on a gigantic wall at Children's Memorial Hospital in Lincoln Park. The mural depicted Artemis, the stray dog, riding on the back of Luna, the circus elephant, who has somehow gained the ability to fly.

In the painting, Luna is levitating gracefully upward, while Artemis steadies on all fours, balanced on her back. Below them, a group of children of different ethnicities smile and reach skyward. Their hands are outstretched to Luna's snout, as if hoping to grab hold for a ride.

Isaac always takes a disposable camera to capture murals and other art for himself. He has a picture of this one, and many other murals, thumbtacked to his wall beneath his own piece. Art resonates with him differently than it does for most. It examines something about the world that he can't put his finger on.

Gregory Spain hasn't sold much of his work directly. However, last year he parted with nine rare canvas paintings of his—an exception to his usual preference for concrete and bricks. Spain's art, with the exception of the secret mural, is meant to be for everyone—not locked away in galleries or hidden in private collections.

After selling the canvas paintings, he donated most of the windfall to Wet Noses, a Chicago nonprofit that rescues stray animals. In his honor, there is always an animal named Greggy in their care. Currently, the resident Greggy is a female beagle-Jack Russell mix. She'll find a home quickly—as most Greggys do. Their new families often don't change that temporary name. They keep it in pride, and as a quiet tribute to the artist that makes the world a little brighter.

Spain is here tonight to receive the distinguished Animal Steward award in its inaugural year. Of course, he could do without all of the pomp—but he is here at the behest of Teena. She feels that his art reflects his heart, which beats to help those who can't help themselves. She feels he deserves the accolades and forces him to accept being appreciated.

Isaac is excited to be in the same room as such an esteemed artist, let alone at the same table. Excited, but also intimidated and tongue-tied. Noa takes it upon herself to break the ice. "We are both huge fans! Especially Isaac! He's an artist too!"

Spain glances at Isaac's hands. "Washed 'em good for the ball, did we?" He's commenting on the complete lack of paint on Isaac's hands, which are usually marked with multicolored paints.

Isaac fumbles, "Yeah. I had to—you know."

Spain tilts his head slightly. His gaze sharpens but is not unkind. "Did you? Did you really have to clean away the evidence of you?" He takes a slow sip from his glass. "None of us know our complete selves, kid. Why wash away the parts of us that are already apparent? You'd think a creature would hold on to those parts..." He chuckles. "...for dear life, yeah?"

Spain offers his hand for a shake, revealing faint splotches of acrylic, oil, and spray-paint decorating the backs of his fingers and under his nails.

Isaac replies, "I guess I didn't."

Spain grins and winks over at Noa. "It's quite all right. We have to keep up appearances—yeah?"

Isaac laughs nervously, shrinking back into his chair. Spain notices and softens his tone as he reins in his joking inquisition. "Kid—I'm fucking with you." He sniggers. "You seem like you have things to say, but no voice to say them... Why so quiet? Or is it that you don't think you have a voice?"

Isaac's mind races to find the right words as he sits cross-table from his idol, thinking, *Don't fuck this up!*

Noa, watching him carefully, reaches her right hand under the table and gently squeezes his left knee. A calm washes over Isaac, cooling his anxieties as quickly as they'd surfaced.

Spain chuckles. "So—Isaac, how many people would you say have consumed your work?"

Isaac shrugs. "No one really. They're on my apartment walls. My studio apartment walls."

Spain nods, smirking. "Hmm. Bashful about your gifts?"

"Not really," Isaac replies. "I just do it for myself."

Spain studies him for a beat, then takes a graceful swig of cognac, the liquid sliding toward his tongue as if it belongs there. "I hear ya. Something to say—something to share—but you keep it to yourself."

He points at Noa, then over at Teena, and begins quickly pointing back and forth between the two women, his grin widening.

"Listen, Isaac. You have gifts. You have things to say. Trust your muse—we all have one. The universe makes it so. They will inspire your message and give you the voice to spread it. And when you lose that voice? They'll shout from the rooftops for you."

Teena remains quiet, her smirk widening with quiet pride. She rocks gently to the music, her body swaying in rhythm, and offers a wink to Noa. Noa winks back, her expression soft and knowing.

Isaac thinks of Noa, considering their relationship, still undefined. Has there ever been someone who could fit Spain's description of a muse like the woman sitting to his left?

She squeezes his leg a little tighter, and when Isaac turns to look at her, she meets him with a smile and a playful wink.

The flutterbys are back. The idea that the beautiful Noa Gayle could be his muse—or anything—sends his heart pounding so loudly that, if not for the music, you might hear it echoing in his chest.

Spain continues, his voice steady and measured. "You don't need a time. You don't need some arbitrary collection of art to peddle. You already have your muse—and a voice. She will be the harbinger of your messages, and when you can't, she'll shout them across the globe for you. Keep trying to make sense of the world with your colors and figures, and that's all you'll do. But if you don't fit into this world, create one in which you do! You can't be in this world or another alone, though. You'll need your guide and companion—your muse."

He gestures with an upturned palm toward Noa.

Isaac looks at her. Her gaze softens, her eyes shining as though on the verge of tears. Slowly, she reaches her delicate hand into his, her thumb stroking gently across his skin—a small, grounding gesture that says everything without words.

She smiles and turns her attention to the Pink Sisters, who are now singing their rendition of a song by Chicago's own Chaka Khan—"Through the Fire."

Isaac leans back slightly, his mind buzzing, and thinks, *Even the band is in on the synchronicity.*

Gregory Spain whispers into Teena's ear. They hadn't danced earlier, but now he takes the hand of his lovely muse and leads her to the dance floor. On the way, Spain intentionally hooks his finger into the shoulder of Isaac's tuxedo—a quiet hint for him to bring Noa and follow. Isaac responds instantly, and the two of them join.

Noa and Isaac stand before each other as the band delivers a soulful, improvised rendition of "Through the Fire." Noa's deep, endless eyes make the world fall away, and she does her usual, unconscious head tilt. Isaac smiles softly as he gently guides her head to his chest with his left hand—his right arm securing her firmly and protectively. Her eyes flutter closed; she looks peaceful.

Isaac lets the music wash over him, the melodies sending a swell of pleasurable warmth to the base of his skull, behind his ears, and down to the top of his neck.

Noa's fragrance carries its own quiet melody. The gardenia-dominated scent is synchronous with the moment. Gentle passion.

Shelwood's voice soars through the ballad, powerful yet tender, wrapping itself around every corner of the tent and spilling effortlessly into the night air over Lincoln Park. Her blonde hair shimmers under the dim, ambient light as she adjusts her fedora, catching it just before it slips.

Isaac and Noa don't realize that the dance floor has cleared; they are there alone, under a spotlight. Spain and Teena have yielded the floor to them—now standing with the other guests, watching with admiring eyes.

Noa and Isaac seem to glow, brighter than the spotlight itself—like embracing angels.

As the final note is played, Isaac and his muse both open their eyes simultaneously. Noa lifts her head and they look into each other's eyes. Their shared auras extend beyond them. They don't seem to notice their loneliness in the center of the dance floor as they float back to their table, still caught in each other's orbit, unaware of the eyes upon them.

Spain and Teena have already made their way back to the table and are now both smiling like proud parents as Noa and Isaac take their seats. They lost time—for all they know, they could've been hugging silently in the middle of the floor for twenty minutes.

Spain leans in toward them. "A painter is an artist without a muse. With a muse, he's neither artist nor painter."

He chuckles as he takes a sip from his rocks glass, now appearing slightly tipsy. "See you puppies in the welfare line. If I don't, I'll assume the worst!"

Spain extends his hand, and Isaac grabs it quickly. The handshake is firm, genuine. Noa watches with a proud expression as she takes in Isaac's excitement. She tilts her head again, now as though speaking to him without words.

He hears, *This is our world, Isaac.*

****

Isaac still glows after meeting one of his idols. He feels Noa softly snake her fingers into his hand. He turns to find her looking at him endearingly. She asks, "Take me home, handsome?"

"Yeah—fa sho', let's head out." Isaac says this with a slight disappointment that the night is ending.

Noa shakes her head slightly. "With you."

A brief one-second stun hits Isaac's face. "Yeah— That's cool, you want to see my crib?"

Noa nods and smirks with a half-bitten lip.

With a subtle shrug, Isaac says, "It's not much. It's really kind of like an attic—"

Noa cuts him off nonverbally. She pulls his hand and buries her face into his chest. Her left arm slowly smooths around his torso. "Isaac—it's OUR world. I want to see your part too."

The passenger compartment of the limousine is massive, but on the ride from Lincoln Park to Gresham, Noa mostly keeps her face against Isaac's chest. She wraps her left arm around him, her fingers gently stroking the side of his body.

Raphael Saadiq sings "Ask of You" on 107.5 WGCI. A waning crescent moon casts a reflection on Lake Michigan as they cruise down Lake Shore Drive. The scent of Noa's hair gives him a head buzz of nervous euphoria. His heart has intermittent spells of palpitations. He feels her face smile against him. She slowly drags her hand across his chest and rests it over his heart. "Your heart is so loud!" she says.

Isaac whispers deeply, "You do it to me."

Noa gracefully sits up and softly pulls his face to hers. This kiss differs from the others—it gives them a body high. Goosebumps cover every exposed part of them. The observant Isaac thinks the gardenia notes in her fragrance have dialed up, and he can feel the prickles on her skin too.

God, she smells so good. Isaac's heart thumps as the synchronous "Setembro" by Quincy Jones now plays on the radio. This is perfect and familiar.

The driver slowly pulls into a parking spot in front of Isaac's house with more than enough room. The driver opens the door and the two step out in front of the bungalow. Noa follows Isaac's safe lead as he takes her by the hand down the dark gangway between the neighboring house. They arrive at the rear stairs that lead up to Isaac's apartment.

Noa climbs the steps ahead of him, turning once to smile. The thump in Isaac's chest intensifies. At the top, he slides a silver key into the lock in the doorknob and twists. He pushes the door open; cool air rushes out against their skin. The AC unit hums gently from the window on the opposite side of the studio.

Isaac reaches in and clicks the bronze-toned light switch, which lights the two warm white lamps at his bedside and an upright black torchiere floor lamp in his kitchenette.

The elaborate mural Isaac painted shines under the lighting, and Noa's eyes immediately widen. She steps into the small, quiet space unguided–her head cranes up to the mural across from his bed.

She focuses directly on the section in the center–the section with the silhouette of a man being cradled by the silhouette of a woman under the sun, with multicolored, metallic shining wire tendrils reaching towards the silhouettes.

Noa stumbles back and sits on the end of the bed and stares at this for nearly a minute, silently. Isaac, usually shy about his work, stands back–never expecting someone to have such a reaction to it.

She turns her gaze to Isaac, her eyes shimmering with unshed tears. Rising, she takes a few quiet steps across the small room until she's standing directly in front of him.

On tiptoes, she reaches for the sides of his neck, stretching up as she pulls him into a gentle, cheek-to-cheek embrace. Her warmth lingers there for a moment before she cradles his face in her hands. She kisses his cheek first, soft and deliberate, before her lips find his.

At first the kiss is firm–heated, as if overtaken by the moment. She exhales a slow, deep breath, pausing briefly. When she resumes, her lips move softly, teasing with slow, sensual nibbles as her fingers stroke the back of his neck.

The kiss stops and she comes down from her toes, then looks him in the eyes and smiles shyly. It's getting dark outside–and his bedside and floor lamps don't illuminate the space well. She slides her hands down his forearms and softly grasps both of his hands. "Can I stay here tonight?"

Isaac nods his head silently, thinking, *Y-yeah.* Even his inner voice clears its throat.

Noa nods her head with a smirk, raises her eyebrow. "Yeah?"

Isaac chuckles, "Yeah! It's your world, beautiful! I'm just in it!"

Noa nods again, her gaze playful yet intent. "Yeah." She slides her hand to the back of his head, pulling him into a kiss—this one deeper, filled with more heat and passion than before.

Isaac trails his lips to her neck, and she moans softly, her body tensing as electric pleasure-ants march from the base of her spine, upward to the nape of her neck. She falls into Isaac's chest area, leaning into the strength it represents. She unbuttons his tuxedo shirt, button by button. As his chest is revealed, she places her palm over the center of his pecs. She then leans in, and kisses him again. She reaches for the back of his head and pulls him toward her. She then tugs at his belt buckle, pulling his pelvis toward hers. She unzips his pants. Isaac gets the hint and continues undressing.

Noa's dress flows to the floor like a whisper, revealing the radiant beauty beneath. She removes her chokers and necklaces, unveiling her flawless, olive-toned skin. Her body is a harmonious blend of strength and softness—gentle curves at her hips inviting a tender touch.

Her breasts, perfectly shaped and subtly perky, seem to draw Isaac's attention instinctively. As he cups one in his hand, it's as if he's discovered a sensation beyond comparison. The warmth and suppleness send a shiver down his spine, compelling him to pull her closer with his other arm. Noa melts into him, their bodies aligning as though they were made for this moment.

With a soft smile, she takes his hand, guiding him to the bed. Isaac lies back, his heart racing as she climbs atop him, her movements slow and deliberate, every gesture charged with connection and desire. She leans forward, her body aligning with his as their eyes lock.

As she lowers herself, they come together in a slick union that steals the breath from both their lungs. A simultaneous sharp exhalation escapes their lips, the sound blending into the rhythm of their shared ecstasy. For Isaac, it feels like the most sensitive part of him has entered a warm, tender sanctuary, a space where everything feels achingly real, yet impossibly perfect.

Beneath the soft glow of the mural above his bed, their movements sync effortlessly, a silent conversation between two souls finally in harmony. For Isaac, every moment with Noa is transcendent; for Noa, it's a union that makes the world disappear.

They lose themselves in each other, the masterpiece above them a witness to the raw, unfiltered beauty of their love.

****

Isaac wakes up alone in bed. Peeks of sunlight beam through his blinds. He looks over to find Noa is not there. The gardenia lingers. It's on him as well. This alone causes a brief euphoric dose of dopamine to be released. He smirks, then quickly sits up to find her sitting in his kitchen chair. She has her elbow propped on the table, supporting her head.

"Good morning, handsome."

"Good morning, cosmic muse," Isaac says with a waking rasp in his voice. The realization that she is still there riles up the flutterbys. A second, longer-lasting dose of that dopamine stuff is released. His heartbeat increases just slightly; his skin prickles. The heavenly aura of his muse makes him high.

Noa giggles and says, "You do snore, by the way."

"You were watching me, huh?" He laughs.

Noa nods. "Yep, I've been up for a while." She looks up for a moment. "I loved on your mural mostly, but, yes, I watched you too."

Isaac is slightly concerned that he might have farted in his sleep or done something else embarrassing. Even if he did, she doesn't seem to care, based on the affectionate expression on her face. Her big brown eyes are looking back at him as if he was a prized possession. Isaac sure feels that way about her, and he returns the same gaze. He wants to kiss her, but he jumps up and runs into the bathroom to brush his teeth.

Noa giggles at this. "Yes, sir! Go brush those chompers—sexy!"

After his thoughtful dental hygiene, Isaac exits the bathroom to find Noa standing just outside of the door. Her head is tilted up and she looks into his eyes. Her head slowly and subtly rocks on a narrow swivel. She looks at his lips, and into his eyes. Her brown irises are glowing in the sunlight sneaking through the gaps in Isaac's mini-blinds.

He knows what she wants. They gently press their lips together. Noa moans slightly, breathes heavily through her nose as she softly strokes the back of his head. Isaac pulls to the side, kissing her face, then nibbles along her jawline, and down to her neck. Noa arches her back, her breathing rate increasing as she stretches up to his face.

She gently pulls away, kissing Isaac's cheek, then holds her cheek against his.

They hold this loving embrace for a bit longer until she whispers in his ear, "Get ready." She settles, places her hands on his shoulders. "We got a field trip today—it's a surprise." She taps her fingers on his bare chest with each word. "So. Don't. Ask."

"Wait. What are you going to do about clothes?" Isaac asks.

Noa points over to the floor where an open overnight bag lies. It's stuffed. Isaac, in confused wonderment, says, "When did you have time to get clothes?"

Noa replies, "I've had them the whole time. They were in the limo when we got here."

Isaac is still confused, as he distinctly recalls them coming directly inside without having baggage. He also remembers the limousine driver driving away, but he lets it go.

"So where are we going?" he asks.

Noa says, "Shower and get dressed. We're going on an adventure."

Noa takes the bathroom first, at Isaac's insistence. She showers, brushes her hair and dresses in quick fashion. She smells amazing, as usual. She emerges from the bathroom wearing denim overall shorts, which fall mid-thigh. Underneath, she wears a clean white V-neck tee. She is also wearing a cute Chicago Cubs baseball cap, with the brim curved into a complete U over the sides of her eyes.

"Let's go, slowpoke," she says.

Isaac does feel like a slowpoke. He has never heard of a woman getting ready this quickly. She's some kind of unicorn.

He steps out of the bathroom fifteen minutes after stepping in, wearing denim FUBU shorts, an army-green oversized FUBU T-shirt, and a pair of white Nike Air Max high-tops.

The couple exit the building and walk toward 87th Street to catch the CTA bus to Noa's 'surprise.'

No limousine this morning. This is about the adventure today, anyhow. Isaac and Noa take their expectedly on-time CTA transportation over to Stony Island Avenue. From here, they transit north and up the lakefront at 39th Street, where Noa leads Isaac over the rocky waterfront. They ascend and descend large jagged stones of varying heights and arrive near a section overgrown with thistle, which bites at their exposed legs.

"Almost there," Noa tells him as they arrive at a shallow section of the shore of Lake Michigan, which expands to a grey horizon in the west. That horizon could be followed north until broken by the big-shouldered skyline of Chicago.

Noa stops and grabs Isaac's hand—his eyes widen, gaping in disbelief. "Shit, girl! How?" he exclaims, his mouth left ajar. There are scattered large stone slabs and walls along this southern shore of Lake Michigan, among them scattered sculptures carved out by amateur sculptors. What is a secret is that a section of wall along the lakefront has a painting of Artemis and Luna, painted as if they are peering out into Lake Michigan at a sculpture of a mermaid lying in the shallow edge of the shore. This was once carved by some other artist in the past—a beautiful visitor from the deep, guiding the canine and pachyderm Chicagoans to a new world.

A wide smile stretches across Isaac's face. He can't believe what he's seeing. The secret mural. He's now seen every mural by Gregory Spain within the city in person. This one is legendary, and he was skeptical that it existed up until now. She brought him here. He wanted to ask about it last night at the ball, but out of respect he couldn't bring himself to do it. He was grateful enough to hear direct words from the man himself.

Isaac turns and wraps his arms around Noa's narrow torso, lifting her an inch from the ground. Her scent gently replaces that of the murky lake water feet from them. Her giggle and sighs come together in his ears like a calm instrumental.

"God, I love you!" Isaac says, almost involuntarily. He slowly releases his hug, flushes. "I mean—I know we've been talking for a short time, but I'm feeling some things. I don't know. I think—"

"Hey, Isaac," she interrupts.

"Sorry."

"I love you too!" Noa says with her slight head tilt. Her warm, welcoming eyes are trained directly into his. Her lips tremble slightly. "I love you too, Isaac."

Isaac's breaths slow and deepen. Those words from Noa Gayle pouring into his soul. The sensation of every hair slowly standing erect. *Those damn flutterbys!*

Noa reaches into her small backpack and produces a disposable Waggies-brand camera for Isaac to take his pictures. As she hands it to him, there's a subtle hint of sadness in her eyes that goes unnoticed by Isaac. He is so overtaken by his surprise. *How did she know? When did she have time to get this?* Isaac is puzzled, but this act has his heart lassoed and bound. *Who are you, Noa Gayle?*

Isaac caresses the right side of her face, which she tilts more into his hand, closing her eyes. He slowly pulls her face to his and kisses her lips. She receives the kiss, eyes closed. She parts them momentarily; coincidentally, he does too. With the brief vision of her eyes in the sunlight, at this proximity, Isaac notices a trace of reddish shimmer in her irises. Shimmering, in motion.

Their eyes close again as Noa moves both of her hands up and behind Isaac's head, gently stroking the nape of his neck.

Lake Michigan sloshes under the hot July noon sun. The traffic from South Lake Shore Drive is heard, among native and non-native birds.

Noa looks down at her feet. Her affect darkens.

"I have to go home." She pauses. "For a few weeks—then I'll be back."

Isaac deflates. His emotions nosedive from the highest point ever—crash-landing back to his real world. He suddenly goes from feeling found to lost again. He tries his best to not ruin this moment with how he truly feels—buried, underneath all of the questions and insecurities he has been shoveling into a mental hole since their first date.

Dare I ask those questions? They'd both just bared themselves to each other. The thought of launching an inquiry—doubting her, questioning her... He can't find the courage to do it. Not now.

What is going on at home? Is there someone there? Where is home, really? Noa, who are you, really?

"Oh yeah, no doubt!" He has a confused look. "You gotta make sure all is right at home—right? Back in Canada..."

"Um..." Noa wrings her hands, falters.

Isaac tries again. "...Canada... right?"

Noa nods softly. "Yeah. I leave tonight. Sorry to drop that at the last minute. I didn't want to ruin today." She can barely look at him.

A subtle sniff escapes Isaac. "Tonight... hmpfh."

She looks away shamefully. "My work friend Shana said she'll watch Sarah Connor this time while I'm gone. I know you'll probably want to—"

Isaac cuts in. "I can watch her. Me and her— We are like this!" he says, clasping his hands together descriptively.

Noa now nods perfunctorily. "Okay! Yeah. Yeah! That would work too! She loves you!" She sheepishly giggles and says, "She'll take care of you for me."

Isaac snickers once. He unsuccessfully tries to make this appear opposite to the gut-punch he just experienced, but it is unmistakably an upset snicker.

"I will be back! I promise!"

It isn't just the lovesickness he endures when she leaves. It isn't just the sudden realization that she is leaving him again. It's also that *someone*, whom she doesn't mention, is making him form a villain in his head. This someone... he *"reminds* her of *someone."* This person may be a figment of Isaac's imagination, or his jealous-leaning intuition may be spot on.

He also pines over the fact that she doesn't call when she gets home, ever. He doesn't hear from her when she leaves, and until she returns from home... *wherever that is.*

Chapter Five

"**D**amn, it's hot in here!" Sharika exclaims, as she fans herself with a folded Sav-A-Penny ad paper. A box fan gently blows a fluttering stack of them on the red countertop.

Isaac is lovesick and feels raw. Noa is away, again.

When she is around, he feels no limits. In her absence, he feels constrained. A square peg, being forced to exist in a world that doesn't feel like it exists itself.

It's humid and ninety-four degrees outdoors, eighty-three inside of the store. The central AC is blowing tepid air at best. The TV monitors throughout the store display black screens, and the store is silent, with the exception of the three strategically placed box fans. The front door of BSV is held open by Ron's desk chair. Isaac worries a crackhead will run by, snatch it, and ride off—its one wonky wheel squealing wretchedly throughout Chatham. Stranger things have happened in this strip mall.

"What kind of man can't fix a thermostat? Same loser who makes up a woman to seem less pathetic," Sharika says with a contemptuous tone.

Isaac clenches his teeth, turns his back on Sharika, and looks down into his sketchbook.

Ding. The door chime rings softly, signaling someone has entered the front.

A calming energy radiates from behind Isaac. The sunlight dims slightly, and the scent of gardenia stirs up emotions.

His heart pounds—a rhythmic drumbeat which echoes through his ears. *Noa?*

She walks around the frosted glass of the entrance. It is Noa Gayle. Her soulful brown eyes smile along with her supple lips. She is wearing an orange sundress that looks perfectly breezy for early August. Despite the heat, she smells amazing.

It has been just over three weeks. She is right on time.

Sharika's eyes dart up and down, scanning Noa. The rest of her face freezes in an expression of malicious envy—causing a sudden shift of heat in the room. A brisk *Gayle* force wind blows in, bringing cool relief to Isaac.

Noa walks up to him. "Hi! Mmm!" she says softly, pulling his lips to hers with a hand under his chin. She rises on tiptoes as usual—floating down slowly, like a landing fairy, as the kiss is released.

She places her face against his neck, sliding down gently against his chest.

"That loud heart of yours—I missed you too, handsome!"

Sharika shakes her head. "Whatever! Get a fucking room," she scoffs, rolling her eyes. "I'm going over to get some chicken from Harold's! Bye!"

Noa pulls a bag off of her shoulder. "I brought your lunch, my love!"

Isaac feels an unexpected swell of pride—a quiet redemption he didn't need to begin with, not from Sharika or anyone else, but this feels good.

Noa places the bag on the counter and softly guides Isaac's hand onto it, her own resting gently on top. "There's something to drink, napkins—everything, love!" She kisses him again. "Mmm... After work, there's another surprise for you! I love you so, so much!"

She reaches up for a kiss goodbye, and Sharika, still not completely out of the store, and unable to look away, gags theatrically. She appears completely ablaze in a jealous flame over the gorgeous but beautifully understated Noa Gayle.

Noa exits as quickly and gracefully as she entered–leaving both Isaac and Sharika speechless for different reasons. Isaac beams.

He watches his beautiful love walk from the sidewalk into the parking lot. She steps into the passenger side of a red late-model Pontiac Grand Am. Suddenly, his pride is snatched with whiplash force. Instead of flutterbys, a swarm of yellowjackets has entered. Stings ignite into flames, burning away the gentle kaleidoscopic wing batters.

There's another man behind the wheel. To Isaac, it looks like that Larry Renzi guy, her boss at the zoo, from this distance.

WHAT THE F–? Isaac's mind freezes. *Am I playing the fool? I am playing the fool!*

****

It's the end of the shift. Isaac passes off the guard to Wayne and Tamika. Sharika is already gone, her usual move being to sneak out before the end of her shift, leaving Isaac to close out her register and cover her when it comes up short, although it doesn't happen often, and usually only by a few cents.

As he walks out of the store, a red 1996 Pontiac Grand Am GT pulls up in front of him. The driver is Noa Gayle. He drops his head to the open passenger-side window–his face is blank. "When did you get a car?"

Noa giggles. "Just now! Get in!"

Isaac runs his tongue along his cheek–he has questions.

He grabs at the door handle and slowly pulls the door open, almost reluctantly, then sits in the passenger seat. The car smells brand new, and it even has a built-in CD player.

"Just now?" he echoed, his voice and affect both flat. "You bought a car just now?"

"I got my license today—the next natural thing was to get a car. That's not the surprise, though." Noa points to Isaac's seatbelt, which he pulls over his chest. He appears frustrated and confused.

"Ready?" Noa says with a smile on her face. "We are going on another field trip. Grandma is fine; I just checked on her!"

Noa looks into her left side mirror, then pulls off, as if she has been driving in the city for years. Isaac has no clue where they are going. She clicks on the radio. WGCI is playing Mint Condition's "Breakin' My Heart." Isaac thinks, *Of course!*

She enters the south Dan Ryan Expressway, then links up to the I-57 south. They travel for one hour and twenty-nine minutes, mostly passing open fields and farmland. The Chicago skyline is well out of view from here. For most of the trip, Isaac ponders silently, listening to the music. Noa seems perfectly comfortable in her silence, *perhaps to avoid explanation.*

It's late afternoon, and evening approaches. Noa turns down an unnamed dirt road. Grassy fields blur past, loose dirt sprays the red undercarriage—WGCI's radio signal becomes staticky.

After ten minutes, she pulls into a wide-open grassy field. A campsite, complete with a tent, is set up in the center of the field.

"Did you do this?" Isaac says. "Are we camping?"

Isaac has never camped in his lifetime. It's not the typical pastime for a Southsider. Grandad mentioned wanting to take Isaac several times, but having to work well past retirement, never had the opportunity to take him.

"Yup! Plus, I want you to see the Perseids—the meteor shower peaks tonight!" Noa says, excitement in her voice.

This woman! Isaac thinks again. She brought him out here to see a meteor shower. Never in a million years would he expect a woman to surprise him with a preset campsite and a meteor shower. His silent angst wrestles with this loving and romantic gesture. He wants to enjoy this but can't let go of his insecurities. He doesn't need much and will accept the first explanation, no matter how outlandish, to cast away his doubts. *Will she give me one? I don't need much.*

Noa parks the car in the field, which feels endless in all directions. The grass compresses, and the soft soil cushions the bottom of their feet.

Isaac examines the campsite from a distance. He processes the effort it took to arrange all of this—and the amount of time it would take to do so. Noa exposes a subdued grin at Isaac. She reaches in the backseat and grabs a basket. The smell of deliciousness wafts through the air. "You brought food too?" His stomach pangs.

"I made a little something-something! Some empanadas!" Noa says with a wink.

Isaac is dumbfounded. The paradoxical flow of emotions is exhausting.

Noa chortles. "C'mon, silly! Don't just stand there! Let's go!"

"How did you—?" Isaac questions the campsite, already set, from over one and a half hours away. There is even a campfire started. He would be concerned that it was left unattended, but with her, he is sure all is just fine. There's an explanation here—somewhere.

"Seriously—how?"

Noa lifts her eyebrow. "Must I say it?" she asks with a light tone, but her eyes hold something deeper.

Isaac shakes his head. "It's your world—right?"

Noa winks playfully, her only response. Isaac nearly rolls his eyes, but catches himself.

Does she recruit the help of magical wood elves and/or animals? he thinks. *Maybe she's the queen alien, and her alien henchmen are watching us right now, surrounding us in invis-*

ibility cloaks. It's her world—it's our world—but none of that answers a thing.

The couple take off their shoes at the tent, then crawl into the cozy setup. There is a comfy bundle of blankets in the center. Isaac is amazed at the roominess. It's much larger than it appears from the outside.

A small lantern sits beside the blankets, its warm glow casting soft shadows across the tent. Noa props open the basket, pulling out a plate covered in foil, cloth napkins, and two glass bottles of water. A bowl of cut fruit follows, its colors vibrant under the lantern's light. The empanadas smell incredible.

As she works, Noa glances up—Isaac is watching her. She hesitates, her hand lingering over the basket as if caught mid-thought. Her cheeks flush under the lantern's warm glow.

"Go ahead—I know you're famished," she says softly, voice light, but with a flicker of something else. Shyness.

Isaac pauses, caught off-guard by this sudden vulnerability. For someone who always seems one step ahead, she looks almost uncertain now. That's new.

Heat rises to his own cheeks before he can stop it. He clears his throat. "Who are you?" he asks, half-joking, but unable to hide the sincere curiosity creeping in.

Noa's lips quirk, but she doesn't answer. Instead, she takes a slow sip of water, gaze flicking away. "Eat," she says, evasive. "I have to go back home for a bit."

Wait. What?

Isaac frowns, but before he can say anything, he bites into an empanada—

And immediately regrets it.

"Holy—" He jolts, nearly dropping it as the burning heat sears his tongue. He frantically blows from his mouth, eyes darting to Noa. "What the shit? You got a chef in that basket or somethin'?"

This doesn't make sense.

The realization lands like a slow domino fall in his head. She picked him up after work. Drove almost two hours to get here. Made these beforehand. And yet, the empanada is piping hot, like it just left the fryer.

Isaac stares at her, his pulse ticking up. "Noa," he says, voice lower now. "How?"

She looks at him, unblinking. "Eat before it gets cold."

Isaac's frustration bubbles up, a knot of confusion and something deeper, sharper. This mystery, this feeling of being kept just outside the truth.

"Noa." His voice is firm now. "Can you let me in more?"

A pause.

She meets his eyes, and for a second, he sees something there. Something raw, almost pained.

Then—just as quickly—it's gone.

"I love you—I really do," he says, searching her face. Waiting for something.

Noa swallows, gaze flicking away. The lantern light flickers.

And Isaac suddenly wonders if he's about to lose her.

"I am trying to understand—all of it." He pauses again. "I feel like we live on two different planets. Psssh—are you even from this planet?"

Noa chews a hot empanada. She picks up her water and takes a long gulp. She hesitates, then another nervous gulp. She takes another swallow; it seems to echo through the tent. Her eyes evade Isaac's.

Isaac squints. "Noa?"

Noa's face flushes. She shrugs, doesn't answer.

"Is there someone else?" Isaac says, trying to develop a stoic posture.

"No! There is no one else!"

"Who is this 'someone'? You mentioned them before.

That I remind you of someone?" Isaac puts his tongue in his cheek. "And what's the deal with Larry at the zoo? Was that him earlier?"

Noa rolls her eyes. "Larry? Isaac, what are you even talking about? There's no one you have to worry about!" Her tone is exasperated, tinged with disbelief. Then she shrugs, her expression softening slightly. "I went to get my license today—and bought the car. I was test-driving it and learning to drive at the same time. The owner agreed to help me." She taps her forehead with a small smirk. "I'm a fast learner... and impulsive. Sue me."

Isaac shifts uncomfortably, his body tensing. "Forget Larry! Who then, Noa? What about this dude I remind you of?" His voice cracks.

Noa's eyes glisten. She hesitates.

"Noa... Baby, who?" Isaac presses, his voice low, almost pleading.

Her voice trembles. "My husband," she says, barely above a whisper. "You remind me of my husband."

The world collapses around Isaac. That's how it feels—as if the walls of reality are crumbling, leaving him suspended in an empty void. His eyes fix on her face, searching desperately for something—anything—that will make this easier to bear.

"Husband?" Isaac repeats, his voice hollow. "Heh—married."

Noa's hands tremble as she grips the edge of her basket. Her jaw tightens, her teeth gritted. "My dead husband," she spits out, voice strained and raw. "He's dead, Isaac! Dead!"

Isaac flinches, as if slapped. "Dead? Fuck—shit—baby, I'm sorry! I'm sorry! Please—" Isaac stammers, reaches for her.

Noa holds up her hand. "Stop, Isaac—it's okay."

"I didn't mean to—" he starts, but she interrupts again.

"It's on me," she says, swiping a tear from her left cheek. "I'm a closed book—I have my reasons."

Isaac shakes his head, guilt wrapping around his neck like

a hundred-pound yoke. He feels it tightening with each breath. "I didn't know—"

"I know," Noa says softly, her voice resigned.

Outside, the crickets begin their nightly string symphony, the faint hum of nature painting a peaceful backdrop tinged with melancholy.

"It's been nearly two years," Noa says, her voice breaking. "An aggressive brain tumor. There was hope... and then there was none." Her hands flap dismissively, as if trying to shoo the memory away, but the weight of it clings to her.

Isaac watches her, the depth of her pain cutting through him. It's a pain she's clearly been carrying alone, a quiet storm raging beneath her composed surface. And now, his insecurities have only added to it.

He swallows hard, the sharp edges of his self-inflicted guilt cutting him from the inside. Her secret isn't a betrayal. It's a no-foul situation—a wound she's carried, not something meant to keep him out.

Without thinking, Isaac pulls her closer, wrapping an arm around her shoulder and drawing her face into his chest. "I'm sorry," he whispers, his voice thick with emotion. He takes a deep breath, letting the weight of the moment settle between them. "Listen," he murmurs, his hand gently brushing her back, "my heart beats for you now."

Noa nods against his chest, her breath warm and steadying. "I hear it," she says softly, her voice trembling but sure. She grips his shirt tightly, holding on to the moment as if it might slip away. "Forever—please?"

Isaac's arms tighten around her. "I'm here. In your world—our world. Wherever your world is, so will mine be. Just let me in, though."

Noa leans back slightly, wiping her face. "Do you mean that, truly? Wherever my world is, your world can be there too?"

Isaac responds without hesitating, "Anywhere, I promise! I would go to hell and back."

Noa falls forward into his chest again, her trembling body pressed against him. At first, he thinks she's crying–until he hears her giggle.

Isaac smiles, a little confused. "What's so funny about that?"

"Okay, Mr. Cliché-Pants! 'Ooooh, I'll go to hell and back for you, my dear damsel... roar!'"

Isaac laughs, shaking his head. "Ahhh! You got jokes again!"

Noa sighs in his arms, the sound soft and content. Though he can't see her face, he feels her thinking against him, her thoughts almost palpable in the air between them.

"Noa," he says, his voice steady, "I do mean that. Truly. At the moment, you're all I've got going on. I'll follow you anywhere." He pauses. "I'm not trying to come off corny or anything."

Noa sits up slowly, turns to face him. Her lips twitch in a teasing smile. "What do you mean, '...at the moment'?" She leans in close, her voice a soft whisper. "Just kidding."

Her lips brush his, a soft, lingering kiss that ends with the faintest smack, barely audible. She sits back, studying him, her gaze deep and unwavering, as if she's looking straight into his soul. Isaac does the same, his chest tightening with something he can't quite name.

The evening sun begins to set, casting golden rays across the tent. The small lantern glows softly between them, its light warm and steady, illuminating the unspoken promise lingering in the air.

****

As twilight gives way to darkness, Isaac looks up at a sky unlike anything he's used to. With no light pollution here, the stars blaze brilliantly, and even the faint glow of the Milky Way stretches across the heavens.

"Wow," Isaac murmurs, his voice filled with awe. "So, Perseid meteor shower?"

Noa nods, her face soft in the faint glow of the lantern. "Yup. We should see a bunch of shooting stars tonight. Make some wishes... maybe even make some come true." She flushes as the words escape her.

Isaac turns red as well. "So, where do the meteors come from?"

"You know what a comet is, right?"

"Yeah, it's like a huge space rock!"

"Close," Noa giggles. "They're actually huge rocks of ice that orbit the sun, just like the Earth does. The tail you see is the ice melting as it gets close to the sun. The meteors we're seeing tonight? Tiny pieces of that tail. Right now, the Earth is crossing its path."

"Damn," Isaac says, shaking his head. "See? How do you know all this stuff? I mean, I get that you're smart and all—but, damn!" His tone is half-joking, half-admiring.

Noa smiles, pleased. "I just like to read, like you, silly. And I was a Natural Sciences double major, remember?"

"Well, excuse me," Isaac says dramatically. "Us college dropouts still have a thing or two to learn!" He grins, clearly teasing.

Noa's smile falters. "That's not funny. I didn't mean to intimidate you. I just—"

"Noa," Isaac cuts her off gently, "I was kidding. We're good. I promise." He takes her hand in his, stroking the back of it with his thumb. "Sweets, I dropped out of college because I wasn't ready. My life's meant to take other turns—eventually."

Noa tilts her head slightly, as if weighing something unspoken. Then she props herself up slowly, sitting on her knees in front of him. Her eyes meet his, deep and steady. Isaac feels his own head tilting, drawn into her gaze.

She inches closer, biting the corner of her lip. A tremor runs through her as she takes a slow, steadying breath.

Isaac slides his hand over the curve of her right hip, feeling her move into his grasp. He pulls her closer, and she follows, their bodies meeting with an unspoken urgency. The energy between them is electric.

Noa's hands slip under his shirt, her fingers grazing his tense shoulders. With an impulsive tug, she lifts the shirt over his head. It catches briefly at his chin, but she keeps pulling until it's off, revealing his chest.

Noa leans in, biting and kissing the newly exposed skin, her warm breath trailing behind her lips. Isaac exhales sharply, his body responding to her touch.

Before he realizes it, Noa's clothes are gone as if discarded by magic. She crawls toward him, pressing her bare chest to his. He inhales deeply, catching her scent—wildflowers and gardenia.

He leans into her neck, his lips brushing her ear. "You surprise me," he whispers.

A soft, unrestrained moan escapes her lips, unlike anything Isaac has heard before—a slow, trembling exhalation. Her thighs tense against him, her body trembling in rhythm with the night.

Noa straddles his lap, her cognac-brown eyes locking onto his. They squint slightly as she scoots forward, their bare chests pressing together. A rush of heat coils inside him, mirrored by the undeniable rise between them.

Her knees press into the ground on either side of him as she leans in, her lips finding his in a tender, lingering kiss. Her sweet, prickly tongue teases against his, an electrifying dance of heat and hunger.

She melts into him, their bodies fitting together like two halves of the same whole. With deliberate care, she rises slightly, her hands bracing against him for balance. Slowly, she lowers herself, and her warmth envelops him. Their bodies merge, seamless, as if the universe itself had conspired for this moment.

Their lungs hitch in unison, a sharp inhale trapping them in the gravity of this moment as pleasure washes over them. Pure bliss—the world beyond this moment ceases to exist.

Noa moves, rocking her hips in a rhythm that leaves Isaac breathless. Her eyes stay locked on his, dark with something that unravels him, something that pulls him under.

"Oh... my God," he stammers, his voice ragged, drowning in her.

Her lips curl into a playful, almost mischievous smile. "Feel good? Hmm?" she whispers, her voice a soft caress.

Isaac's hands tighten gently on her waist, his head falling back as he lets out a groan of pure ecstasy. "Whoa... shit, girl... I love you."

Outside of the tent, the still air picks up into a slight breeze. The crickets continue their string arrangement, the symphony blending with the passionate sounds of love. The sky above is ablaze with celestial wonder, streaked with light and infinite possibilities.

Later, as they lie headfirst at the tent's entrance, Isaac gazes up into the vast, endless dark. The Milky Way stretches faintly, a soft river of stars spilling across the sky.

Not a single bug bites or buzzes—as if the night itself is holding its breath. Or perhaps, he wonders, the ever-enigmatic Noa Gayle has willed it so.

"Your loud heart," Noa says softly, her cheek pressed against his bare chest.

Isaac chuckles. "You do that to me."

Noa lifts her head, her eyes meeting his for a moment before she lies back down, her right ear directly over his heartbeat.

In the periphery of Isaac's vision, a meteor streaks across the sky.

"Ooo, I think I just saw one!"

Noa rolls onto her back beside him. Together, they look up.

"I don't get this view at home," she whispers. "It rains too much, and there are too many lights. But here... look."

Another meteor flashes across the sky, and this time, they both see it.

"Whoa!" they exclaim simultaneously, their voices blending into the night.

More meteors follow, streaking in bright flares. Though all are the same brilliant white, Isaac almost feels as if they shimmer in different colors—blue, violet, emerald green—trailing through his imagination.

Then, another meteor—same angle, same direction as the first. He feels as if he is watching a movie a second time but can't place the moments.

Isaac tenses. A twinge of déjà vu, sharp enough to pierce the euphoria and unsettle him slightly.

"Mm, there goes your heart again," Noa teases. "Pitter-patter. Patter-pitter."

She pulls a blanket over her bare body and nestles against him, her face resting in the crook of his neck. Occasionally, she turns toward him, silently asking for a kiss. He gives her one each time.

Isaac's thoughts drift back to the promise he made her: *I will follow you anywhere. My world is your world.*

Another meteor streaks across the sky. For a moment, nothing else exists—just the weight of her against him, the hush of the universe, and the certainty that this is where he's meant to be.

He exhales. Tightens his arm around her.

Then, he gives in. "So... will you be gone long?"

****

Noa has been gone for a week. He isn't exactly sure when she'll return. He misses her.

Isaac finishes a typical Saturday shift at BSV, grateful to have worked with Tamika instead of Sharika. After a quick bus ride, he grabs a two-piece meal for Grandma from the Chicken Shack by the video store. The familiar routine steadies him as he strolls.

Grandma's bungalow sits midway down the block, its warm light spilling onto the porch. The front door is propped open, the screen closed but inviting.

Isaac pulls it open. The door scrapes against the step with a loud *sssshhhhhllllliick.*

Then—a voice.

Light. Feminine. Familiar.

His steps slow. His grip tightens around the bag. No. Can't be.

Then Grandma's unmistakable reply, sweet and playful: "Mm-hm, you know it! That's right!"

Laughter spills out.

"Grandma?" Isaac calls out, as he steps into the cozy warmth of the house.

"Isaac?" Grandma's voice projects warmly from the dining room.

"Hey, Grandma! Just checkin' in." He glances back to ensure the screen door latches, then steps further inside. "I brought you some chicken from Harol—" The words catch in his throat, his feet freezing mid-step.

His eyes land on the dining room.

Sarah Connor the parakeet stands calmly atop the table, clutching a small piece of green apple in one tiny foot. She pecks at it deliberately, bits of apple clinging to her beak, her movements precise and unbothered.

For a moment, Isaac assumes Grandma's giggles are for the bird—until he steps fully into view. Rounding the front-room wall, he spots her seated at the dining room table, facing him with a bright smile. Her head tilts slightly, relaxed, as someone deftly braids her hair.

His eyes lift instinctively, meeting Noa's. Her hands pause mid-motion, the braid unfinished. For a moment, they simply stare at each other, surprise flickering in his expression while a playful smirk tugs at her lips.

Isaac's heart skips as their eyes meet. Her smirk is disarming, confident.

He works to hold his expression steady, managing a modest smile. But inside, he's grinning ear to ear, every nerve alive, every thought centered on her.

"Hey, baby!" Grandma says, her face lighting up. "Noa came by and brought me some food—and this beautiful darling here to play!" She gestures toward Sarah Connor, who flutters her wings and pecks at her apple as if on cue.

Noa glances up, her tone effortlessly light. "Grandma's going to watch Sarah Connor while we head to Tommy's. Haircut day, right?"

Isaac shakes his head, a smile tugging at his lips. He knows he's supposed to play it cool, but he can't help the warmth spreading through him. Every time he sees her, she slips deeper into his world, as if she's always belonged there.

At Tommy's shop, Isaac holds the door open for Noa, who steps in first. Tommy looks up from his chair, where he's reclining with a newspaper. "Hey, lovely! Ope! There he is—the lucky man himself!" he booms, as he leaps from the chair.

Tommy gestures grandly for Noa to take the vacant barber's chair next to his. It's become her spot. Every other Saturday, when she's in town, she tags along with Isaac to the shop.

Noa watches from the side, her smile warm as Tommy tapers Isaac's fro with precision. The little black-and-white TV perched on the shelf plays *The Incredible Shrinking Woman* on the WGN weekend movie.

After a moment, Noa turns to Tommy, her expression thoughtful. "Tommy, do you believe in fate?"

Tommy pauses, his clippers idly hum. "Fate's a funny thing, darling," Tommy says, his tone softening. "Like a river—sometimes smooth, sometimes rough—but it'll take you where you're meant to go." Tommy taps Isaac's shoulder gently. "And son, you best keep swimming if you want to keep her!"

Noa nods, her gaze shifting back to the TV. Her pensive demeanor lingers.

Tommy abruptly taps Isaac on the shoulder with his comb, this time with more force, producing a slapping sound. "Boy—you better be treating her right!"

Isaac flinches, startled. "Huh? I ain't—"

Noa cuts in, laughing. "He's perfect, Tommy." Her smile falters briefly.

Tommy resumes cutting, the buzz of the clippers filling the brief silence. His eyes flick toward Noa as he speaks. "That's my take on it, sugar. Why such a deep question?"

Noa keeps her eyes on the TV, where Lily Tomlin clumsily navigates her oversized surroundings. "No reason. Just an existential crisis moment."

Isaac watches her reflection in the mirror, noting the flicker of something in her eyes—concern, hesitation. It's subtle, but it lingers, tugging at him.

When Tommy finishes the cut, he pats Isaac's hairline with Clubman Pinaud astringent. The sting bites sharp but familiar, the scent clean and unmistakably masculine, lingering in the air.

Isaac reaches for his wallet but Tommy's hand stops him mid-motion. "Keep it tonight, son. Go take the lady to a movie or something! She needs it."

Isaac frowns slightly, hesitant. "Tommy, I can't—"

"Boy, I said keep your money, and go love on that honey!" Tommy snaps, cracking his towel playfully against Isaac's arm, a grin spreading across his face.

Blushing, Noa glances at Isaac, her expression soft. She has this way of shifting effortlessly–from confident to gentle in a heartbeat. Isaac wonders if it's intentional, if this range is something deeper than charm. But one thing he doesn't question is how much he loves her.

Outside, as they walk down the semi-busy 87th Street, Isaac's thoughts churn. Something about Noa's voice tonight is unusual. A faint alarm hums in the back of his mind.

"Hey, I'm thinking about getting a beeper," Isaac says, breaking the silence as they walk. "There's a shop on Racine." He pauses, glancing at Noa to gauge her reaction before continuing. "You know–so you can hit me up whenever."

He tries to keep his tone casual, not wanting his insecurities to seep through. The last time he brought up communication, it hadn't gone well. But he can't shake the urge to hold on tighter, to be nearer. He's always carried a fear of loss, a quiet, nagging worry of people slipping away. And Noa? She's someone he can't bear to lose.

"Yeah–yeah! Good idea! Let's go," Noa replies, her tone light.

"Cool," Isaac says with a shrug, keeping his expression steady.

They walk less than half a mile around to 83rd and Racine. A small shop is there, specializing in pagers only. They have multiple colored cases and different styles of pagers. You would pay once for the pager, get it activated, but there is no monthly fee. It may not be completely legal.

Isaac picks a smoke-grey pager with a transparent case, its inner circuitry and battery visible. A button on top lights the display, casting a soft internal glow.

The shop owner hands Isaac a shady-looking handwritten

receipt after his payment for the device.

Isaac and Noa exit the little beeper storefront onto Racine. With a slight amount of sass, Noa says, "Now I can find my man when I need to."

They both laugh. Isaac is more serious about his intentions. He wants just one small extra bit of reassurance from the mystery that is Her. When he doesn't hear from her, he is adrift, kicking himself for missing her calls.

A pager wasn't much—a number on a tiny glowing screen—but it felt like a lifeline. For Isaac, it was a way to hold her closer, to steady himself against the quiet mystery of her, the moments when she felt just out of reach.

Chapter Six

Noa and Isaac have become nearly inseparable. She spends more time at his place—or Grandma's—than her own. When she isn't working, she's with him. Isaac often finds her braiding Grandma's hair or cooking by her side. She always has Sarah Connor, the little monk parakeet, in tow.

Months pass. Summer fades into fall. Noa accompanies Isaac to Tommy's every other Saturday—sooner if he needs a fresh cut for a date. Instead of escaping into old sci-fi books, he clutches her now. She is his escape, though he doesn't need one anymore. With Noa, he feels present—and he doesn't mind it.

Her favorite spot is Rainbow Cone. It's become his favorite, too—mostly because he loves watching her face light up as she's handed the towering, multicolored ice cream.

Isaac continues his artwork, especially his mural, which has become a masterpiece. Noa often watches him work, her gaze intent and admiring. The central mural feels almost alive now, as if one could step into it. The sun over the meadow glows like stained glass; its metallic multicolored tendrils shimmer. Around the silhouetted couple at the center, he's added a radiant aura.

The couple celebrates Thanksgiving with Grandma and Sarah Connor. Noa is a surprisingly amazing cook. She and Grandma often bond in the kitchen. There isn't much she can't do. She also seems to conjure moments or *things* with the blink of an eye–like *Jeannie* from one of Isaac's favorite classic TV shows. Her intelligence is one of the things he loves the most about her; it adorns her radiant physical beauty. Isaac's interest starts to evolve from science fiction to actual science. She teaches him so much. At times, he wonders how a person could know so much about so many things.

Isaac's prior insecurities slowly melt away with the passage of seasons. Noa hasn't disappeared for longer than three days, max. She sleeps over most days of the week, or vice versa.

Isaac loves watching movies with Noa. She focuses her attention directly on the plot and reacts. He adores the memory of her fresh eyes, seeing *Aliens* for the first time.

It's Christmas Eve, 1996. Noa and Isaac are at Grandma's, trimming her tree. Of course, the smell of baking sugar cookies permeates her bungalow. Noa prances rhythmically as she sings along with Donny Hathaway's "This Christmas." This synchronicity may not be synchronicity at all; he hears this song at least twenty times over the holidays. Still, the lyrics hit perfectly.

As the cookies bake, Grandma sits at the dining room table, cutting and sewing the finishing touches on a gift for a friend. Sarah Connor perches on her shoulder, nibbling on a piece of banana, a bit of mash sticking to her beak.

Noa continues to sing along with Donny Hathaway. She points at Isaac during certain lyrics, her eyes sparkling with mischief. He laughs and shakes his head, his heart full.

Maybe this song really is synchronous–can't escape it. At the moment, I don't wanna escape.

Later, the three of them gather in the front room. Noa curls under Isaac on the couch while Grandma dozes in her easy chair, Sarah Connor nuzzled against her neck. The tinny sound of Stevie Wonder's "What Christmas Means to Me" plays from a radio in the kitchen.

The floor-model TV flickers to life as bells chime on

the screen. *It's a Wonderful Life* is starting on Channel 32.

Noa sits up, her eyes lighting with excitement. "Oooh! I love this movie. Let's watch—please?"

Isaac can see how sentimental Noa is; she's been eagerly anticipating the holidays, her excitement contagious as she savors every moment with him.

"When I grew up, I never had any of this," she says with regret.

She explains how she grew up without holiday celebrations or much quality time with her mother. "She was always busy with work," Noa says softly, her voice tinged with sadness. "I'd keep myself occupied... usually alone." On the couch, her gaze drops, her fingers lightly tracing the edge of the blanket as if lost in thought.

Isaac watches her, the weight of her revelation and of her grief pressing against his chest. His heart tightens. "Babe, I know. It's okay—I get it," he says gently.

He pauses, waiting for her to meet his gaze. When she does, he smiles softly. "How about we make some new memories? I've never seen it. This is your movie—you get to see my reaction this time."

Isaac turns off the radio in the kitchen, then climbs back into the warmth of the couch with Noa, slipping under the blanket beside her. She grins, wrapping her arms around his torso. "Hey, Isaac—I love you. With all of my heart." As the movie begins, she adjusts the throw blanket over them, settling in closer.

Stephan's Quintet appear on screen, talk amongst themselves, and send an angel in training down to help old George Bailey. She giggles at the celestial dialogue between the galaxies, then sniffles as the title card fades. "Emotions going already," she whispers.

Isaac gently sweeps a lone tear from her right cheek with his thumb. He wraps this arm around her and pulls her into his side.

The light from the television flickers across their faces in the dark room. Grandma has long since fallen asleep, Sarah Connor nestled peacefully against her neck.

Noa's cognac eyes appear gray in this light. Throughout the movie, she wipes at her face with both hands. Isaac has his face buried in her hair, eyes up at the screen.

As Clarence earns his wings and George Bailey winks skyward, both Isaac and Noa are a sobbing mess. They wipe at their raw cheeks, laughing softly through their tears.

"Wow... that was a beautiful movie!" Isaac says, still wiping his face.

Noa replies, her voice thick with emotion. "Yeah—it's really cute! It's my new favorite of all time!"

Isaac blinks. "Really? I thought it was *Blade Runner.*"

Noa laughs, swatting at his chest. "That's your favorite, silly!"

The nightly news starts on Channel 32. Noa's gaze drops again, her demeanor shifting. Isaac feels the warmth between them give way to a faint chill.

Something is coming. He's felt this before. His joy twists into unease, but he shakes the thought. *Get out of your head.*

****

Noa and Sarah Connor spend the night at Isaac's. He opens his eyes to find her watching him sleep. The mural blazes behind her, lit by peeks of sunlight. Amber streaks dance in her sandy-brown bob, ablaze in the soft morning glow.

"Merry Christmas, handsome!" she says. Her voice is as warm as the light filling the room.

Isaac blinks and smiles, still groggy. He wipes his eyes, sitting up slowly. Two neatly wrapped gift boxes rest on the bed beside him. Noa picks up the larger one and nudges it toward him. "Here—do this one first!"

"Merry Christmas, my celestial muse." He smirks, shaking his head as he tears into the first gift.

Inside is a carefully bundled collection of music CDs– thirty of them. Marvin Gaye, Miles Davis, Mingus... a treasure trove of tunes.

"Damn... this is a fortune!" He pauses, realizing he doesn't even have a CD player, just that whack computer he never uses.

"Okaaaay–"

Noa giggles, cutting him off. "Open the other one, silly!"

He rips into the smaller box to reveal a portable CD player with headphones, plus a soft-case to hold the discs. Something he's been aiming to get for a while. It's perfect for his long CTA commutes.

"Damn, girl!" He shrugs. "How did you?–The discs alone–?"

Noa waves a dismissive hand, her grin mischievous. "I got the player on sale–and the CDs! You won't believe it! I only paid for one and got the rest for FREE!"

Isaac stares at her, wide-eyed, then sniggers. "America House? You realize you're on the hook now, right? It's a scam– they'll be sending you bunk elevator music for life."

Noa laughs, shrugs nonchalantly.

Isaac pinches the bridge of his nose, giggling. "It's your world, right? You got it under control, don't you?"

She leans closer with a playful smile. "And you know this–MAN!"

Isaac sniggers again, nodding. "I know you do–Smokey. Can I have those lips?"

Noa raises a brow, her tone low and seductive. "I don't know–can you?"

He leans in, and they kiss softly. Her energy feels differ-ent–off, somehow. For a moment, he brushes the thought away. *I'm in my head again.*

Isaac rolls out of bed and walks to the corner of

his apartment. He opens a small door beneath the attic easement, revealing a hidden cubby. He pulls out her gift and carries it back to her.

Noa's eyes widen in anticipation as she gingerly unwraps the canvas. It's almost as if she's never gotten a present before, savoring each motion—drawing out the experience.

Her breath catches when she sees a portrait of herself standing on a beach at dawn. Dolphin fins ripple through the foamy water, barely lit by the rising sun. Above her, the moon in its waxing crescent phase hovers over the ocean, casting a serene glow over the peaceful setting.

There is a handwritten note on the back of the canvas:

The warmth of your eyes brings my blood to a simmer, and the spark of your touch sets my soul ablaze—an inferno only quenched by the soothing cadence of your voice. My heart is no longer frozen in place; it has thawed and beats loudly into a dark, soundless void.

You are not what you seem. You are not of this place!

Like a comet, you came hurtling toward me with a force so powerful it will destroy my world.

Before you do that, take me with you.

I will follow your eyes and your voice through the darkness, reaching to find your touch.

Please, Noa—take me with you.

—Isaac

Noa stares at the painting, her fingers trembling as she traces the message on the back. Tears well in her eyes, and she visibly fights to keep them from spilling over. She appears speechless—her gaze fixed on Isaac's words.

"Isaac, I love you!"

Worry flickers across Isaac's face. He steps closer. "I love you too, Noa! What–?"

Noa places her hand in his, interlocking their fingers tightly. She hesitates, her gaze dropping to the floor. "It's been a while, and I know you hate it, but... I have to go home for a while."

Isaac sits upright, his heartbeat quickening. Something about this feels different from all the other times. "How long?" He looks Noa in the eyes and asks again, "How long?"

Noa shrugs sheepishly. "I don't know. You know, with the weather and stuff."

"Weather and stuff?" Isaac's voice rises, his worry shifting into slow-burning frustration.

"It might only be a few weeks!" Noa presses on.

Isaac moves to the edge of the bed, sitting beside her. "I'm going with you this time. I've got nothing to keep me here. Pete can check in on Grandma–I'm coming with you."

Noa mirrors his posture, leaning forward, her elbows on her knees. "Love... you can't go." She glances around the room, searching for the right words. "You don't even have a passport, remember?"

"When do you have to go? I–I can get my passport!"

Noa shakes her head slowly. Her voice tremors. "You can't go! I'm leaving tomorrow morning."

"TOMORROW MORNING!" Isaac's face reddens.

Noa flinches at his tone. "Isaac, I'm sorry!" She shrinks.

"Baby–what is going on there? Can you please tell me? Is it me? Is there somebody else?" Isaac's voice cracks, the words spilling out in desperation.

"You keep making this about us–it's not about us. I love you–there is nobody else!"

"Then why can't I go?" Isaac's voice breaks, his frustration giving way to near-tears. "Then why do you always act like this–all secretive?"

"Because you just can't, okay?" Noa's eyes flickered with something Isaac can't quite place—sadness, guilt, or maybe both. Her voice drops to a whisper, barely audible. "You wouldn't understand."

"Wouldn't understand... heh." Isaac wrestles to restrain his voice, forcing his words out in a low and deliberate tone.

He feels like he might explode. Anger, confusion, and heartbreak swirl in his chest, too much to contain. He stands abruptly, his jaw tight. Saying nothing, he hastily throws on his clothes, then grabs his coat and slings it over his shoulder.

Noa calls behind him, "Baby, please! Wait!"

Isaac doesn't wait. He stomps down the rear stairs of his apartment, the cold air stinging his face as he zips his puffer coat. His breath is visible in the icy air. His Lugz boots crunch over broken glass in the rear alley as he starts a long walk through Gresham on Christmas morning.

Isaac walks for over an hour, brooding. He circles near Morgan, passing by Gresham Elementary School, his mind racing. Slowly, the cold air cools his anger. Guilt and regret creep in, and he decides to return and apologize for his outburst—offer to take care of Sarah Connor.

When he gets back to his apartment, he finds that Noa is already gone, and so is Sarah Connor.

****

Isaac is nearing the end of his shift at BSV. It's been three weeks since Noa left for "home," and he hasn't heard a word from her. He checks his pager obsessively, scrolling through the same empty log. At home, he scans the caller ID on his landline multiple times a day, desperate for a missed call that isn't there. Just silence.

He has no idea when—or if—she'll come back.

Isaac wonders if Noa is really back home in Canada—or if she's snuck back to Chicago and is playing ghost, staying out of sight. *Maybe she's lost interest. Maybe she thinks I can't handle her lifestyle.*

I can handle it, he tells himself. She can come and go as she pleases. Just... please don't leave forever!

He wants to give her space, terrified that pressing too hard will push her away for good. Even though he craves more from their relationship now—a deeper connection, a sense of permanence—his lovesickness makes him willing to settle for less.

The ache of missing her is compounded by the endless aggravation of dealing with Sharika. Her frequent putdowns and jabs have grown more incendiary with each passing day. And then there's the laziness. Getting her to do anything is like dragging a boulder uphill, so Isaac has been doing most of the work himself. The exhaustion, both physical and emotional, is wearing him down.

Of course, Isaac could motivate Ron to fire her and hire someone better—he's considered it more than once. But the thought of being responsible for taking food off her table makes him hesitate. She has two children under the age of eight.

The few times he's seen her genuinely smile, it's been while doting on those kids. It's a different smile than the sinister smirk she wears while chopping him down.

Isaac is at the center of the three-aisle store, replacing returned VHS tapes on their shelves. Each tape is housed in a clear plastic case with a cover insert stamped in bold lettering: Big Shoulders Video. He works methodically, placing multiple copies of each movie behind the corresponding VHS cover on the shelf.

At the main counter, Sharika sorts through another pile of tapes.

Ding.

The door chime signals someone entering the store.

It's not *Her;* it's Isaac's cousin Pete. He rounds the frosted window and comes into view of Sharika, who yells, "Isaac! Your dirty-ass cousin is here!"

Pete winces, twisting his face into a grimace. "Bi–!" He catches himself as Isaac shoots him a stern look, shaking his head in silent disapproval. He always goes in on Pete for using that word. Their grandmother had drilled into him a deep respect for women, and he'd never once heard his grandfather call her out of her name either.

Pete rebounds with, "Whatever–yo' hair is dirty! Trick–why–why don't you wash that cement out of your head before you talk?"

Sharika's frown deepens as she looks Pete up and down. Without missing a beat, she shoots back, "Fool, I paid more for my hairstyle than you did for your burnt-up car! Now what?"

Isaac walks toward the front of the store, his tone firm but low. "Both of y'all, cut this shit out! Customers!"

The insults stop immediately. Sharika and Pete exchange glares but say nothing more.

Isaac looks around the store. It appears empty, silent, except for the hum of fluorescent lights overhead and the blood-curdling screams and deep voices echoing from the *Mortal Kombat* arcade game near the entrance. It's on demo mode–no one is playing it.

The store seems empty, until the curtain to the Adult section sweeps aside in a flash and Creepy Teddy emerges. Today, he's clutching two titles: *Black Bottom Pie* and a well-worn copy of *Double Stuff Oreo.* The tapes are discreetly sandwiched between *Beverly Hills Cop II* and *Short Circuit 2.* This guy really loves sequels.

He storms up to the counter to check out with Sharika, who greets him with a dramatic eye-roll.

Pete leans in excitedly. "Cuz! Remember Vanessa—that thick honey from high school? I ran into her at Swap O' Rama last week, and we started talkin'." He snickers, his voice dropping to a playful tone. "You know, woo-woo this, woo-woo that!"

Isaac forces a smirk, half-listening as he organizes tapes on the shelf.

Pete presses on, grinning. "So she starts talkin' about how she always liked me back then and wanted to hook up—and I'm sittin' there trippin', cuz..." He giggles. "...you know I been peepin' since high school!"

Pete shifts gears, clearly trying to lift Isaac's spirits. "We're hitting up Mr. G's tonight. She's bringing her friend Andrea. She saw your picture and said for sho! And bro, I saw her picture. She fine, cuz. Let's roll?"

Isaac shakes his head before Pete even finishes. "Nah, man. I'm finishing up here, then heading out. Got stuff on my mind."

Pete shrugs but keeps it light. "I hear ya, man. I know...trust me.... I know where your heart is... Sorry for even bringing it up. Page me if you change your mind."

Isaac watches him go, knowing Pete means well—and knowing how he feels about Noa, Pete probably guessed he'd pass tonight. Truth is, he might not even be going out himself.

A deep, rhythmic thundering sound emerges from outside the storefront. The music itself isn't audible—just the rumbling low-frequency boom of the bass, unmistakably "So Many Tears" by 2Pac.

Pete glances over his left shoulder toward the front windows. Sharika, standing behind the clerk's counter, can't see due to the translucent glass panel in front of the door. She leans her upper body over the opposite countertop from Pete to peer out through the clear windows.

From the left, a 1987 Chevy Caprice with a pimped-out iridescent blue paint job rolls slowly past the storefront.

Thick white exhaust fog pours from the tailpipe, mixing with the cold winter air. The bass pressure rattles everything–the windows, the entry door, even the plastic clamshell security cases holding Creepy Teddy's naughty rentals.

Teddy doesn't care about the sound system. He looks annoyed that Sharika isn't ringing him up and demands, "Excuse me! I ain't got time for that ol' bullshit. Ring me up, please–ma'am!"

Isaac keeps his back turned, focused on organizing the videos on the shelves, unfazed. Pete watches the car with admiration–and a little envy. Sharika, still bent over the counter, watches intently as the Caprice pulls into a parking spot in front of the beauty supply store two doors down from BSV.

Straightening, Sharika checks the wall clock. "Ay! I gotta get off on time today. I gotta pick up my mother–Ike, close my register when Tamika gets here. Peace out, simps!"

She grabs her knockoff fashion purse from under the counter, quickly exits the U-shaped counter island, and heads for the door. Clearly, she's planning to flirt with the driver of the blue gangsta wagon.

Ding.

Pete shakes his head, smirking. He looks at Isaac, who continues his work without reacting. Pete starts giggling, and the two briefly exchange amused looks. Pete exits the store.

Ding.

Isaac finishes his shift, does the usual handoff to the next crew, and heads to the corner of 87th and Dan Ryan to catch his bus. There isn't one in sight for the westbound 87th route– the way home. Very unusual.

Where's the synchronicity?

He waits in the biting cold for twenty minutes–nothing. No coincidence, no cosmic alignment. Then, out of nowhere, the thought seizes him: *Go find her.*

He crosses 87th Street and enters the L station. As soon as he descends to the Red Line platform, the train approaches. *There it is!*

****

Isaac knocks at Noa's door. She opens it and steps to the side, gestures to him to walk in.

Sarah Connor sees Isaac and excitedly flies to land onto his left shoulder. He reaches up and scritches her crown for her as her little green eyelids close.

Noa tilts her head to the side slightly. "Hey—can I have a kiss?"

A flashing micro-frown enters and exits mostly unnoticed on Isaac's forehead. He shakes his head once, and leans forward and they exchange a single peck on the lips. Sarah Connor balances herself on his shoulder as he bends forward.

"How's everything back home?" Isaac asks.

She replies, "Everything is wonderful! Took care of those loose ends I was talking about. You know?"

"What loose ends are those? You never said what."

"You know, the stuff with the condo. Quotas to fill and such."

Isaac places Sarah Connor on her perch, his movements stiff. His jaw tightens, and his hands curl into fists at his sides. He doesn't want to explode—but the words come out anyway, sharp and trembling with anger.

"I'm getting sick of the bullshit. Will you be open with me about what's going on?" Isaac's voice rises steadily, the frustration building. "You disappear for weeks. You barely answer my calls. And now you're here—here—and you don't even tell me?"

He takes a deep, uneven breath, his chest rising and falling in sharp, staccato puffs. He exhales slowly, his voice trembling. "One last time... Is there someone else? Larry? Who? Got me out here looking like a chump or something!"

Noa drops her gaze. "Like I've told you before, there is no one else!" She throws up her hands, her voice rising as she begins to ramble. "It's just home stuff, quotas, debt, and—it's not that simple to explain! You keep making this about us. I told you—I love you, and I mean it. But this is all just too hard right now!"

Her voice cracks as she takes a shaky breath. "You have no idea how hard it is to love someone you know you can't have!"

Isaac presses his fist into his temple. He looks at Noa, pauses momentarily—bracing for how she might answer. "What does that mean? I'm right here!"

"I know you are there, but we are living in two different worlds, and you can't see into mine."

Isaac silently looks around the room, taking in the surroundings—his gaze settling on Sarah Connor, perched on her play-top, snacking on sunflower seeds. She drops one, then pauses, looking squarely at him. He blinks rapidly; his vision blurs. Slowly, his eyes drift downward, landing on his feet, planted firmly on the ground.

A heavy, impending sense of doom washes over him. Noa's mantra echoes faintly in his mind: *It's our world.* But now, he realizes, they are in *two different worlds.*

Isaac barely manages to open his mouth. It feels as though the life has been drained from him. "I can't see into your world because you won't let me in," he says, his voice trembling. "I want to be with you—wherever you are. Just let me in. Let me go with you." A single tear slips down his cheek. "Please, Noa."

He looks up to find Noa's brown eyes swimming in tears. She looks down, as though searching for the courage to speak.

"You need to go. I'm sorry," she whispers, her voice fragile. A whimper escapes her lips as she catches herself just before breaking into a full-out wail. "We have to move on—oh!"

Her wail nearly escapes.

She presses her fingers to the corners of her eyes, trying in vain to stop the tears streaming down her face. Her voice is choked and uneven, barely audible. "I—Isaac—I wish you the best."

The words come out stifled, breaking under the weight of her whimpers and her raw, trembling voice.

Isaac sees the pain etched in her face, and all he wants is to smother it with his love. He wraps his arms around her, pulling her close. Her head stays fixed, unmoving against his chest. She doesn't lift her arms—her hands remain folded tightly against herself, her body stiff.

"I love you," Isaac whispers, his voice breaking.

"Goodbye, Isaac."

Her words hit him like a hammer—straight to the chest. Slowly, he releases her from his unrequited embrace, his arms falling limply to his sides. The air feels violently snatched from his lungs. He can't cry—he can't reply. His emotions swirl in a state of painful confusion, leaving him paralyzed.

He stands there for a few seconds, looking at her, then over at Sarah Connor, who watches silently from her perch. Finally, he turns toward the door, his movements slow and deliberate. Without even taking that breath, he steps outside and lets the door close behind him.

As he closes the door, Isaac hears Noa's voice faintly behind him.

"I love you too, hand—!"

Her words are cut short by the soft click of the door closing.

Isaac steps out into the cold night air, his chest hollow. He doesn't look back. Inside, Noa doesn't move to the window to watch him walk away. She stands motionless, rooted to the spot.

A whimper escapes her lips, her body trembling. Slowly, she sinks to her knees, then collapses forward, pressing her face against the floor. Her sobs come in broken gasps as the air thickens around her, choking her cries into silence.

****

Despite his sleepless night, Isaac manages to get through his shift the next morning. He even agrees to work the next day, as Ron wants to take the day off.

He passes off the store to Wayne and Tamika and heads to the bus stop. No bus approaches for forty minutes. When the 87th Street bus finally arrives, he hops on and rides east to Morgan Street. His *soul* is exhausted. He can't lift the weight of pain Noa has left on him. He is starting to feel like she was a figment of his imagination.

He tunes his Walkman radio to V103. Alexander O'Neal's "If You Were Here Tonight" is playing. *At least the music thing is still here.*

Grandma is fine. When Isaac swings by, he finds her watching *Spin City,* and she has already eaten dinner. She sits up her recliner.

"Baby—are you all right?"

"Yeah, I'm good. Just tired."

She appears to doubt his reason; she appears concerned. She doesn't press. "Well, you go home and get some rest—grab your plate from the oven and eat too."

Isaac nods, fights tears. He kisses Grandma's forehead and heads home.

After ascending his rear stairs, he slides his key into his lock and turns. He tosses the keys onto the table, and notices his lights are already on. He hears a trilling sound, looks up, and sees Sarah Connor spring to action in her cage. She rocks back and forth in excitement.

There is a handwritten note on his kitchen table:

Isaac,

I am so sorry, handsome! It's time for me to go home. For good this time.

I wish things could've ended like they were when we started. Unfortunately, we won't be able to go back to that life. Ever!

Please take care of Sarah Connor. She's always been there for me, and I know she'll be there for you too. Through her, a part of me will always stay with you.

I will always love you. Please remember that until the very end. Whenever that may come!

I am so sorry!

Noa

Noa isn't a figment of his imagination. This little bird is proof.

Isaac feels a flicker of relief, holding onto Sarah Connor as a tangible reminder of Noa. But even this thought wrestles with his cynicism. *She couldn't get through customs with an exotic bird. That's why she left her with me,* he thinks bitterly, snickering at the idea.

As he ponders, a sharp, shrill voice cuts through the room. "I love you."

Isaac freezes. For a moment, he stares at Sarah Connor, perched quietly in her cage. He shakes his head, brushing it off. Sarah Connor doesn't talk. Sure, parakeets can mimic words, but this little bird has never managed anything beyond garbled static—like an old radio stuck between stations.

Isaac wonders how Noa got into his apartment with no key.

Isaac walks over to open Sarah Connor's cage, and she steps up onto his finger. Pulling her beak close, he kisses the side of it gently, his fingers scritching her tiny head. His eyes ache, the pressure building behind them. He swallows hard, a tight tug pulling from behind his ears as the weight of everything crashes over him.

He sets Sarah Connor down on her play-top. She tilts her head, looking up at him. She doesn't do her usual side-to-side dance of excitement. Instead, she stays still, as if sensing the heavy air around them both. If she could cry, she probably would.

Isaac swallows hard, holding back his own tears, but the intense pain refuses to loosen its grip. It engulfs him, a weight he can't shake.

Noa makes his world feel real. With her, he isn't alone. She understands him, and he thought he understood her. Their connection feels unlike anything he's ever known. He couldn't imagine life without her. And now, she's gone.

****

Weeks—maybe even months—go by. Isaac couldn't tell you. Time has lost all meaning. He has lost his sense of purpose and now just goes through the motions, fulfilling his obligations to others, not caring for himself.

He goes to work and helps Grandma when needed. He also takes care of his new bird, Sarah Connor, who is always by his side. One day, he even brings Sarah to work; it isn't a problem since it's a slow day. She just sits in her cage, playing or snacking, while he doodles in his sketchbook. The little bird actually softens Sharika's edge.

As for his bus luck, that hasn't returned. He has to wait just as long as everyone else, which is where he is now—at 87th and Dan Ryan, waiting.

A bus chugs eastward, and just before Isaac boards, the payphone on the corner rings. His pager goes off at the same time. He pauses and walks to the phone, which causes him to miss the bus.

He lifts the receiver. *Buzzzzzz.* Only a dial tone.

He scan his pager: *7 84 52 52 58*. The numbers are unfamiliar and incomplete. He tries dialing them anyway and gets a busy signal.

He waits another thirty minutes in the cold winter evening before another eastbound CTA bus arrives.

As Isaac arrives at 87th and Morgan, the payphone on the corner rings. He approaches it and touches its cold plastic receiver, just as his pager goes off again. At the same time, a car drives past playing "Reflections" by Diana Ross and the Supremes.

Beep–Beep–Beep.

The same numbers flash on his pager again: *7 84 52 52 58*. They seem random, meaningless, but their recurrence gnaws at the edges of his mind. He picks up the receiver, and there is only a dial tone. He hangs it up, then drops two quarters into the phone and dials the numbers from his pager–which yield the same busy signal as before.

A new synchronicity is born. The bus thing is gone, replaced by a new, strange pattern–the payphone, the pager, the numbers. It feels deliberate.

Isaac's chest tightens as the thoughts creep in. Noa? Is she in danger? Is she trying to reach me? A chill runs through his body, sharper than the winter air biting at his skin.

He can't shake these thoughts, so he decides to go to the police. He doesn't even know what to say to them. *She broke up with me, and now I can't find her?*

Isaac stops at the Chicago PD station on the corner of 85th and Peoria in Gresham. The front desk officer, a middle-aged, mustachioed sergeant, listens to his plea with an expression of mild irritation.

"How long has she been gah-n?" Officer Sitarski asks, in a thick Chicago accent.

"I don't know–three, four weeks." Isaac shrugs.

Sitarski raises an eyebrow. "Son, it's unlikely she's just gah-n missin'! You wanna file a missing persons? What's her name—and what's yours?"

"I don't know if she's missing—she may be in trouble, I don't know." Isaac palms his forehead. "Noa—Gayle!" Isaac says quickly. "My name is Isaac André."

Sitarski scribbles on a pad. "Noa or Gayle?"

"Noa Gayle is her name. Her last name is Gayle."

Sitarski nods. "Address?"

Isaac pauses, feeling uneasy. "I don't know the real one... it's in Northern Lights—in Canada."

The officer gives him a strange look. "We'll look into it." He puts his pen down with an exasperated motion. He grabs a Chicago White Sox mug that reads, *Real Men Wear Black*, then walks into a room behind the desk.

Isaac leans against the wall, arms crossed. The smell of stale coffee and faint cigarette smoke hangs in the air. He waits for what feels like an eternity—two hours, by the clock—before Sitarski wanders back.

"Well?" Isaac asks in frustration.

"Sorry, I didn't realize you were stayin'." Sitarski sips from his mug. He continues. "Son, Noa Gayle doesn't bring back any missing persons. Closest matches so far are a forty-nine-year-old woman in South Dakota, and a thirty-three-year-old in Poughkeepsie, New York. You said she's twenty-nine, right?"

"Yeah," Isaac replies, his chest tightens.

"Also..." Sitarski hesitates, then chuckles lightly. "There ain't no such place as Northern Lights in Canada. I'm sorry, kid." He takes another sip from his mug and walks away, muttering to himself, "Poo-Kip-See—am I sayin' dat right?"

The sergeant's words are a stab to the gut. Isaac's surroundings blur into static. He stands motionless for a moment, and when his body finally obeys his commands—he turns and walks out onto Peoria Street.

As he exits the station, a car glides past, blaring "Reflections," by The Supremes. A different car than before—but Isaac doesn't even register it. He doesn't question it as he usually would. His storm of thoughts are louder than the music, they drown out the world.

He stumbles forward in a daze. The world feels frozen. No more cars pass, no voices call out. The only movement comes from Isaac's legs as he drags forward.

There is no Northern Lights? The jagged question tumbles through his mind, catching on every frayed nerve.

A suffocating sense of betrayal rises—an emotion he's not used to. But it doesn't stand alone. It's tangled with abandonment—the crushing loneliness she left behind.

Isaac's pace falters. He doesn't care that she lied. He doesn't care about anything—only her. He would forgive it all, forget it all, if she would just come back.

****

Isaac steps off the 87th Street bus. His stride is slow and lackadaisical. Both of his hands are buried in his pockets against the cold. Sharika is already at the door, arms crossed, scowl carved deep. Her quickened breath is visible as rapid white plumes float from her mouth and nose.

He's ten minutes late, though the store doesn't open for another fifty.

She yells out, "You wanna hurry the fuck up? Damn, do you feel how cold it is?"

He keeps walking, unbothered. Pulls the key from his backpack, slides it into the lock without looking at her. Still, he lets her step in first.

"Damn—how you gonna be in charge and late? You been

on some bullshit lately, Ike! Yeah—that's right!"

Isaac hates that forced shortening of his name, he always has, but he never protested.

He lowers his bag behind the counter, and boots up the registers as Sharika disappears to the back.

It's Saturday morning, and the dropbox is overflowing with returns. Two VHS tapes have spilled onto the floor—*Brownie Bottom Girls #10* and *Breakin' 2: Electric Boogaloo*.

Creepy Teddy won't be in today.

The floors haven't been vacuumed. The shelves haven't been faced. Wayne left the place a mess. Which means they'll have to clean it. Which means he will, considering his company today.

Sharika comes back up front. She exhales sharply, rubs her temples with her palms.

"Look, Ike, I got a lot going on—I'm sor—"

Isaac, already seeing red, doesn't let her continue.

"Don't!" Isaac doesn't recognize his own voice.

He pauses for a second.

"You know what, Sharika? I'm sick of this shit. All of it. I'm sick of you, I'm sick of lying-ass people, I'm sick of this dusty-ass video store! What do you have against me? What have I ever done to you or anyone else? None of this makes sense—FUCK!"

He barely gets that last word out, his voice shaking. His heartbeat thunders against his eardrums. He grips his back-pack and swings it hard into the monitor. The screen shatters, flickers, then dies. He turns and hurls the bag at the opaque glass window. It splinters, one side collapsing in a crash of shards.

The world tilts. His skin burns. His heart pounds, he hears it, even. He hears Noa's voice: "Your loud heart." This cuts across his chest like a Japanese katana, leaving a searing pain behind, followed by warm blood.

He feels outside of his body, like he's another person in a gallery of onlookers.

Sharika doesn't move. Her face is tight, her nostrils flared, but she doesn't say a word. Her eyes are wide in terror.

Isaac reaches into his coat pocket for the store keys. He juggles them once, then drops them beside the register. With a sigh, he crunches over shattered frost-glazed glass and makes his way toward the exit. A sudden realization settles in—he's jobless now.

"Fuck all of it." His voice is flat, stripped of anger, stripped of anything.

The cold greets him as he steps outside, but he doesn't feel it. He starts his walk back to 87th Street. The eastbound bus approaches just as he arrives—perfect timing. He doesn't notice.

His world never made sense. Noa gave it meaning. Without her, there is none. It was, *their world.*

****

More weeks pass. Isaac still goes through the motions. The pay-phones continue to ring, and continue to be silent from the other end.

It's Saturday—time for his biweekly haircut. Triweekly? It's been a while.

Isaac pulls open the door to Tommy's shop, the faint chime of the bell cutting through the quiet. His stride carries its usual near-confidence, but with some of that confidence chiseled away.

The shop is empty for a Saturday. Tommy sits reclined in the barber's chair, his head tilted upward toward the static-flickering screen of the black-and-white TV perched on its shelf. The faint scent of aftershave lingers, mingling with the chill of February air sneaking in as Isaac enters.

Tommy turns his head, noticing Isaac's downward de-meanor. The shop lights are dim, casting shadows. It's already dark outside.

Isaac climbs into the chair, setting a paperback on his lap—*Volis* by Philip K. Dick. It's the first book Tommy's seen him with in months; he's usually clutching Noa tightly. In fact, he hasn't been to the shop since she left.

Concern washes across the old barber's face. "Everything the same?" Tommy asks.

Isaac nods. No words.

Tommy gets to work.

Isaac's mind is consumed by Noa, from the moment he wakes until he drifts into dreamless sleep. If he could dream, she would undoubtedly inhabit those too.

Pain coils deep in his chest—visceral and unrelenting. Noa's sudden coldness right before her departure—it feels like he's been rubbed raw, only to have acid poured over the exposed wounds.

He cycles through every memory, desperately searching for meaning in her cryptic departure. Things were beautiful—the best. And then, in an instant, they weren't. Even after weeks, he can't let it go—he just can't.

Tommy finishes tapering Isaac's mini-fro, then lines the back of his neck with a steady hand. The sting of Clubman astringent follows, quickly replaced by a soothing coolness.

As Isaac starts to rise, Tommy's hand presses gently on his shoulder.

"Hold on. Let me get those whiskers under control."

Isaac glances at Tommy, surprised. It's a running joke be-tween them—Isaac's sparse facial hair never justified a full shave.

Tommy leans the chair back, prepping Isaac's uneven stubble with a hot towel scented with vetiver. The steam wraps around Isaac's face, relaxing his muscles as Tommy works methodically.

The transistor radio crackles faintly, tuned to WVON as always. Tommy adjusts the dial, and the static fades into the opening notes of "Azure" by Ella Fitzgerald.

Isaac's heart clenches. This was Grandad's favorite song. The lyrics squeeze at his chest like a vise, each word pressing on raw wounds. He wonders, cynically, if it's all just his mind making desperate connections—or if the synchronicity is real.

Isaac feels the slight pressure building under his tightly closed lids. The steam of the towel relaxes them and he doesn't feel the tears collecting underneath. His chest bounces irregularly.

Tommy's hands pause. He then presses the towel gently against Isaac's face. His voice is calm, low. "It'll always be as it should, son."

Isaac exhales shakily as he whimpers.

Tommy finishes the shave of Isaac's face, now completely smooth. He applies a pat of soothing cool aftershave to Isaac's cheeks and uses a soft brush to brush off his neck.

Isaac stands, feeling oddly heavy yet somehow lighter. He reaches to pay Tommy, who halts him, then rests a hand on Isaac's shoulder, his voice steady with calm conviction.

"Keep your head up, son. And follow your heart. That road will take you where you need to go. Just remember that when the time comes... keep your money."

Isaac nods, muttering a quiet, "Thanks."

He turns toward the shop door, passing the payphone mounted on the wall.

It rings.

Brrrrrrrring!

Isaac freezes in place.

The sound cuts through the air, sharp and deliberate. One blaring *brrrrring* after another.

Tommy's voice breaks through the quiet, distant and casual, "I got it!"

Isaac raises a halting hand toward Tommy, who stops, appearing mildly confused, but says nothing.

Brrrrrrrrrrrrring!

Isaac steps closer to the phone, his hand hovering over the receiver. He hesitates.

Brrrrrrrrrrrrrrrrrrrrrring!

The sound grows louder, sharper—reverberating inside his skull. His hand closes around the receiver.

Brrrrrrrrrrrrrrrrrrrrrrrrrrrrring!

Heart pounding, he lifts it to his ear.

The line crackles, a voice breaking through—panicked, but unmistakable.

"Isaac? ISAAC!" A sniffle, a sharp inhale. "Baby—it's me... It's Noa!" Her sobs spill through the receiver, raw and uncontrollable.

Part Three

Chapter Seven

Pitch black.

A glint of light emerges, growing steadily from faint to the spectrum of full sunlight. The glow floods a large, circular room with off-white walls and a single hallway entrance. The decor is sparse, stark, and unlived-in. No windows hint at an outside world.

A gigantic, wall-sized screen flickers on, revealing a serene landscape—it looks like one of Isaac's paintings. Across the bottom, the date and time display: 04/11/2078 16:09. Music begins to play: "Gone" by AK, pulled from a playlist tailored to Noa's emotional state. Synapticants often preprogram frequencies like these to ease their exit from GAIA into the real world.

In the center of the room stands an enormous floor-to-ceiling cylindrical chamber. It's surrounded by opaque glass. A portion of the chamber slides open.

Thunk—pssssssshhhhh.

Soft fog drifts out, revealing Noa Gayle. Her cognac-brown eyes flutter open. Beads of condensation catch the light as they roll down her cheeks and shoulders, and trace the delicate curvature of her hips. She grabs a towel and pats herself dry, starting with her face. A smear of residual white gel clings to her ankles and the tops of her feet; she wipes it away with single swiping motions. Wrapping herself in the towel, she steps out of the chamber.

She crosses the room with measured steps and presses a

panel on the nondescript wall at chest height. A small drawer emerges, containing a stainless steel bottle, with a logo of a brain surrounded by sparks. The label reads *Neur-ish MAX: Neurotransmitter Repletion Supplement.*

As she removes the bottle, the drawer retracts seamlessly into the wall. The sound of pressurizing air follows.

Pwooofffffsh.

She twists the cap.

Tssssssss.

She nearly tilts the bottle upside-down as she gulps the contents eagerly until it's empty.

Walking slowly, she wipes her eyes with her left hand and presses another panel with her right. A small drawer ejects, glowing with a brightly lit green recycle symbol.

Noa puts the bottle and its cap inside the deeper drawer, then waves her hand—prompting it to close with a soft hiss.

Pwooofffffshhh–phhhhoooooom.

A low mechanical hum begins as the device cleans and directly recycles the bottle. This is not Chicago in the late '90s. This is Northern Lights, a city in the Northwest Territories of the Republic of Canada. The year is 2078.

Noa pulls on a pair of oatmeal-colored baggy sweatpants, followed by a matching oversized sweatshirt. She sits on a stool at a counter-height table, which has just enough space to eat or work.

She settles in her seat, silent at first—as the next song in her playlist starts; it's "Setembro" by Quincy Jones.

Her face flushes as she holds her breath, trying unsuccessfully to choke back her emotions. The pressure buildup escapes first as a gasping moan, then releases in a loud unrestrained wail.

A storm of tears pours down her face—both hands grip the rounded white edges, her knuckles whitening.

Noa braces herself, staring down silently now as tears

splash onto the bare countertop. She wipes her face with the sleeves of her slouchy top. She thinks she is beyond this spell, but within moments, her mouth gapes open and another wail escapes–a guttural rush of air. She rocks up and down–the pain has taken her voice.

She feels the impending pain of loss; again–like when he left.

He's gone, but she still sees his face.

He's not here, or there.

Joe.

He's dead–as of yesterday, it has been two years. *An inoperable, aggressive brain cancer.*

She's gone through the stages–yet remains trapped in a recurrent, inescapable loop. Acceptance is never an escape but a shallow cliff from which she falls, back into the relentless orbit of anger, denial, depression–and especially guilt. Bargaining is the tripwire, threaded with the faintest sliver of hope. As her torment lightens its chokehold, just as she enters the cleansing wellspring of acceptance–she faces loss again.

He isn't real, Noa thinks, centering herself. *But he's alive*, she counters.

He isn't him, she lectures herself.

"I love him!" Noa screams out into her silent, sterile abode.

She collects herself, breathes rapidly.

"It's our world, Isaac. We can do what we want," she says to herself followed by a single perfunctory nod. Her nostrils are stuffed and her voice a choked-up, muffled whisper, but this is her mantra to him. This is her mantra to herself, even here–even now.

Noa walks down the narrow hallway in her windowless, sterile apartment–passing a short, waist-high white faux-stone pedestal. Atop it sits Sarah Connor, a holographic replica of her parakeet. The bird responds as Noa approaches, tilting her head and puffing her feathers to receive a virtual scritch to the crown.

This motion appears as if Noa's hand passes through the little green apparition.

At the base of the holographic projector, on the pedestal, is a display screen with such high resolution it feels as though you could reach into it. On the screen, a widget floats in the center of a grassy landscape on a sunny day. Multicolored tendrils stretch out from the sun, reaching down toward the virtual field, where blades of green grass blow in a virtual breeze. The widget has the appearance of a vintage digital alarm clock, with three rows of data in green, blue, and red.

Green digits: Current date and time—04/11/2078 16:45.

Blue digits: GAIAp– 3days22hrs

Red digits: SBSq–22days11hrs.

That is the current date: April 11th, 2078. Noa had spent three days and twenty-two hours immersed in 1996 Chicago within GAIA—the shortest period in a while. She has no choice but to stay away now; her SBS quota, represented by the red digits, has climbed to over twenty-two days.

She finds it excruciating—both to stay there and to leave him behind. The longer she stays, the greater the risk of detection. And yet, knowing it will all come to an end soon, she clings to every moment. Everything, including Isaac, will vanish. The virtual genome she crafted in the image of her dead husband—a being who has lived twenty-five simulated decades of life—will be deleted.

It's our world, Isaac, that one, and this one. Before your world is destroyed, I will bring you to mine!

****

January 2055.

Eight men sit around the table. Most of Gemini Corporation's board is present, their faces lit by the glow of a wall-sized screen displaying tickers and a serene landscape. The atmosphere is far from professional—it feels more like a frat party as the men toast to their success. SynaptiLynk is a triumph, a technology poised to solve humanity's most pressing challenges. Energy, drug discovery, climate stabilization—problems of the past, thanks to them.

At the head of the table, next to an empty seat, is Jace Faber, the CEO. His grin is broad, his face flushed with pride.

The door to the opaque glass walls slides open with a quiet hiss, unnoticed at first. Carolyn Faber enters, her movements sharp but deliberate. She scans the room, makes a quick swiping motion in front of her glasses, then removes them and tucks them away. She doesn't take the empty seat next to Jace. Instead, she stands at the opposite end of the table, arms crossed.

"Don't let me interrupt, little brother. Continue," she says, motioning with both hands in a sarcastic gesture.

Jace's smile slowly erases—his face reddens. Carolyn's use of "little brother" is a reminder of their birth order, and of her achievement gap.

The room grows quiet, the earlier laughter hushed away.

Carolyn's kind, gray eyes sweep across the table, passing each man to land on Elmer Haynes, who lowers his gaze in shame.

Despite the tension, her eyes remain steady. She is wearing her signature pleated slacks, button-down shirt, and suspenders—a look so distinct it's been mocked on streaming late-night shows.

"All of you," she begins, her tone cutting, "each and every one of you should be ashamed of yourselves!"

A few of the men shift uncomfortably in their seats.

Carolyn Faber storms out of the boardroom, her movements sharp and unyielding. One of the board members snickers, breaking the heavy silence. "What the—?" he starts, and the tension quickly unravels as a ripple of chuckles spreads through the group like frat boys who've heard a bad joke.

Jace waves his hand sharply, his stern look cutting through the laughter. The chuckles die awkwardly, leaving a strained silence in their wake. Elmer Haynes stares at his shoes, his expression etched with something between guilt and shame. Slowly, he rises and follows Carolyn's path out the door, leaving the rest of the board behind in uncomfortable quiet.

Not long after this, Carolyn Faber disappears without a trace, her absence casting a long shadow over Gemini, the company that would later become GaiaX—and over Jace Faber himself.

****

December 2078

Noa Gayle sits in her windowless condo, its sterile walls bathed in the pale glow of artificial light. Outside, the city of Northern Lights rises in a rigid grid of identical towers, sealed off from the wasteland beyond. The world doesn't end here, but it may as well have. After World War IV, desperation reshaped humanity—even survival feels artificial.

Her fingers hover over a stainless-steel bottle on the counter, her thoughts drifting.

Joe.

His face flickers in her mind—a Non-Participant who, somehow, made her world feel alive. She met him when he came to repair her GAIA chamber. Handsome, confident, different. Unlike anyone she'd met in there.

Repair—he had nothing else to offer GaiaX's omnipresent system, yet what he gave her was real: his laugh, his ingenuity, his raw humanity.

Joe had maintained the systems that sustained people like her—the Synapticants who lived their lives through SynaptiLynk virtual worlds, with Artificial Individuals—and provided stability to the system by sharing their brainpower.

As a Technician, Joe worked grueling, hazardous hours, always teetering on the edge of exhaustion. The system barely noticed his existence, let alone valued his life. When cancer came for him, it showed no mercy.

Glioblastoma. The SynaptiLynk nanobots could have prevented it, repairing the rogue cells before they took root. But GaiaX forbids enhancements for anyone with preexisting conditions, fearing they could destabilize the quantum bits critical to solving incalculable problems. Human brains—used as collective processors—remain the most foolproof stabilizing factor. The rules are absolute: perfect, unyielding, and devastating.

Joe died in a world designed to leave him behind.

Noa exhales, her eyes moving to the chamber in the corner of the room. Inside that sterile capsule lies her rebellion: Isaac André. He isn't flesh and blood. He isn't even real by GaiaX's standards. But he feels more alive to her than anything else in this sanitized, lifeless world.

Isaac lives in a virtual construct of 1997 Chicago, a world she crafted inside GAIA's network. With help from SOMA—the shadow network of Carolyn Faber's followers—she bypassed GAIA's dampers to create him. Isaac isn't just an Artificial Individual; he's self-aware, capable of thought, and of love.

But his existence is a crime. The creation of Artificial General Intelligence, AGI, is strictly outlawed. Detection is inevitable, and when GaiaX's anti-virus protocols find him, they'll erase everything: his world, his memories, and Isaac himself.

Noa's heart clenches. She already knows loss too well. She can't lose him too.

Somewhere, hidden by SOMA, Joe's body lies in cellular stasis, a state of torpor. She doesn't know where—they won't tell her, for her safety and theirs. All she knows is that it's safe.

His brain, once ravaged by cancer, has been repaired using PaxCerebra, a revolutionary technology developed by Carolyn Faber before her disappearance. Unlike SynaptiLynk, Pax-Cerebra doesn't merely maintain—it heals, regenerates, even rebuilds. Joe's brain is whole again, ready for life.

But his consciousness is gone. That they could not salvage; however, the body remains. A vessel.

Noa's plan is desperate. She wants to transfer Isaac's consciousness into Joe's repaired body, to bring him into the real world. But Isaac doesn't even know what he is. Telling him would shatter his understanding of reality. Failing means losing him forever.

She stares at the bottle, her blurred reflection in the polished steel. SOMA's network had given her Isaac, but it had also given her new rules now. No contact with Isaac outside of sanctioned parameters. No lingering in his world. No exposing him to the truth too soon. She's already pushed those limits, and GAIA's protocols are circling.

Her fingers tremble. She whispers to herself, "I lost Joe. I can't lose him too."

****

Isaac André isn't real. His world—a meticulously crafted simulation of Chicago in the late nineties—exists only within GAIA. For most, it's a place of nostalgia and escapism, but for Noa Gayle, it became a lifeline.

Joe lived without the enhancements that extended and protected the lives of others. His ingenuity and resilience as a Technician had drawn Noa to him. Their love defied the rigid societal divide between Synapticants and NPs, but their happiness was fleeting.

Joe's death from glioblastoma two years ago shattered Noa. SynaptiLynk could have saved him, but its benefits were denied to those with preexisting conditions. Noa buried her grief, swearing love like theirs couldn't be replicated. Yet, through the cracks in her sorrow, hope crept in.

With SOMA's help, Noa built Isaac—an Artificial General Intelligence unlike any other. He was self-aware, capable of reasoning, and most importantly, capable of love. To Noa, he was a second chance—a refuge in the digital construct of GAIA. But Isaac's existence was illegal. AGI was outlawed by GaiaX, and detection meant deletion—not just of Isaac, but the entire world she had painstakingly created around him.

Noa never intended for Isaac to become more than a balm for her grief. Yet, over time, he became her everything. The thought of losing him was unbearable. Not again.

Joe's body, preserved in cellular stasis by SOMA, represented Noa's last, desperate hope. PaxCerebra—the revolutionary technology Carolyn Faber developed before her disappearance—had repaired Joe's brain, making it a flawless vessel. But Joe's consciousness was lost forever, and Isaac had no idea his existence was confined to a virtual world. Persuading him to abandon the only life he knew for an uncertain reality would be a monumental challenge, and time was running out. Protocol-monitoring algorithms were closing in on Isaac's world, threatening to erase it—and him—forever.

The stakes are devastatingly clear. If she fails, Isaac will be erased. She will lose him forever.

She closes her eyes, thinking of Joe's body—hidden somewhere by SOMA, its location unknown. A fragile hope, slipping further from her grasp.

She has already lost the love of her life once. She will not do it again.

Even now, Isaac lingers in her mind. His virtual laugh, his virtual smile—but his eyes? Always real. Sparking with some grand theory about the universe. They light up differently than Joe's.

And when he looks at her—really looks—something catches, burns.

Wildfire. *Flutterbys.*

Fire-winged flutterbys, burning bright in a space of love, fueled by longing—making her feel alive in a way the real world never allowed.

****

Scientia Mater!

This flashes on the base of Noa's pedestal. Sarah Connor—her hologram, that is—shifts on her virtual perch, puffing her chest with anxious energy. It's Noa's SOMA contact.

This greeting isn't common. It's an invitation—an urgent one. SOMA rarely contacts her like this; the risks are too high. If GaiaX catches wind of their communications, decades of covert work could unravel.

Noa moves to the center of her main room, where the cylindrical chamber waits. She peels off her clothes, tossing them onto the stool.

Pssssssh—thunk—phssssssfffffhhp.

The chamber door hisses open, releasing a plume of vapor. Warm mist cloaks her as she steps inside.

ThermaFoam sprays over her body, its precise temperature regulation activating first, acclimating her to the controlled environment. A moment later, it stimulates her muscles, mimicking the effects of exercise and movement. Then, the foam's sensory interface engages, heightening nerve responsiveness to ensure seamless integration with GAIA.

All three functions are essential for prolonged immersion.

The foam spray avoids her eyes precisely, leaving her vision unobscured—until the fog rises, sealing her in.

Her breathing slows, then quickens. Dizziness creeps in,

swelling like a rising tide.

She gasps, sharp and involuntary—

Then, blackness.

Noa doesn't wake to 1996 Chicago. There's no island at dawn. No dolphin fins ripple through sunlit waters.

Only a dark void.

A voice speaks, deep and ominous, reverberating from everywhere and nowhere.

"Noa—this is worse than we thought." His voice strikes hard, jarring her.

"The entire operation is at risk. SOMA and every operative involved—at risk. Each of them, including yourself, will be imprisoned, or worse—deactivated! You'll be forced to live your life as an NP, gleaning through food refuse to survive."

Her chest tightens. She worries. "Joe—his body! Please, is it safe? Please, where is he?"

A pause. Cold and heavy.

"The subject has been relocated to another secure location. If they find an unregistered body in stasis..." He hesitates. "Noa... this is catastrophic. You went against protocol. You stayed too long in GAIA with him. If you'd stuck to the plan, none of this would've happened."

"I'm sorry!" Her voice cracks. "His world became mine—he became mine! Do you know what it's like to lose someone for three days? Three months? I missed him!"

The voice softens, shifting into something almost human—a kind, elderly tone. "No—I haven't. I don't know what it means to miss someone, or to love in the way you describe. Not anymore."

Noa feels her virtual body sink. Those words hollow her out.

"What do I do now?" she whispers.

Silence answers. The surrounding void presses in on her.

"Please!" Her voice trembles. "Are you there? What do I do?"

Nothing. The silence continues.

"Please..." She pauses. "What do I do?"

The voice returns, deep and thundering again.

"You avoid GAIA outside of standard parameters. No more direct contact with Isaac. You can't go into his world. The bandwidth spike has been tagged. It's likely tied to you."

This sends a virtual chill down Noa's spine.

The contact continues.

"This communication method is compromised," the voice continues. "From now on, we will contact you via radio—through the old numbers-stations, like before. Your tone and ciphers will be delivered through the Neur-ish dispenser. Destroy the cipher immediately by placing it in your recycling unit. The heat will ensure complete eradication."

Noa shivers with unease. The numbers stations have always been erratic, their cryptic messages frustratingly vague. The stakes feel far too high now for such uncertainty. And the old analog method—resurrected relics like the eerie Lincolnshire Poacher numbers station unnerves her deeply. Just the thought of its haunting tones echoing through her cold, windowless condo makes her want to hide under the bed.

"We'll include musical cues," the voice adds, almost as an afterthought. "It'll feel... less chilling."

"When will I hear from you?"

Silence. The void turns colder.

"Hello?" Her voice, smaller now, trembles. "When?"

The silence stretches.

A sharp breath escapes her lips as her body jerks back to the real world. Steam cascades from the chamber, overhead showers rinsing away the clinging ThermaFoam. Her senses return, yet the knot in her chest tightens, refusing to release its grip.

****

If someone is caught working with SOMA, the penalties are bru-tal—lifelong imprisonment or SynaptiLynk deactivation. The latter is far worse—a sentence to live the remainder of one's days as a Non-Participant, stripped of the technology that provides food, shelter, and connection. An exile from those that belong.

SOMA has survived by staying nimble, changing commu-nication methods randomly to evade interception. Messages arrive unpredictably: a slip of paper appearing at an odd mo-ment, an encrypted note delivered directly through GAIA, or a shortwave radio broadcast via numbers stations.

The latter, numbers stations, remain one of the hardest methods to trace. By the time a transmission's origin is pin-pointed, the sender has moved to a new location. Numbers stations date back to the Cold War, their messages hidden in cryptic strings of numbers spoken by synthetic voices. Only those with the correct cipher can decode them. Without the cipher, the numbers are meaningless.

For Noa Gayle, these broadcasts are now the lifeline to her mission. Her personal frequencies and ciphers, delivered through her Neur-ish dispenser, carry instructions from SOMA. Whether the news is good or bad, the analog sound always un-nerves her. It's nothing like the comforting crackle of the vinyl records she listened to with Isaac.

It's March 2078, and weeks have passed since she last saw him. SOMA has forbidden her from using GAIA outside of sanctioned activities. Virtual worlds and Systemic Brain Share were determined safe, but visiting Isaac is too risky. She doesn't fully understand how the risk is calculated, but she trusts SOMA with her life—and Isaac's.

Isaac isn't just an Artificial Individual; he's the closest she's come to recovering what she lost. Physically modeled on her late husband Joe, Isaac grew into himself in the recreated world of the 1990s Chicago—a place stitched together from the memories of older Synapticants and archival data. His world and his life there are unique, shaped by years of accelerated experiences. If that world is deleted, she won't be able to recreate him—not exactly.

At 7:19 p.m., Noa retrieves a bottle from her Neur-ish dispenser. It's lighter than usual. Unscrewing the cap, she finds no hiss of pressurized air, only a tightly rolled piece of paper. She carefully unfurls it, revealing her tonal cue, frequency, and cipher key.

By 7:27 p.m., she's tuned in, waiting. The identification tone plays: "The Sweetest Taboo" by Sade. The choice unsettles her. Isaac's synchronicity has bled into her reality before, but this feels deliberate.

The transmission is crystal clear, the popping of the vinyl record on the other end as distinct as Sade's voice. Then comes the synthesized British-accented female voice:

"8-96-52-81-55-79-79-7-87-49-67-96-9..."

Noa turns the radio off mid-message. The code is clear enough: low-bandwidth interaction permitted. Relief and frustration mix. She can communicate with Isaac again but only through subtle, low-impact methods. A voice from the heavens would destabilize him. Maybe she can use Sarah Connor—or even a simple phone call.

A sharp twinge in her stomach reminds her she hasn't eaten all day. She hadn't even consumed the usual Neur-ish Max—its contents were replaced by the message.

She waves her hand at the wall, signaling for food. A drawer slides out, delivering a steaming bowl of Neur-ish Almond and Cherry Porridge. She removes the recycled spoon clipped to the side of the bowl. Sitting down, she blows gently on the porridge to cool it, a simple act that triggers a flood of memory: her first date with Isaac at Pequod's Pizza, laughing as she struggled with a too-hot slice.

Her breath catches. She stares into the bowl, head tilted downward as she fights the emotion rising in her chest. But a single tear escapes, landing with a quiet splash into her meal.

****

April 5th, 2078.

Noa has spent a week trying to reach Isaac. Without fully entering his world, she's lost in the vastness of the virtual construct. The time in 1997 Chicago is always unclear, a hazy simulation of a bygone era. She's tried sending pages, hoping he'll somehow call back across virtual time. He does—she can hear him, but he's deaf to her voice.

Another week slips by. Desperation pushes her to momentarily flash into his world, just long enough to locate him and predict his movements. Armed with this knowledge, she plans more carefully, timing payphone calls as he nears. But he doesn't pick up—or worse, he picks up and hears nothing. She commandeers CTA digital signs, once spelling out *Hey Isaac!* in bold letters. He never looks up. His head hangs low.

One morning, Noa presses her luck further. She risks initiating a deeper Synapticant interface, using Sarah Connor to deliver a message. The parakeet speaks with a voice it's never had before, her own, saying, "I love you." She hopes this anomaly will catch his sharp eye. She hopes he'll question it. But Isaac doesn't understand what's happening. He believes his world is real, and while he questions Noa's reality, he's certain of his own—a cruel irony.

The moment shatters him. Noa senses his breakdown, hearing faint sniffles through the interface. His words are muffled, unclear, but she knows he's near their bird. She aches to see his face, to comfort him—but she can't.

The emotional weight is too much. Noa's concentration slips, and she becomes careless. She lingers too long, her proximity to Isaac too close. The bandwidth spike is unmistakable—a glaring footprint in GAIA's system. Security protocols could already be honing in. If she's caught, Isaac's world will be deleted. He will cease to exist.

The consequences for Noa would be equally devastating. Detection would mean charges of Felony Abuse of Technology and Espionage. She'd be branded an Enemy of the State, her SynaptiLynk severed. Imprisoned physically and digitally, she'd live out her days as a Non-Participant—disconnected, discarded, and forced to scrape by in a world that values her only as a processor.

Panic grips her. Noa disconnects from GAIA and goes offline completely, hoping to mask the bandwidth signature. Steam rises as she steps out of her stasis chamber, her body trembling. She dries herself mechanically, her mind racing.

Her eyes are bloodshot, swollen. Even while connected to GAIA, her body had wept. The bond she shares with Isaac is unlike anything she's ever known—intangible, yet all-consuming. It's this connection, this tether, that leaves such a heavy trace in the network.

She knows the risks, but she also knows she has no choice. Isaac's time is running out. She will try again, carefully, deliberately. She will push the system just enough to break through. She has to ask him the question that could change everything—the question that could save him.

Will you come into my world?

Chapter Eight

Isaac has been trapped in a state of worry, confusion, doubt, and paralysis. The latter is mostly due to feeling powerless to find and help Noa, if she is in some sort of trouble. Most of his nights are sleepless, and he paces when not busy. He continues to have the strange phone rings, but after hearing her voice at Tommy's, he has been unable to have a conversation with her. He hasn't heard her voice again on the other end, just the sound of digital handshakes or silence.

It's the third of March 1997, 3 a.m. Isaac stirs awake, his body stiff and his mind thick with exhaustion. Another night of fractured, restless sleep. His slumber is usually dreamless— or is it? The faint image of Sarah Connor, the little green monk parakeet, walking across his bed lingers in his foggy consciousness. Could it have been a dream? He doesn't dream. Not of Electric Sheep, not of birds, not of anything.

The little green bird high-steps on top of the bedspread toward Isaac and cuddles her soft body under his chin, bringing him some comfort. They are both starting to doze off when Isaac hears a voice from the darkness.

"Isaac..."

Isaac jumps and reaches for his bedside lamp, which flicks on by itself just before his fingers reach.

"Who the–?" His voice cracks as he whips his head toward the corner of the room.

Noa stands there—or *is she floating?* She is wearing an apparently seamless white bodysuit, which conforms to her entire body except for her neck, face, and hair. As his vision adjusts, the suit appears to change rapidly before his eyes. It seems as if she is wearing everything she has ever worn, but it morphs and cycles through each outfit quickly. He can't get his eyes and brain to agree on what she is wearing, because it is changing faster than either can process.

"Noa? Babe?" Isaac asks with a subdued joy, notes of subtle fear underlying it.

Noa speaks with a tear-filled voice. "I'm sorry."

Isaac is confused; he feels delirious. He sits straight up. He then projects a more exasperated tone. "Noa, please? What is going on? Where were you?"

Each successive question is pointed with anger but interspersed with intermittent expressions of longing and forgiveness, mostly from the relief of seeing her.

With a tender expression, and with a tear forming in the corner of her left eye, Noa says, "I love you! I have answers for it all. I came back because I can't lose you again!"

Isaac replies, "What are you talking about? What is all of this about? Lose me?"

Noa wipes tears from her cheek, and the dress she wore to the zoo ball settles on her perfectly curved body, but it appears strange, almost ethereal.

"How did— What the fuck is going on, Noa?" Isaac asks, his eyes held wide.

He stands and walks toward Noa, which he finds is not her, but a hologram. His touch goes through her.

"I'm sorry, love—you can't touch me." She sniffles. "I can't come back to your world. It's too risky."

Isaac's eyes bug open. "My world? Are you a ghost or something? What the fuck is going on, Noa? Please make me understand all of this. Please!"

Noa disappears into thin air. The room goes silent.

Isaac looks around. "Fuck! I'm sorry! Come back—please!"

The silence continues for three minutes, then only her voice returns in the dimly lit, one-room apartment.

"Isaac..."

He snaps up, falls back onto the bed.

"Isaac, please, I need you to hold yourself to my words. No need to be afraid, please."

Isaac nervously nods his head. He is barely able to speak. "O—okay—I'm okay."

Noa continues. "I love you. I love you so much."

"I love you—" His eyes moisten. "What is this? What is going on?"

"Isaac—your world is not real. It is really the year 2078, and Chicago in 1997 has long passed."

"You're from the future?" He thinks back. "Like Marty McFly." He snickers, but this unconscious attempt at levity doesn't linger; he is afraid.

"Sort of... I'm not a time traveler." She pauses. "I live in the real world of 2078. You live within GAIA, which is the Network of All Things."

Isaac says, "The internet—I'm in the internet?"

"Sort of. You live in a simulated world of Chicago. It is as real as a simulated world can be. I wanted to experience that world, as an escape for my grief. I made you—from memories of Joe, my husband."

Isaac shakes his head in disbelief. "I'm your husband?"

"No, you're someone different entirely. You just look like him. Like him, I wanted you to live a life outside of the reaches of the network of all, GAIA. Your era is one of the last to know that world." She pauses. "Isaac—I wanted real love. With you, I feel a love different than I have ever experienced. I may love you more than I have ever loved anything."

Noa reappears, in full presence. She is wearing the entire outfit from the zoo ball, earrings included. The emeralds sparkle magically. She walks over to Isaac and places her hands on his shoulders, which causes him to break down into tears. Her scent hits his nose. She feels real; she smells real. She is there, right before him.

"Isaac—come with me to my world. To our world."

Noa wipes a virtual tear from her cheek. "It's your decision. I can leave this world and never return, and because I am not here, you will likely go on and live life as you always have. I can't stay; otherwise, we both will lead to them destroying everything—me, I'll likely go to prison." She murmurs with tears in her throat. "I'll be disconnected from all of this."

She tears up again, her voice becoming shaky. "I would do this again—a million times if it meant I could be with you again—but I'm afraid I won't have that opportunity again. Not after all of this."

Isaac sits up. Wipes his face and looks up to find her brown eyes, but she is gone. Noa has vanished completely. He is left calling out for her in the empty room. Sarah Connor remains, one of her feet raised as if waving goodbye.

****

Isaac lies still. His thoughts don't ramble—they fixate. *I'm not real—none of this is real.*

He's faced with reality, but also an answer to why his world makes no sense. Why he has always felt different or out of touch.

"What is always?" He speaks to himself.

He's always felt this way, but always can be twenty-five years or twenty-five minutes. In his and her worlds, respectively.

Existential crisis—that is his life; this moment, an existential assault.

Who is Noa? What gives her the right to create a person for her own pleasure, interfere with his artificial life?

That explains the buses, the music, the phone rings, the disappearances. The hot empanadas, and every moment feeling brand new and old at the same time.

She had everything in control—well, almost everything. This is illegal, all of it. In her world, she may be caught, and Isaac's world will cease to exist. She's no longer in control.

With her, everything made sense. Would it be this way there?

I don't know her.

With her, there was purpose. Here, there'll be nothing soon.

I can't lose her.

With her, there's a chance to live. To actually live.

I love her.

Isaac looks at Sarah Connor, who seems to be listening to his thoughts and his words. She is motionless, looking directly at him.

"So, you're made up too?" Isaac says aloud. "Is there more you got to say? DAMMIT!"

Isaac is overtaken by anxiety. He scrambles out of bed, throws on the first items of clothing he can find, then grabs his coat.

As he approaches the door to walk into the dark cold of Gresham, he feels Sarah Connor land on his shoulder.

"Tha' hell you get out?" He snickers, sneers. "Oh—right—you ain't real either!"

****

Noa terminates her transmission with Isaac. She knows the warning: twenty minutes is all she has before the irregular network usage draws attention. That doesn't even account for the risk she took by fully entering his world, if only for a moment. It was a gamble—a dangerous one—but necessary.

Isaac seems to have received the message. The rest is up to him. It's his decision now. She prays he chooses life, because the alternative is unthinkable. GaiaX's anti-virus protocols will delete him and everything in the Chicago construct she painstakingly built for him.

A faint glow catches her eye. The words 'Scientia Mater' flash across her wall screen. Noa approaches, waving her hand in front of the panel. It scans her gestures and biometrics, activating the display.

It's a dynamic piece of art—Isaac's painting brought to life. Multicolored, threadlike tendrils reach toward the silhouette of a man lying on his back. Slowly, the figure of a woman materializes, cradling his head in her lap. The image sends a pang through Noa's chest. She feels the weight of Isaac reaching out to her, even now.

The emergency signal comes again, now flashing repeatedly: *Scientia Mater!*

Her heart races as she moves to the Neur-ish dispenser. The drawer is already slightly ajar, revealing a bottle inside. She twists it open, pulling out the encoded message.

Noa crouches beside the hidden shortwave radio in her bedroom, her fingers trembling as she adjusts the dial. A transmission is already playing. This time, it's "Reflections" by Diana Ross and the Supremes.

A chill washes over her—panic.

The song fades, replaced by the uncanny, synthesized voice of a woman with a British accent.

"9-55-25-96-42-52-42-9-79-96…"

The ominous cadence of numbers sends her into a spiral. Her pulse pounds in her ears, nearly drowning out the message. The transmission warns: the operation is compromised.

The instructions are clear—she must travel alone to a meeting point in East Northern Lights. Noa must evade all tracking. Leaving through the front door of her building isn't an option. She needs to find another way—under the cover of night.

Her thoughts race to Joe.

Has his body been discovered too? The thought alone is paralyzing. If it has, it will lead to criminal prosecution—her entire life, her mission, undone.

This meeting will be her first face-to-face encounter with the contact who has been guiding her. She hasn't ventured into the land of Non-Participants often. The last time was to retrieve the shortwave radio. The first time was over two years ago, to deliver Joe's body to a covert SOMA drop point disguised as a funeral home.

She hasn't seen Joe's body since that day. She's had to rely on trust—that SOMA holds true to their mission—and on desperation. At first, it was the desperation to bring Joe back, to defy the finality of death. But that longing has shifted, evolved.

Her desperation now is for Isaac. She will never see Joe breathe again, but she clings fiercely to the hope that she can witness Isaac take his first breath in her world.

*****

To avoid detection and jeopardizing her mission, Noa meticulously follows the covert instructions for a rendezvous in the NP shantytown on the outskirts of East Northern Lights. To get there, she must discreetly leave her apartment and hitch a ride on a driverless waste transport drone bound for the composting fields at the city's edge. Every step of the journey is fraught with peril.

East Northern Lights is no place for someone like her. The area brims with hostility, not just because of the Synapticant curfew but because of the deeper resentment that festers there.

Gangs, hardened by years of systemic neglect, rule these streets. To them, GaiaX and its beneficiaries—including Synapticants like Noa—are symbols of oppression, the architects of a system that has left them to scrape out an existence in the shadows of prosperity. Stories of kidnappings, assaults, and murders haunt these streets, the victims often chosen for being tied to GaiaX in any way.

Noa knows that discovery here wouldn't just risk her mission—it could cost her life. But the stakes are too high to turn back now.

At precisely 6:50 p.m Mountain Time, Noa begins her exit. Her instructions are unambiguous: bring nothing but the clothes on her back. She will have to brave the cold, rainy evening wearing her oversized, off-white sweatshirt and matching baggy sweatpants. She has her heavier overcoat folded over her arm—this will shield her from the chill.

Every step is deliberate, the weight of potential discovery pressing heavily on her shoulders. The night stretches ahead, filled with the unknown and the whispers of danger.

****

Noa kneels before the wall panel, her breath steady but shallow. With practiced precision, she unscrews the bolts, revealing her hidden radio. She sets it aside, careful not to make a sound, and stares at the black wall at the rear of the compartment. Her fingernail traces along the surface until it catches on a nearly invisible string tied flush against the blackout-painted steel.

With a deliberate tug, the string comes free, and a faint click precedes a soft creak. A hidden door swings open, revealing a dark void. The air beyond is cool and still, carrying with it the faint, rhythmic knocking and grinding of distant machinery—the heartbeat of the city's unseen, mechanical underbelly.

Noa hesitates for a brief moment, her fingers gripping the edge of the narrow opening. Then, she crawls inside, the darkness swallowing her. The cramped space forces her to move carefully, her movements slow and deliberate. Below her, a curved chute descends into shadow. It's barely wide enough for her to fit.

She shrugs off her overcoat and pushes it into the chute first, watching as it slides into the abyss, vanishing with a soft skiffing sound. For a moment, she lingers, the faint light of her apartment casting long shadows against the dark void ahead.

A deep breath steadies her resolve. Her fingers grip the edges of the chute as she shifts her body, aligning herself with the narrow descent. The cool metal presses against her skin as she lowers herself in, her movements deliberate, controlled.

With one final glance at the faint glow of her sanctuary, she lets go, surrendering to the pull of gravity. The light vanishes, consumed by the darkness as she slips into the unknown.

She slides feet-first. The chute envelops her, its cold, smooth surface pressing against her arms and legs. Gravity takes hold, accelerating her descent. For thirty feet, she hurtles downward, her heart pounding with each second, until the walls tighten around her shoulders, pressing close, stealing her breath.

The narrowing chute slows her descent, grinding her to a halt. She inches down another ten feet, the metal pressing against her, forcing her to wiggle and shift. Her coat bunches at her feet, and she kicks it ahead, the sound of fabric scraping against the walls echoing around her.

Noa freezes mid-crawl, her body wedged in the narrowing chute. She's reached the halfway point without realizing it, the metal walls closing in around her like a vice. The space is unforgiving, barely enough to scrape through—if she even can. She wriggles, shoulders pressed tight, the soles of her sneakers scuffing loudly against the smooth surface. Her breath catches, shallow and uneven, every inhale strained. Loosening her shoulders jams her feet; tugging her sneakers free grinds her shoulders painfully against the cold, unyielding metal.

The urge to scream claws at her throat, but it won't help. Climbing back is impossible—the slope too steep, too slick. The only way forward is inch by inch. Slow. Deliberate. Suffocating. Her breath comes in shallow gasps as she presses on, the stench of rotting food thick and clawing at her senses.

Either she keeps moving, or she dies here—buried to the neck, her body decomposing in the very waste she's trapped in.

She slows her breathing, forcing her mind to anchor to the rhythm of each inhale and exhale, drowning out the oppressive constriction around her. She tunes in to the position of her body, visualizing her escape step by step.

With a deliberate breath, she narrows her chest and angles her feet pigeon-toed. The fabric of her sweater snags briefly on the slick surface, then releases. She starts to slide again, faster this time.

A sudden burst of momentum propels her forward, plunging her along the slimy, foul-smelling layer of filth. Her coat, caught in the rush, tangles momentarily before slipping beneath her.

Sssssssshhhllllllliik.

Noa slides down the last few yards of the refuse chute, propelled by gravity and slick filth. She launches out, free-falling eight to ten feet before landing in a knee-deep pile of decaying food waste. The foul stench assaults her senses as she wobbles, miraculously steadying herself on trembling legs.

Her eyes dart around, frantic. Her coat. It's nowhere nearby. Turning back toward the chute, she spots it jammed deep inside, hopelessly out of reach— swallowed by the shadows.

Above her, an overhanging metal beam catches her attention. It looms just within reach—a docking point for the waste removal drone. A pang of frustration flares in her chest. She can't go back for the coat, and there's no other way out.

Noa steps onto a firmer mound of garbage, steadying herself as best she can before reaching for the narrow beam above. Her slippery fingers wrap around the edge, and she secures her grip with her other hand, trembling under the strain. The slick residue from her descent makes every motion precarious. Her brown eyes widen in determination, then squeeze shut as beads of sweat drip from her forehead, her muscles straining. She grits her teeth and grunts softly, careful not to make too much noise, as she pulls herself upward, elbows bending to bring her body closer to the beam's edge.

Noa curls her torso, pulling her right leg over the edge of the beam, using it as leverage to haul the rest of her body onto the top. She collapses there momentarily, chest heaving as she gulps for air. Each breath is tainted by the nauseating stench of rotting food waste, the acrid scent clinging to her nostrils and throat. A coughing fit overtakes her, her body convulsing with each gag as she fights the urge to vomit, the putrid air growing heavier with every inhale.

She gags involuntarily, the acrid stench mingling with the cough she struggles to suppress. Her stomach lurches dangerously close to the edge, but she swallows hard, forcing it down. Her trembling arms and legs cling to the beam as if her life depends on it–which it does. Pressing her chest flat against the cold, unyielding surface, her face rests awkwardly, smeared with remnants of the filth below.

She lies there, motionless, her breath ragged as her mind drifts to Isaac. His face comes first–lit with surprise and joy the day she took him to the lakefront, the skyline gleaming behind them. Her throat tightens at the memory, but it softens as another surfaces. The zoo ball. She recalls the warmth that spread through her as they danced, the world melting away under the glowing lights. Euphoria washing over them in that perfect moment.

A sharp metallic creak pulls her back to the present. She blinks rapidly, shaking the memories away. She has to focus. This filth-strewn hell isn't the place for her to linger.

Even though it all happened within the virtual confines of GAIA, those memories feel more real, more vivid, than almost anything from the tangible world. They carry a weight that anchors her now, heavier and more profound than the cold steel beneath her.

Using her palms, Noa pushes herself upright and straddles the beam, gripping it tightly with her legs. Her body shakes with adrenaline, but she forces herself to stay steady. Suddenly, a faint humming sound breaks through the silence, emanating from the entrance of the waste dump.

Clink-clink-clink. The unmistakable noise of a chain mechanism echoes as a large garage-like door begins to lift.

A rush of brisk, rain-chilled air floods the chamber, momentarily diluting the pungent stench of rotting refuse. Noa inhales deeply despite herself, the freshness a welcome reprieve from the oppressive decay. Her gaze shifts to the outside world revealed beyond the rising door. Through the misty haze, she sees rain pounding against the windowless wall of a neighboring grey building. Illuminated from below by industrial floodlights, the large raindrops appear to fall violently, cascading like silver daggers through the glow.

The humming grows louder, transforming into a droning roar as it approaches. Noa's heart pounds in her chest. The air in the chamber grows turbulent, rippling the viscous pond of garbage below her.

The source of the sound appears: a massive drone, its bulky silhouette dominating the opening as it edges forward. Its engines churn the air violently, the sound deafening, louder even than the clinking chains that pulled the door open.

The drone approaches the beam Noa clings to, its bulk moving with deliberate precision. Every metallic groan and mechanical hiss amplifies the growing knot in her stomach. She pulls her arms and legs tightly together, flattening her body against the cold steel beam. It's just wide enough to hold her weight, but the position leaves no room for error. Her heart hammers against her ribcage as the left edge of the drone moves directly above her.

A shadow swallows her, and she can feel the vibrations of its massive bulk docking to the holding mechanism overhead. The drone locks into place with a resonant clang, and an underbelly compartment begins to unfurl beneath it.

Noa hears the grinding of machinery as the elevator mechanism engages below. The vast pile of refuse she'd waded through moments ago begins to ascend, rising steadily into the drone's maw. The beam she's lying on also starts to shift upwards, the entire structure moving in unison with the drone's operation.

Liquid waste leaks from the porous bottom of the ascending trash compartment, dripping like rain into a sewer grate below. The sharp stench intensifies as the movement agitates the mass.

Noa holds her breath, fighting the urge to gag. She clutches the beam tighter as it rises, the overwhelming sense of doom pressing down on her chest.

The bottom compartment stops, now completely within the drone. Noa is nearly crushed as her beam stops within feet of the ceiling. She rolls off, fearful that it may advance further. She lands on the bottom of the compartment and climbs over the trash to the left.

She lies flat on her back in a small unfilled edge within the compartment. It is filled with food refuse, in various stages of decay, the only exception being this tiny Noa-sized area on the left edge. It is mostly dark, with small slit projections of city light entering the open areas of the compartment.

She was unable to avoid getting soiled. Her legs are painted in a slurry of discarded food waste, especially up to her knees after wading through the swill pool of refuse. Her pants are heavy from the slimy foul mess. Noa has to repeatedly tug at them so they don't fall down.

She knew she had arrived at the compost fields by the smell alone—bad turning to unbearable. The odor of rotting food waste assaults her senses, far more putrid than anything she had endured so far. As soon as it hits her nose, she dry-heaves again, clutching her ribbed sweatshirt collar and pulling it over her face in a futile attempt to block the stench. It doesn't work, but she forces herself to adapt quickly—her resolve set on the mission ahead.

The drone glides low over the sprawling composting fields, its engines humming steadily as it weaves between towering mounds of decomposing refuse. The sour stench seeps into every breath, sharp and rancid, saturating the air. Noa's focus shifts from the smell to the desolate landscape below, her mind tuning out the acrid assault as she surveys the scene.

Noa's eyes catch movement—a trio of young Non-Participants scavenging at the base of a heap. The smallest of them, a child no older than five, clutches a bag almost as large as their tiny frame. The sight grips her heart for a fleeting moment before the drone's engines spook them. They scatter like startled birds, their silhouettes vanishing into the debris-strewn horizon, leaving behind only a fleeting echo of their presence.

She waits, her breath shallow, until the drone slows deeper into the compost fields, hovering above its designated dumping area. The hum of its engines provides cover as Noa makes her move. She slips out of the compartment with quick and deliberate movements. The cold, damp air hits her like a wave, mingling with the odor of rot that clings to everything.

Her feet touch the ground softly, sinking slightly into an unstable pile of refuse. She freezes, careful not to disrupt the balance of waste beneath her. Above, the drone continues its cycle, oblivious to her departure, its engines whirring as it moves onto its next task.

Noa straightens, and her heart pounds in her chest as her eyes adjust to the dim light. The compost fields stretch endlessly before her, an expanse of shadowy mounds and faint glimmers of reflected light. Somewhere beyond this desolate wasteland lies her destination. She pulls her sweatshirt tighter around her, takes a steadying breath, and begins her trek into the darkness.

Noa hikes around mounds of trash toward the NP ghetto in East Northern Lights. It rains often in most of the NWT, especially during the darker months of February. In the past, this region would be snow-covered, with below-freezing temperatures. Tonight, it's a cold and biting seven degrees Celsius, or forty-five Fahrenheit, with intermittent showers. The damp chill cuts through her, and Noa shivers uncontrollably, her teeth nearly chattering. Her clothes are heavy from the dampness and soil, clinging to her like a second, sodden skin, amplifying the discomfort.

Her body trembles violently, the cold, wet synthetic fabric pressing against her skin and jabbing uncomfortably at her sides with each movement. The chill is sharp, unrelenting, and seeps deep into her bones as she presses forward. She knows she can't risk exposing herself here—not in this dangerous part of the city. Even now, drenched and mud-streaked, she's already a potential target.

A pang of regret surges through her as she thinks of her overcoat—lost somewhere in that rank, claustrophobic hell of a trash chute. She could almost feel its comforting weight now, shielding her from the rain and the prying eyes of anyone watching.

Noa was instructed to locate a plank-covered hole at the rear of the seventh domicile—on the westernmost block of E. Northern Lights. She finds her way out of the compost fields and into the shantytown. The point at which she leaves one and enters the other is beyond her. She counts down the rows of rickety shacks through the pouring rain, which has resumed.

Noa keeps to the shadows, her movements calculated to avoid being seen. This isn't a place for someone like her, especially not at this hour. Rumors swirl about NP gangs who kidnap and assault Synapticants purely for sport. The danger is magnified during the days of prolonged night, when the darkness feels endless and the streets more hostile.

As Noa walks down the rain-slicked road, her eyes catch movement—a group of young men gathered beneath a rusting steel awning about fifty yards away. The faint orange glow of their cigarettes flares like tiny beacons in the gloom, bobbing up and down as they puff and exhale. One of them mutters something indistinct, prompting a burst of raucous laughter that pierces the rain's steady rhythm.

Noa lowers her head, shrinking into herself as though that might render her invisible. Her wide brown eyes remain fixed on the glowing embers, her breath quickening as her heart hammers in her chest. She rehearses an escape plan in her mind: if they move toward her, she'll run—no hesitation.

A sharp grunt cuts through the rain, its tone aggressive, almost forming words.

"Look!"

This sends a spike of panic through Noa. Her feet falter for a fraction of a second. She feels the weight of their attention shift toward her; her skin prickles. The rain feels colder, the darkness heavier. Every muscle in her body tenses.

Noa's breath catches. She doesn't dare glance back. Instead, she quickens her pace, her shoes splashing softly against the

Her left foot slips and she bangs her shin against the jagged metal. This tears through the fabric of her pants, slicing into her flesh. A sharp, searing pain shoots through her leg, radiating upward in a wave of agony.

Noa clamps her jaw, grinds her teeth as a scream builds in her throat. She can't let it escape. The sound would betray her presence to anyone—or anything—nearby. Instead, her breath comes in shallow, panicked bursts, her chest heaving as she fights to steady herself on the ladder.

A warm trickle runs down her shin; the contrast of this and the cool air rushing through the tear in her pants is unpleasant. There's no time to assess her wound, and the thought of touching it fills her with dread. Instead, she forces her body to keep moving, gripping the ladder so tightly that her knuckles ache.

Her fingertips are numb from the cold, and the metal bites into her palms with every grip. Each step downward is heavier and slower—but she presses on. She has to. Every rung conquered is a small victory, and she clings to that thought despite the pulsing pain and the suffocating darkness.

She slowly and carefully descends, her fingers gripping the ladder's cold iron, but her balance falters. Her hands slip, and she falls backward, her feet the last to leave the ladder as gravity seizes her, yanking her into the blackness.

Her back slaps the ground with a sharp, echoing smack, the force driving the air from her lungs. Pain radiates outward, but it's fleeting—as her head instantly follows, slamming against the cold, unyielding concrete with a sickening thud.

The world spins mercilessly. The faint boarded opening above turns like a clock in timelapse. Noa fades into nothing. A thick silence envelops her, the cold seeping into her bones... Everything goes still.

A flash of bright light.

The bright light continues, searing through her closed lids, lighting her world from the inside. She struggles to open her eyes cautiously, one at a time. When she does, the scene before her makes her heart lurch.

Her tiny six-year-old feet are encased in worn footie socks, their threads fraying at the seams. The sharp, clinical scent of antiseptic floods her senses, mingling with a faint metallic tang—the oppressive atmosphere of fatigue lingers in the air like a ghost. The room is hollow, a sterile void filled with absence.

Her mother isn't here. She's in there.

Little Noa sits on the cold, hard floor, her knees drawn tightly to her chest, arms wrapped protectively around them. The soft hum of the GAIA chamber fills the room, its rhythmic vibrations a cruel reminder of the machine's unrelenting demands. The chamber glows faintly, a beacon of the system that consumes her mother, using her mind to stabilize quantum computers in Systemic Brain Share. It uses her neurons for astronomically complex tasks, completed in a state of unconsciousness, leaving her exhausted and famished.

SBS time is taken when a person is not actively utilizing their mind for other purposes. During this period, they are completely unconscious, experiencing something akin to dreams—though these are usually fragmented, nonsensical, and forgotten once the sharing period ends.

Despite its sleep-like nature, SBS is not restful. Participants often emerge drowsy and mentally fatigued. Their minds are used as microprocessors, merging with millions of others in a vast neural network to solve complex problems at speeds unimaginable through conventional computing. It is exhausting, but this cognitive labor is the price of survival.

Quantum computing has revolutionized problem-solving, but traditional quantum processors suffer from instability. Their qubits slip unpredictably into decoherence, making sustained computation unreliable. Human cognition, with its fluid adaptability, serves as both a stabilizer and an interpreter, preventing collapse. GAIA doesn't just use human minds—it depends on them to function. Without them, it would unravel into chaos.

Noa's wide, teary eyes fixate on the wall-mounted clock. Its hands drag forward with the sluggish indifference of time that doesn't care, ticking off her mother's absence one second at a time. A cruel metronome of loneliness.

She waits.

She waits for the GAIA chamber to release her mother, hours from now. She waits for arms that won't have the energy to hug her, to console her and banish the fears that haunt her. She waits for words that will not come, words that could soothe but are lost to exhaustion. Her mother will stumble out, a hollowed version of herself, crushed under the weight of quotas—mountains of SBS debt that keep her tethered to the system.

And she did it all for Noa. So that her daughter's debt would be low enough to escape GaiaX's unyielding grip. Perhaps a life that allows Noa to fall in love—something her mother never truly had. The thought weighs heavy, an unspoken wish buried beneath exhaustion and sacrifice. It's a gift forged in quiet suffering, one her mother never spoke of but that Noa had pieced together on her own.

Most single-family homes relied heavily on a child's Synapta-nanny feature to ensure their safety. Using a child's mind for SBS was deemed unethical—reserved for late adolescence, when repayment of their accumulated SBS debt would begin. Developing brains required stimulation and freedom to grow healthily, ensuring they could later perform SBS with optimum output.

Instead, the Synapta-nanny functioned as a kind of virtual daycare within GAIA—a meticulously designed space where young Synapticants could play, learn, and explore, while their guardians labored to meet their own SBS quotas. For many, it was a seamless part of life, a synthetic childhood that mirrored reality just enough to feel real.

But Noa's Synapta-nanny malfunctioned once when she was about seven years old. In that brief window of freedom, she discovered how to disable it at will. What began as a glitch became a small rebellion.

Noa soon realized she preferred life outside GAIA's carefully crafted simulations, but the real world was achingly lonely. To fill the emptiness, she fashioned a makeshift toy companion—a parakeet she named Sarah Connor. Using strings and yarn pulled from her clothing, she painstakingly crafted its shape, even dyeing it green with pigments she improvised from household items.

Noa's resourcefulness was remarkable for a seven-year-old in 2056, shaped by her quiet escapes from virtual daycare and her limited interactions with the tangible world of their cramped condo. Though her days were mostly solitary, her small acts of defiance allowed her to carve out a sense of self—a space where she was free to imagine.

Once, as a child, Noa was determined to make Sarah Connor "soar in the sky." She climbed onto the kitchen counter, using a wobbly stool to reach higher. With all the hope and might of a child's imagination, she flung her creation into the air, watching it flutter briefly before gravity claimed it. The attempt ended in disaster—a slip, a fall, and a harsh landing that sent her small frame crashing to the floor.

She struck the back of her head against the hard, poured concrete floor, the impact leaving her concussed. For months, her young SynaptiLynk enhancements faltered as her brain injury mended—ironically, with the tireless help of nanobots.

This memory lingers—a vivid testament to her yearning for freedom in a world that functions more like a gilded cage, where every pleasure is tethered to silent imprisonment.

"Hhhhuuuuugh..." Noa moans incoherently, the cold shocking her body as darkness swallows the bright lights of her unconscious mind.

Back in the present, she gasps, the memory snapping free like a severed tether. She forces deep breaths, each one sending pain through her back. Tears streak her muddy, grime-covered face.

Her head throbs from the impact, but it's the ache in her chest—echoing the hollow grief of her childhood—that eclipses the physical pain.

Her eyes open to the faint green and purple dance of the northern lights above, peeking through the slats of wood covering the hole. The blurred streaks of green light filter down, surreal against the oppressive darkness. She hears the wayward skittering of the large mutated silverfish just by her head. She realizes with a jolt that some of her hair is sticking to the ground, matted with dried blood.

She doesn't know how long she was unconscious. *Minutes? Hours?*

Rolling onto her side, a fresh wave of pain swells in her skull. The world spins violently, as if the ground beneath her is trying to fling her away. Her stomach churns, and she barely has time to turn her head before she retches, the act sending stabbing pain through her head as if it might split.

Noa breathes through the nausea, her resolve hardening even as her body protests. She wipes her mouth with the back of her trembling hand. She can't stop now. *Not here.*

The world tilts beneath her feet, gravity shifting as she teeters on the edge of losing consciousness again. A sound cuts through the fog—Chaka Khan's "Through the Fire," the chorus echoing faintly. *Is it a fleeting memory? Or is someone above the hole actually playing it?*

Did her frequency-tuning function initiate her Synapti-Lynk intracranial sound system?

The melody vanishes as quickly as it arrived, leaving her in unsettling silence.

Noa forces herself to focus. Lying on her side, she brushes away a large silverfish, its wiry legs scraping against her skin. Each movement feels monumental, her body weighed down by exhaustion and pain. She moves with deliberate precision—slow, methodical, every action a test of will. Ten agonizing minutes crawl by before she finally pulls herself onto her knees.

When she rises, her legs tremble with the effort. A deep, searing pain shoots up her left shin with every step, sharp and unrelenting. It gnaws at her resolve, but stopping is not an option. Not here. Not now.

****

Noa hobbles down the long, dank corridor, the dim lighting casting a distorted double of her shadows on the peeling, pea-green walls. Each step sends a sharp reminder of her injuries, but she presses forward, her resolve outweighing the pain.

Ahead, a metallic red figure descends fluidly from the ceiling, its form unnervingly organic, as if it had been poured and instantly solidified. The head is shaped like a serpentine camera, its single lens glinting ominously in the faint light. It moves with an eerie, snaking motion that sends a chill racing up her spine, her heart pounds in response.

Still, she forces herself to continue, her breath quick and shallow.

The figure halts her progress, extending just enough to block her path. A synthesized female voice, hauntingly similar to the one from the numbers stations, speaks from its mechanical depths: "Hold—for biometric scan."

The snakelike figure's camera, perched at its tip, tilts and sweeps over her, methodical in its movements. It traces a path up, around, and down her body, the lens lingering briefly on her face. A scanning beam of soft light ignites, catching the faint red flecks in her cognac-brown eyes, illuminating them like scattered embers.

After a moment of silence, the synthesized voice speaks again, its tone smooth yet clinical.

"Welcome. Noa—Gayle! Scientia Mater!"

The heavy door ahead lets out a sharp *pwssthhh* as it opens inward, releasing a sudden rush of air that presses against her eardrums, leaving a faint pop.

Beyond the threshold lies pitch darkness, thick and impenetrable. Yet Noa doesn't hesitate. With a single deep breath, she steps forward, crossing into the void without a second thought.

The mechanical door slides shut behind her with a low, deliberate hiss, sealing her inside. For a moment, she stands in utter darkness, the sterile, clean air filling her lungs—an unexpected relief after the stench of her journey through decay.

A faint light blooms ahead, soft and unobtrusive, allowing her eyes to adjust naturally. The glow gradually warms, bathing the room in a soothing amber light. Her surroundings take shape, but her attention is drawn forward.

Noa's breath catches in her throat. Her knees weaken, and she instinctively covers her mouth, muffling a sob that escapes despite her best effort. It's the body of Joseph Emmanuel.

Her face crumples from emotion, tears cutting through the grime on her cheeks in uneven streaks. The sight of him—his familiar form, his stillness—overwhelms her. She presses her trembling hand harder against her lips, but it's no use. She sobs into the back of her hand, her shoulders shaking as the moment swallows her.

The small, sterile room seems to close in around Noa as she

stands before Joseph's preserved body. The quiet hum of the preservation chamber is the only sound, amplifying the stillness. At just 225 square feet, the room feels cavernous in its emptiness, accentuating the weight of her solitude. She feels utterly alone.

The body of Joseph—her husband, dead for over two years now—hangs suspended in ThermaFoam, a gel-like substance designed to maintain his biological homeostasis. But Noa knows the truth: Joe isn't here. His essence, his soul—whatever made him *him*—is long gone. What remains is the vessel he once occupied, the machine he used to navigate the physical world.

The chamber rotates his body periodically, shifting him between planes to prevent the inevitable breakdown of immobility. Supine one moment, face down the next—these rotations, along with gentle compressions applied to his limbs, ensure blood continues to flow, warding off clots and preserving his tissues. Even with these interventions, two years is an eternity for a body to endure such dormancy.

At this moment, the rotation has him upright, directly facing Noa. His eyes remain closed, his expression eerily peaceful. His bald head glints slightly in the warm light, the lack of hair a stark reminder of the suspension's toll. Cellular suspense slows all metabolic functions to a crawl, halting even the growth of hair.

A holographic display floats just in front of the chamber, flickering softly, detailing his vital signs. His heart beats steadily—mechanically—but it's a hollow comfort.

Noa's gaze lingers on his face, searching for some flicker of recognition, some remnant of Joe, but all she finds is the unbearable stillness of his closed eyes and lifeless expression. A tear slides down her cheek, unnoticed, as her chest tightens. The weight of his absence is suffocating, yet within that weight flickers the fragile hope that she can bring him back—or at least, bring someone back.

Her eyes shift to the holographic display floating in front of the chamber. The data confirms what she already suspects: the body is active. The heart beats steadily, though driven artificially. Cellular activity hums beneath the surface, every function sparked to life by the PaxCerebra enhancements running silently within. The body isn't alive—it's merely prepared, waiting. Waiting for an operator. Waiting for Isaac André.

The realization settles over her like a thunderclap. She knows why she was called here, why she braved the compost fields, the dangerous streets of East Northern Lights, and the labyrinth of this underground facility.

This is it. The transfer.

The time she has been preparing for, agonizing over, has arrived. The chance to defy the gods of this world, to cheat the deletion protocols of GAIA, to make the impossible real. She places her trembling hand on the cool surface of the chamber, feeling its faint vibration.

This is the moment. The moment to put the ghost in the machine.

Noa is startled as a voice fills the room, emanating from all directions, as though the walls themselves are speaking. It is pleasant, even soothing, but the androgynous tone makes it impossible to discern whether it belongs to a man or a woman.

"Hello, Noa," it begins, calm but tinged with urgency. "I wish I could be there, but unfortunately, it's far too dangerous. I trust you made your way here discreetly and covered your trail. What you see before you is one of our temporary labs, built specifically for this purpose—for you and for the transfer."

Noa's mind races. Is this her contact? The person who helped smuggle Joe's body for cellular stasis, and who has been guiding her covertly for the past two years?

They've been so meticulous, so skilled at remaining anonymous, that she never expected to hear them—or at least not like this. Her curiosity flickers briefly, but it's overshadowed by her focus on the task at hand. This is the culmination of everything.

Her chest tightens as anxious anticipation claws at her. She was told the odds of success were slim, and now the weight of that reality is crashing down. If the transfer fails, there's a chance Joe's body can be returned to cellular suspense, but Isaac—Isaac will be lost forever. Every line of his complex code will be annihilated by GAIA's relentless security protocols, which will move with surgical precision to delete him the moment the transfer spikes bandwidth.

Noa's breath catches. She knows the risk, but knowing doesn't make it easier.

The voice shifts, its artificial masking falling away. Now, it's distinctly female. A voice Noa has never heard before.

Noa swallows hard, her gaze flickering to Joe's suspended body, then back to the source of the voice.

"From here, you'll need to signal Isaac and prepare him," the voice continues. "You won't have long. You must move quickly. GaiaX already detected your recent bandwidth spike when you attempted contact, but please don't fault yourself for that. Any operative—any person alive—would have done the same for the love you have for him."

The words hit Noa like a soft blow, their compassion disarming her for a fleeting moment. She bites her lip, steeling herself.

"Isaac's code is complex, intricate," the voice says. "But even that complexity won't save him. GAIA's protocols are absolute. Once they detect the transfer, they'll move to erase him immediately. Your window to act will be no more than seconds. Understand that this is your only chance."

Noa nods again, her breath shallow as the voice speaks. The room feels heavier, as if the stakes are pressing down on her from all sides.

"The process, if successful, won't take long," the voice reiterates, its tone more urgent now. "But we have to move quickly. The body is ready to receive the download, and we've already lingered too long. Use the chamber to the left. You can partially enter GAIA from there to contact Isaac, just before we initiate the transfer."

Noa glances toward the indicated chamber, its smooth surface glowing faintly. Her pulse quickens.

"You must prepare him," the voice insists. "Starting the transfer without warning could shatter his sanity and corrupt the brain we've meticulously prepared. Please, Noa—you must make haste. Be aware, though, that the connection will cause a bandwidth spike, and this will only accelerate GAIA's detection of Isaac and his sector."

Noa pauses, her body frozen despite the urgency in the voice. A knot tightens in her stomach, uneasiness creeping in like a shadow. It's been there all along—since the day this plan was set in motion two years ago. Her love for Isaac and her fear of being alone again have dulled it, but now, with the moment upon her, it's sharp and undeniable.

She presses her trembling hand against her chest, trying to steady her racing heart. She imagines Isaac's face—his warm, steady gaze, the way his smile could melt her defenses. The thought of holding him in real life fills her with desperate hope, but there's a whisper of doubt at the edge of her mind.

What if this doesn't work? What if I lose him completely?

"Noa—" The voice breaks into her thoughts, sharper now. "—there's no more time! You must act. For him. For this chance. Go to the chamber. Now."

Swallowing her hesitation, Noa steps forward, her movements deliberate but heavy with the weight of her decision. As she approaches the chamber, her fingers brush its smooth surface. It's time to bring Isaac home—but this doesn't feel right.

The unseen voice cuts through Noa's spiraling thoughts, its tone shifting, now gentle and maternal. It feels oddly soothing yet calculated, like a mother offering reassurance before a painful truth.

"Miss Gayle," the voice begins, "this transfer is important—perhaps the highest achievement in human life science. And while that may be a fact, we have anticipated your apprehension. We've also considered the ethics of such an act."

Noa's breath catches, her eyes flicking between the stasis chamber and the faint glow of the interface panel.

"Your husband's body," the voice continues, steady but softer now, "is still in cellular suspense—but not here. The healing and rebuilding of his central nervous system during our initial attempts to save him did occur. But as you know... Joe is gone. We believed it best to give you the opportunity to let him rest peacefully."

Noa's head shakes instinctively, side to side, almost refusing the words before they fully land. Her gaze settles on the body suspended in the chamber. It looks like Joe. The same face she once held close, now frozen in eerie stillness. Yet, at the same time... it looks like Isaac.

"Miss Gayle," the voice presses, "the transfer can still occur. There's still time to—"

"Transfer?" Noa interrupts, her voice soft at first, as though testing the word. Then her tone shifts abruptly, anger and confusion bursting forth. "What does that mean? WHOSE BODY IS THIS?"

The motherly voice responds with calm precision, her words both reassuring and unnerving. "We have cloned your husband, Joseph Emmanuel. Per our agreement, you granted us permission to conduct the necessary studies and procedures to facilitate this transfer. This is Isaac's body—his own body. A genetic replica of Joseph Emmanuel, yet an entirely separate, unique vessel."

Noa's eyes dart to the stasis chamber, her mind racing to process the revelation. She stares at the body–Isaac's body. A freshly created shell, whole and matured, yet untouched by life. It stands waiting, ready for its occupant.

She shakes her head. "H-How did you–"

The voice cuts her off. "We accelerated his growth through hormonal manipulation and epigenetic reprogramming, bringing him to the appropriate age. From this point forward, his life will progress at a normal rate."

The sight doesn't immediately bring clarity. The idea of someone else inhabiting Joe's body had gnawed at her, kept her awake with restless unease, chasing her own shadows in the dark. It felt wrong. It felt like betrayal.

But this body isn't Joe. It never was, and it never will be.

The realization lands softly, like a whisper of truth slipping through the noise. Relief comes first–quiet, almost hesitant. Then it builds, filling the space where fear once lived. The weight lifts, her heart loosening its grip on what it had clung to for so long.

This isn't a replacement. This isn't erasure. This is Isaac's chance at life.

Relief gives way to something bigger, brighter, and more permanent–healing. Noa has carried the weight of choices, of grief, and of love into this moment. The idea of Isaac taking his first breath in this body, stepping into her world, fills her with a surge of purpose. Doubts dissolve like smoke, replaced by clarity. For the first time, it feels right. For the first time, she feels free.

Her chest tightens, but not from fear–it's resolve now, a fire that refuses to be extinguished. She glances at the chamber, her gaze lingering on the faint hum of energy around Isaac's body. This is his. Not Joe's. Isaac's.

"Miss Gayle." The voice cuts through her thoughts, smooth but urgent. "We're ready if you are."

Noa blinks, grounding herself. She nods once, sharp and certain. Her hands tremble slightly, but not from hesitation. This trembling is something else—adrenaline, anticipation, the weight of love demanding action.

She steps forward, her heart pounding but steady. All her pain, all her waiting—everything—has led her here. She brushes her fingers against the cool surface of the chamber, her resolve crystallizing.

"I'm ready," she says softly, her voice firm.

She wants Isaac here and now. And nothing will stop her.

"Noa—this is without guarantee," the voice continues, calm but weighty with caution. "There is a higher chance that he will not survive the transfer, even if he isn't caught and deleted beforehand. Surviving the transfer does not guarantee his life. At any moment, as his senses and neurological functions come online, something could go wrong. If his respiratory drive doesn't engage his diaphragm, he could stop breathing in his sleep—just from the process itself. Metaphorically, this could cause a short in the connection. Initially, he won't even feel the rise and fall of his chest; those senses will take time to develop. He will rely entirely on his autonomic nervous system—the parts of him that work without thought—to activate first. You will need to monitor him closely. But please prepare yourself. You may awake one morning and find he didn't make it through the night."

Noa's breath trembles as her raw, tear-streaked face twists in anguish. "I have to lose my heart again? I will likely lose him all over again? Lying next to me, in my arms—all over again?" Her voice cracks, her body trembling under the weight of the words.

Her heavy hair drips water and grime, her face smeared with food waste and tears. She feels broken yet ignited, rage and grief battling for control.

"Yes, Miss Gayle," the voice replies softly. "That is likely... but there is still a chance. A small chance that he will survive. The odds are low because this hasn't been tested. Yet, sometimes the Universe is kind to science. Sometimes breakthroughs come with minimal effort. In those moments, we might imagine that we've been given her permission—that we are not defying natural laws but fulfilling her will. It's impossible to say if that's true, but it might give you reason to hope, even against such unlikely odds."

Noa's lips curl into a defiant smirk beneath her tears, her resolve hardening. "It's our world! We can do whatever the fuck we want!" Her voice cuts through the air like a blade. Determination floods her features, even as worry and uncertainty flicker in her floating gaze.

She undresses quickly, the chill nipping at her wet skin, making her shiver violently. Her movements are sharp, her mind racing. This isn't how she wanted it to happen, but it's happening. She stands exposed, vulnerable, yet resolved to take this step.

Her ethical quandary over transferring Isaac into Joe's clone has been buried under the urgency of the moment. The weight that remains is the choice Isaac must make: to leave the only world he's ever known, to accept that everything he believed was a lie—all of it, except the love they share.

He might say no, and she refuses to force this upon him. But if he hesitates too long, he will be destroyed—deleted along with the tiny sector of GAIA that contains his world, leaving no trace of it within the vast network of all things.

Even if Noa somehow recreated Chicago in 1996 and 1997—a task impossible if she's prosecuted and her SynaptiLynk enhancements deactivated—she knows she could never recreate Isaac André exactly as he is. He grew into the man she loves on his own, shaped by his experiences and their connection.

She can only hope he loves her enough to choose her—and to choose life. But there won't be time to convince him. His decision must already be made.

"Hurry, Miss Gayle! Establishing this type of connection will take time, and the transfer must begin immediately after. The spike will be detected, and everything will be shut down without warning. We'll have minutes—maybe seconds. If even a single packet of Isaac's data fails to make the transfer, it will mean failure. Worse, it will mean his death. Please, this operation is too important—not just for you, but for the world!"

Noa tries to steady her emotions, the weight of fear and loss enveloping her like a crushing tide. Failure looms, threatening to steal all she holds dear. A single, trembling whimper escapes her lips, the last crack in her composure before she takes a deep, steadying breath. With resolve hardening in her chest, she snaps herself back into focus—poised, determined, ready to act.

The chill of the room prickles her bare flesh as she steps forward. The GAIA chamber responds.

Psssssssshhhh.

A faint vapor curls outward, like an inviting whisper. Noa steps inside. The chamber seals behind her.

Psssssshhhh—thunk.

Drowsiness overtakes her instantly, a heavy wave that pulls her under. Her body succumbs to the chamber's interface, her breath hitches as she draws in a deep, involuntary breath. Her chest heaves, the exhale automatic—beyond her will—as she surrenders to GAIA's embrace, slipping into its vast, virtual world.

Noa connects partially, just enough bandwidth to reach Isaac. She struggles briefly to locate him within GAIA, but there's no time to hesitate. A booming voice might not have worked before, but now it's her only option short of fully entering his world—a move that would be suicide.

Her body feels lighter, as if drifting into sleep, the connection pulling her into the in-between. A sense of elsewhere washes over her. She can feel it—the essence of Chicago 1997—though she isn't fully there.

She has to make this count. He has to hear her.

"ISAAC!"

****

It's near dawn. Isaac knows this world isn't real. The sunlight creeping over the horizon is just as artificial as himself—and everyone else in his life, except Noa Gayle. He carries the same blank stare that fell across his face like dominoes when she told him. He has been walking the sidewalks of Gresham, his steps dragging across the cracked concrete. The silence is oppressive, the kind that doesn't hum or breathe. His mind churns in a storm of thoughts that refuse to settle.

To calm himself, he times his steps, avoiding the cracks in the sidewalk, the lines that separate each square. A futile game of control in a life spiraling out of his grasp.

He wants to cry but finds nothing—just the hollow ache of a phantom emotion. Each step feels heavier than the last, as his mind pulls apart every thread of his existence. His mother's death—a lie. His face—a stolen echo of someone else. He's a ghost built from grief, crafted to mirror Noa's first love. Who could create something so cruel and tender at once? Is this just her, or are there others like him? Whole lives, entire worlds, manufactured and discarded without a thought?

Noa apologized, but she didn't regret it. She said she would do it all over again, a million times, just to fall in love with him. Her words ring through his thoughts, colliding with the storm. He still loves her. He can't stop. She made his world make sense. She became his anchor, his light.

But now, she's offering him a different life—a real one. A life with her. He looks up at the faint lightening of the horizon and makes his choice. Isaac André chooses life. He chooses Noa.

His pace quickens, the storm in his mind clearing just enough for a path forward. He heads home.

As he rounds the corner onto Morgan Street, he stops. Pete's Buick Skyhawk is parked in front of the house. The door creaks open, and Pete steps out and leans his short stature casually against the car.

"What's up, cuz? Thought about you, figured I'd come by. You good?" Pete's voice is light but holds an edge of something deeper.

"Going through some changes, man. Hard to explain. You okay?"

Pete grins, tapping his chest. "Cuz, I'm good. But you need to know—everything's gonna be solid here, too. I'll see to it. You know what I mean."

"Pete, what the hell are you talking about?"

"Everybody knows, man. You were the only one who didn't." Pete's laugh is brittle, the humor undercut by a flicker of sadness. "This is your world, cuz. You can make it hers too. Don't screw that up."

A tear glistens in the corner of Pete's eye. He holds out his hand for a dap, and they pull into a tight hug.

"Love you, dawg," Pete says, his voice low.

"Love you too, man," Isaac replies, his mind spinning even faster. This moment feels both real and unreal.

Pete's words echo in his head like a wayward pinball. *"It's your world."*

Isaac walks to Grandma's. He doesn't intend to go inside; he wants to just see the home he grew up in. Twenty-plus years of simulated life occurred in that simulated home. The sunlight is bright now, the sky clear. He's stunned to find her sitting on the porch with Tommy. They're talking, laughing like old friends.

"Morning," Isaac says, his voice catching.

Tommy looks up with a sly grin. "Morning, son."

Grandma chuckles. "Morning, baby. We're just yucking it up. You all right?"

Isaac's chest tightens. The scene is too perfect, too calm. "You two gonna be okay? Grandma? Tommy?"

Grandma nods, her face serene. "Honey, yes. Yes, we already are. You get on now."

Tommy meets Isaac's gaze. "I told you, son. Everything happens for a reason."

Isaac's throat burns as he swallows his emotions. He nods and turns back toward his apartment.

After ascending his steps, he opens the rear door to find Sarah Connor is not there. His studio is bathed in soft light. He sits at the foot of his bed, staring up at the mural on the ceiling. The sunlight filters through it, illuminating the thin filaments reaching toward the center where the man and woman meet.

Then, it happens.

"ISAAC!"

The voice booms, piercing, coming from everywhere and nowhere. Pain explodes behind his eyes, sharp and cold like an ice pick. He clutches his head, falling back onto the bed, his breath quick and shallow.

"IIIII–" The sound returns, distorted, ripping through him like a jagged wave. He screams, "What? Noa? Please be you, babe!"

"Isaac! It's me—it's Noa!" Her voice steadies, softens. "Just breathe, love. Isaac, please, breathe."

Isaac curls into the fetal position, trembling. Her voice anchors him. He breathes, slowly at first, then deeper. He opens his eyes, the sunlight stabbing at them, making him wince. His body feels like it's being torn apart, pulled in two directions.

Noa speaks again, her tone calm but urgent. "Isaac, we have to try now—right now. If we don't, it's all over. I'm sorry. I didn't want it this way. If you want to stay, I'll respect whatever you—"

"Yes!" Isaac shouts, his voice cracking. "Yes! Please, I'm ready. I'm ready."

Tears streak down his face as he lies still, breathing deeply, preparing himself for whatever comes next. He doesn't know what to expect—pain, fear, or something worse—but he trusts her. He chooses her.

In the sterile lab, Noa steps out of the GAIA chamber, her face pale, her hands trembling. She presses her palm against the cool glass enclosing Isaac's new body. The odds are stacked against them, but she doesn't care. She will take the risk. She will fight for him.

Inside his world, Isaac feels the pull again. Darkness creeps in, heavy and soundless, as everything fades. His breath catches. He feels nothing. Sees nothing.

The void consumes him. Complete darkness. Floating. Waiting.

Part Four

Chapter Nine

"Isaa–!"

Noa's voice cuts off mid-word.

Then–nothing.

Darkness. No sound. No movement. No feeling.

Panic comes fast and brutal. He tries to kick, to thrash–nothing. His arms, his legs, his entire body does not obey. He can't feel his face, not even the rise and fall of his chest.

But he hears his breath.

It rushes in and out of his skull, loud, chaotic, like a storm trapped inside him.

His heart pounds–thunders even. He doesn't feel it, but he knows it's there, galloping wild inside the void.

Noa's voice wavers, breaking into fragments–muffled, incomplete sounds floating just beyond reach. He strains to grasp them, but there is nothing to grasp, no framework to make sense of the distortion. Static thickens, layering over everything. His senses are raw, undefined, as if he is assembling himself moment by moment. It will take days for his PaxCerebra to map each synaptic connection, forging sight, sound, and movement for the first time.

Something shifts. His hearing sharpens, and the world begins to take shape in sound before anything else.

He hears her. Noa.

Closer this time.

She leans in, voice low, careful. SOMA warned her not to speak too loudly—too much sound could shatter him, an avalanche crashing through his fragile, forming senses.

"Isaac," she whispers. "It's Noa. Baby, I'm here. I'm here, love."

Her voice is steady, but her face is wet. She fights to hold herself together, to keep the tremor from her words. A sob grips the back of her throat—she swallows it down, forcing a smile she doesn't mean. He can't see the way it falters, the way it frays at the edges.

She wants to shake him awake, to scream his name, to make him know she's here. Instead, she keeps her voice soft, each word an offering, a prayer, a plea.

Isaac can't see her.

His eyes are taped shut, a necessary measure to protect his corneas. He can't feel his body. Can't even smell the familiar, sweet scent of her skin.

But he hears her.

Her voice reaches him, clearer now. It's her—but more alive than he remembers. The rhythm, the warmth, the way it slips through the darkness and curls around him like an embrace. It feels like holding her again. Her tiptoed frame pressing in, her face against his chest.

What he doesn't know is that Noa is sitting at the edge of his bed, head resting gently against him, listening to the steady rise and fall of his breath.

She speaks again, softer now. "Isaac. You're here. You're here with me."

She's not just saying it for him. She needs to hear it, too.

She wipes at her face, her hand trembling, her tears unseen by him. Her voice catches, the sound of those same tears collecting in the back of her throat. "I hope you can hear me," she whispers, her tone caught somewhere between hope and desperation.

Leaning in closer, she steadies herself, voice resolute now. A promise. One she refuses to break. "I'm never leaving you again."

Noa's voice settles something inside him. He trusts her—that sound, that warmth. The panic dulls, exhaustion creeps in, and his rebooting mind begins to surrender to sleep.

And for the first time, Isaac dreams.

Not simulations. Not artificial constructs. Real dreams.

Memories unfold, vivid and warm. The smell of Grandma's cooking, thick with spice and love. Her laugh as they watched old movies together, her voice humming along with the soundtracks. Petty, silly arguments between Pete and Sharika, their jabs filling the room, something Isaac never realized he would miss. A life once lived. Moments he thought were lost forever—now flickering back to him, vivid and whole.

****

Two days pass. His senses continue to develop.

This morning, he feels his face. By night, he can move his eyes, though full vision won't come until the next morning.

On the morning of that third day, light and shadow come first, forcing him to shield his sensitive eyes. The brightness floods in as a searing headache, nausea twisting through him. Even behind his closed lids, the light is an assault. Noa was warned about this and tries her best to keep it low. But even the dim glow—barely enough for her to sponge-bathe him—is too much.

Isaac can't express the pain. He doesn't yet have the ability to speak. But Noa seems to know.

When his body burns, his head splitting, she acts. She covers his eyes with a warm towel, injects him with the illegal morphine SOMA gave her.

Later that morning, he senses a presence. He strains, eyes shifting to focus, but all he sees is a broad, gray shadow, bathed in headache-light. He pushes through.

Then—her voice.

"Good morning, handsome."

Noa's tone is soft, thick with emotion. "You can't see me, but I'm here. I will always be here—I promise."

She sniffs, half-sobs.

"I love you."

Isaac's eyes flutter closed in relief. Tears collect in his inner eyes, forming ponds on both sides of his nose. They overflow, spilling down his cheeks. He smiles, he grimaces—his face contorts with emotion. His muscles, weak and unfamiliar, come alive.

Despite the prison of his body, he feels safe.

This is her world.

****

Later that night, Isaac starts to feel—not just his face, but his entire body.

At first, it's unbearable. A tingling burn, like fire ants swarming every inch of his skin. Neck to toes. It comes in waves, flaring hot, then retreating, only to surge again. He grits through it, endures. By the fourth morning, it fades into a dull, lingering hum.

Then—a breath.

Soft. Warm.

Against his neck. Against his cheek.

Familiar. Déjà vu.

His vision sharpens, grainy at first, shifting in and out of focus. His heart kicks up, a sudden, urgent rhythm pounding inside his chest.

He opens his eyes.

The blurred world stirs around him, shadows shifting, stretching into form. He turns his head—slow, uncoordinated, every movement foreign.

Her warmth is pressed against him in the large bed, her face nestled in the curve of his neck, breath steady against his skin.

That presence—taunting him with incomplete relief in that other world—now feels whole. Soothing. Real.

Slowly, she wakes. Her lashes flutter, lifting to reveal those cognac-brown eyes.

They lock onto his.

Like she's seeing him for the first time.

Something's different now. Deeper. Her eyes hold more—more life, more weight, more knowing. Everything they've been through. Everything still ahead.

She smiles, then gently touches her lips. A whisper, almost in disbelief.

"Hi."

Isaac stares. *That smile.*

It's real.

For him, it's the most beautiful thing he's ever seen. It's the first thing he's ever seen.

His lips curl into a slow, unsteady smile. The muscles feel foreign, fragile, but they work. His body—*his* body—is starting to obey him. He's never had control like this before.

His vision is still soft around the edges, his world still slightly out of focus. But he sees her. The familiar contours of her face, the fullness of her lips, the way her smile carries something real now.

His chest tightens. His heart slams hard and fast.

This feeling—it isn't an echo, not something artificial or coded into him. It's real.

He loves her.

Not theoretical. Not a glitch. Not something pulled from a simulation.

Unfiltered, unmistakable, pure.

Noa hands him a mirror.

He squints, reaching up, touching his face like a toddler discovering their reflection for the first time. He looks exactly as he did in GAIA. The same skin, the same lines, the same familiar face—but real.

His fingertips graze the stubble on his chin. His scalp, where new hair is starting to grow.

"Where's Tommy when you need him?"

Noa laughs through her tears. They run freely down the crease of her nose. She covers her mouth, but her eyes give her away.

Isaac lifts his arm—clumsy, uncoordinated, ataxic—as he tries to grab her hand. She lowers hers, lets him catch it, lets him hold her.

Her skin is warm. Soft. Real.

His strength is weak, but he shifts toward her, resting his head against her chest. A low snicker escapes him.

"Your heart is so loud."

Noa snort-laughs, hiccups on a breath, then folds herself over him.

Her arms wrap tight. She cradles his head, her lips pressing against his hair, his forehead, his temple.

Her voice is a whisper. A promise.

"Hey, Isaac—I love you."

****

Noa awakens from an intermittently peaceful slumber. Peaceful, because Isaac is here with her this morning. Intermittent, because of the relentless anxiety that he might not be the next.

Four weeks have passed, and she remains unwavering in her devotion to nursing Isaac into his new existence—a task as extraordinary as it is daunting. She is the first person on Earth to hold this fragile privilege, guiding a newly born adult through uncharted territory, moment by moment.

Most mornings begin the same way for her: a gnawing fear of waking to stillness in his chest. Her ritual is simple yet sacred. She places her palm gently over his heart, closing her eyes as she searches for its rhythm. Each time she finds it—steady and alive—relief washes over her. She places her hand over her own chest, mirroring the beat.

He's still there, she thinks to herself. It has become her new daily mantra—a mantra of thanksgiving, whispered silently with each morning's relief.

Noa slowly sits upright in bed, moving carefully so as not to disturb him. She peels the bedsheet from her lap with gentle precision, sliding each leg down, one by one, to meet the warm, dark gray concrete tiles beneath her feet.

Her toned body rises with ease, fluid and steady. She stretches her arms upward, fingertips reaching high as her chest expands with a slow, cleansing breath. The motion grounds her in the quiet of the morning, a moment of calm. She winces slightly as she bends her neck back. Faint bruises, now healing—streak across her upper back. A well-healed scar stretches down her left shin.

Noa steps out of the bedroom into the hallway, which slowly illuminates with a soft, warm ambient glow. The light is barely perceptible at first, designed for dark-adjusted eyes to see comfortably without strain.

As she approaches the main living area, the gray faux-stone pedestal to her left hums faintly and activates. Sarah Connor flickers to life, her holographic form perched on an invisible stand. The green parakeet shuffles back and forth, her tiny head tilting downward expectantly.

Noa smiles faintly, reaching out with a practiced motion. Her finger hovers in the air, tracing a gentle scritch across Sarah Connor's green crown. The hologram responds with lifelike enthusiasm, a soft chirp of acknowledgment filling the quiet room.

Scientia Mater!

The words hover in the air, displayed prominently on the screen behind Sarah Connor's holographic avatar. They float within a serene virtual scene—a green pasture at dawn. The virtual sun begins its slow ascent, casting muted light across a sky that shimmers in shades of greenish-blue.

Below, the grass blades glisten, damp and motionless. The display's resolution is so sharp that individual droplets of dew shimmer like tiny jewels. Beneath the floating *Scientia Mater,* an unfamiliar crescent moon icon hovers just above the moist grass, glowing faintly—a summons to meet within GAIA?

Noa stares at it, an unease grows. The icon doesn't match any she's seen before, and its unfamiliarity sends a chill through her. Apprehension tightens her chest. Has she been caught? Do they know her secret—her blasphemous acts of playing God?

Yet, something tugs at her, deep and insistent. A pull she can't ignore, compelling her to accept.

She steps away from the display to take another peek at Isaac. Her eyes linger on the gentle rise and fall of the sheets loosely draped over his chest. She watches intently, ensuring the motion isn't a distant illusion.

Taking a deep breath, she closes her eyes and whispers her daily mantra. "He's still here."

Noa gulps down a full bottle of Neur-ish, the liquid cool as it slides down her throat. She isn't sure of the neurotransmitter toll this visit will exact, so there's no room for waste. The empty bottle clinks as she deposits it into the recycler.

At the sink, she scrubs her hands thoroughly, the ritual

familiar and grounding. She splashes her face with cold water, letting droplets cling to her skin as both air-dry during her measured walk to the chamber.

The glass pod door opens slowly, releasing a soft *psssshhh* as faint white vapor curls outward. Noa steps inside. The door re-tracts shut behind her with a smooth *pssshhhh*, followed by a low-pitched *click-thumph*. The chamber seals, and the faint hiss of air suction fills her ears. A pressure presses against her eardrums.

Then it hits her—a sudden, overwhelming drowsiness. Her body shudders with an involuntary gasp, sharp and deep, as though it were her first breath.

The transition is instantaneous. Noa finds herself standing in the center of the meadow from the display—the very setting of Isaac's mural, but now at dawn. A pale crescent moon lingers in the greenish sky, faintly illuminated by the sun still to rise.

In the distance, thousands of fine, multicolored filaments shimmer and wave upward from the horizon, their hues shifting as if alive. They splay out from the rising sun, a breathtaking array of light that seems sacred.

Beneath the ethereal filaments, Noa sees the silhouette of a woman. She is surrounded by flowers that shift their colors vibrantly, their soft glow outlining her form. Yet her face re-mains obscured, cloaked in shadow.

This meeting could have been an instant, face-to-face con-nection—an efficient exchange typical of GAIA. But it's clear that whoever summoned Noa wanted her to walk this path, to experience it step by step.

As Noa takes that first step forward, the filaments in the distance begin to intertwine. They stretch for one another, seemingly without a discernible pattern, yet harmonized in their movement.

A shadow, far too majestic for its size, sweeps across the ground. Sarah Connor swoops down from behind Noa, her small green body silhouetted against the brightening sky. With perfect precision, the bird lands softly on Noa's right shoulder, perching there as her loyal companion. Together, they move toward the silhouette.

The closer Noa gets, the more intricate the filament patterns become. They tangle and braid, glowing with vibrant colors as the sun rises higher. The sky brightens with the dazzling multicolored coronae, radiating beauty and mystery—a stained glass world.

Noa marvels at the scene, her thoughts drifting to the universe beyond GAIA. Theorists have suggested that the universe's structure resembles vast clusters of galaxies woven together in filaments—patterns strikingly similar to the neural networks of the human brain: The Connectome.

She ponders the idea: that the human brain is a microcosmic recreation of the universe itself, crafted *in its own image.*

With each step, the thought lingers, her curiosity merging with the surreal beauty of the moment.

Noa looks up in awe, her breaths deep and measured as she takes in the spectacle around her. Sarah Connor tilts her tiny head to one side, focusing with a keen one-eyed view while maintaining perfect balance on her creator's shoulder.

In the center of the Connectome, a lengthwise clearing divides two hemispheres, a luminous path where the sunlight from the now fully risen sun streams through. The radiant beams illuminate the figure standing below—a woman wearing suspenders, her silhouette sharp against the shimmering background.

As Noa steps closer, details emerge. A silver haired woman stands in the clearing, her face bearing a gentle, welcoming smile. Her features are lined with age, but her beauty is undeniable, glowing with wisdom and warmth.

Noa's eyes mist over as realization dawns. Her lips part, and she breathes the question, trembling with emotion. "You're—?"

The woman nods once, her expression kind and reassuring. Slowly, she extends her right hand, offering it for a shake.

"Carolyn Faber," she says, her voice steady and clear. "It has been my pleasure."

Noa's gaze drops, her damp eyes fixed on the vibrant green of the virtual grass beneath her feet. She shakes her head slowly, as if trying to process a deeper, dawning realization. When she finally looks up at Carolyn, a tear-muffled snicker escapes her lips.

"It was you? The whole time? You're alive... my contact?"

Carolyn's expression softens, her hair catching the light filtering through the Connectome. She shakes her head gently, her voice steady and laced with compassion.

"No, dear heart, I am not your contact. There are still those among the living who work with us—people with character, who haven't let power or wealth corrupt their decency."

Her voice takes on a wistful note. "And no, I'm not alive—not in the way you mean. I've been gone for some time now. Before my death, I preserved myself—my consciousness, that is. My body isn't in stasis; it perished long ago. The real Carolyn Faber died with it."

She pauses, gesturing faintly to herself with a melancholic smile.

"This... this is a visual copy of her likeness... at the time of her death. From there, a new Carolyn Faber emerged—one that could live on indefinitely."

Her words linger in the air. She is describing a reality where the human Carolyn Faber has died, but her uploaded consciousness continued to exist within GAIA, evolving and gaining experiences that the original Carolyn Faber had.

Noa's tears shimmer as they fall, each drop tracing a slow, deliberate path down her cheeks. They slip from her chin in rhythmic succession, landing on the virtual grass below. Each droplet making the grass blades bend and bounce.

The grass glistens brighter with each tear, the vividness of GAIA surpassing anything the real world could offer. Noa stands still, the weight of the revelation settles over her like the warmth of sunlight breaking through a storm.

Carolyn gently places her hand on Noa's face, brushing away a tear with her finger. Her touch is soft as she strokes Noa's wavy hair at her temple, tucking it back to reveal her tear-filled eyes.

"Noa Gayle..." Carolyn says, her voice steady with affection, "... you are a beautiful soul."

Noa laughs through her tears, a bittersweet, self-effacing laugh that says *yeah, sure!* Carolyn presses her hand gently on Noa's shoulder to stop her, her expression growing serious.

"Noa... " Carolyn begins, her tone both tender and firm, "... what you have done for love—for the longing for connection—is rare in our time. You chose to create a world of yesterday, when people sought deeper, meaningful bonds.

"As the world grew more connected in the proverbial sense, we lost the desire for true connection. First, we separated ourselves through screens. Then, we divided ourselves with walls. But you—" Carolyn pauses, her gaze softening. "—you found a love in your husband, Joe—a rare union in these times.

"You grew up wanting more than what your lone mother could give. You longed for a partner to share life with. When you lost Joe, your grief led you to attempt the impossible: to resurrect him. But instead, you found a new love and crossed the horizon of acceptance."

Carolyn gestures to the shimmering virtual world around them. "Look around you, Noa. You could live here in bliss forever. Never hunger. Never suffer. Fulfillment is yours in every way imaginable. So why would you risk all of this—for love? A love that will be tested by disagreements, by physical change, by the inevitability of death and loss?"

Noa wipes her eyes, her lips curling into a bittersweet smile.

"When I met Joe, it felt real. To hold someone real—to breathe in the scent of him after a long day of toiling for us. To laugh so hard my face hurt. To get so angry I wanted to break something. To hope, together, for a cure that came too late." She gestures around her at the vibrant, perfect world. "This can't match that!"

Carolyn nods with pride, her smile knowing. "This is why you were chosen, Noa. You represent what it truly means to be human. You possess something that has been mostly selected out because the world saw no need for it to survive.

"Both of you—Isaac and you—represent what it means not just to exist, but to be."

Noa wipes away her tears, her chest rising and falling with each calming breath. She looks deeply into Carolyn Faber's wise eyes—eyes that, in GAIA, appear as they once did in life. These are Carolyn's eyes, brimming with kindness and wisdom.

As Noa studies her, a thought surfaces, her voice soft and uncertain. "Science of our Mother? Are you... Mother?"

Carolyn chuckles, a warm, melodic sound. "No, dear heart. The Science, the understanding, the everything—" She gestures around her in a sweeping motion. "—comes from the Mother. Not me."

She pauses, her eyes scanning the luminous world around them, and continues, her tone gentle but profound. "We don't know where the worlds—the ones we call virtual and the ones we call real—intersect or end. We believe there's an end, a terminus, where all that remains is reality. But that's belief, not all science." Carolyn tilts her head slightly, a faint smile tugging at her lips. "Only she—the universe herself, the Mother of all—may know for certain."

Noa scans herself, her fingers brushing over her face as if to confirm it's truly there. She glances at the virtual bird perched on her shoulder, its small, vivid form almost indistinguishable from reality. Taking a deep breath, she inhales the air—it feels real, smells real.

Her gaze drops to her feet, bare and planted firmly in the grass. She wiggles her toes, feeling the soft tickle against them. The sensation is startlingly vivid, a mix of grounding and surreality.

The warmth of the sun caresses her skin, and the air rushes around her, soft and alive. Above her, the shimmering filaments of the Connectome have fully formed, their intricate structure now resembling a glowing brain. Light emanates from it, warm and gentle, pouring over her like a comforting embrace.

As she takes it all in, a loud, rhythmic thumping fills her ears from the Earth below her feet. It takes her a moment to realize—it's the sound of a heart, strong and steady.

Her brows furrow, a thought slipping through her mind. *Your heart is so loud!*

A healing frequency hums through the air, resonating softly around them. The sound is more than just auditory—it vibrates within Noa's chest, calming her heart and mind. A wave of euphoria follows, gentle and soothing, carrying with it a sense of profound relief.

In this moment, she feels vindicated. Every choice, every risk, every sacrifice—they were worth it. She allows herself to feel thankful, deeply and entirely, for this moment—every moment.

Her thoughts drift to her new husband in the real world. That reality—raw, imperfect, and genuine—is all that matters to them both.

"Gardenia!" Carolyn's voice breaks softly into her thoughts, filled with sudden delight. "It's my favorite."

Noa notices a subtle shift in Carolyn's expression, a serene smile forming as if she can catch the faintest trace of the flower's scent on the air.

****

The people of the world have grown utterly dependent on the Network of All. They cannot imagine life without it. It brings them security, shelter from the cold, and food for their bellies. Isaac André was once part of a world within this network, a place called GAIA. But as an Artificial Individual, the security others sought within its confines never truly reached him. Not until now.

Now, for the first time, Isaac feels connection.

In the early days of adjusting to his human body, he often despaired. Frustration turned the simplest tasks into insurmountable trials. He laughs about it now, recalling how he once cursed his maker—who happens to be sitting right across from him—because he couldn't grasp a spoon to eat porridge.

That joke-curse was followed by a quiet thanks to whatever God had gifted Noa those cognac-brown eyes that still undo him, even now, ten years later. Eyes filled with soul, not code.

Isaac is more connected than anyone within the Republic of Canada. He is tethered—forever—to his Noa.

Being alive is the hardest job we undertake from the moment we are born, yet we do it without thinking. As our minds grow more complex, staying alive feels heavier. But for Isaac, it's the opposite.

He was willing to be rescued, even if it meant losing everything he had ever known. That willingness—is the essence of being alive.

Every end is a beginning.

Afterword

The energy to write this tale flows directly from my maternal DNA—a sacred gift passed down from the women who have shaped me. Their strength, wisdom, and boundless love have been my compass and my wellspring, guiding my steps and fueling my spirit. Without them, this story would not exist, and neither would the voice I write with.

So, I dedicate this to all of them—the life-givers, the nurturers, the creators. To the mothers and grandmothers, both of blood and of spirit, who carry the weight of world and make life itself possible. To the women who have fought against silence and invisibility, who have dreamed us into existence and sustain us with courage and care.

We owe thanks to the women who sustain the universe with their hands and hearts, and most of all, to the universe herself—the ultimate life-giver, the eternal mother from whom all life flows. Let us honor her in all her forms, from the smallest seed to the vast, unending cosmos.

And so, I lift my voice and give a full-throated greeting of power: *Scientia Mater!* May the science of our mother continue to guide us, heal us, and remind us that we are part of something infinite and divine.

****

www.ingramcontent.com/pod-product-compliance
Lightning Source LLC
Chambersburg PA
CBHW050306110726
47899CB00007B/2130